Praise for *Quiver*

"The apple doesn't fall far from the tree. But the reader's impulse to compare does nothing to spoil *Quiver*'s pleasures, which are legion."
—*The Toronto Star*

"A spare, violent, and grittily humorous crime novel . . . with some cracking dialogue, clever plotting, and an enjoyably bloody climax."
—*The Times* (London)

"*Quiver* is a spectacular debut . . . With a large cast of characters—each presented as meticulously as an Andrew Wyeth portrait—and numerous points of view, all funneling inevitably to a stunning conclusion, you will be holding your breath until the final page. Peter's dad should be proud."
—Otto Penzler

"A strong debut that combines a tight plot (about a deadly double-cross in the woods of Michigan) with memorable characters and dialogue—come to think of it, not unlike what Leonard's father, Elmore Leonard, creates."
—*Seattle Times*

"The best parts of the novel concern the crooks, who, if not as gloriously quirky as those in Elmore Leonard's novels, are sometimes funny and sometimes scary."
—*Washington Post*

"You'll be sitting in the air off the edge of your chair more than once during your reading of *Quiver*."
—*Bookreporter.com*

"Peter Leonard's first novel, *Quiver*, amply shows that he's the great Elmore's son. This book is a wicked trip with the creeps and pukes that inhabit the criminal world who collide with a convincing heroine. The setting in the rural north of Michigan is unique and engaging. I salute Peter Leonard at the beginning of what will obviously be a fine career."

—Jim Harrison, author of *Returning to Earth*
and *Legends of the Fall*

"*Quiver* is terrific. . . . I have to make the corniest admission of all: Couldn't put it down."

—Mike Lupica, *Daily News* (New York) columnist
and author of *Dead Air*

Trust Me

ALSO BY PETER LEONARD

Quiver

Trust Me

Peter Leonard

Minotaur Books
New York

This is a work of fiction. All of the characters, organizations, and events portrayed in this novel are either products of the author's imagination or are used fictitiously.

A THOMAS DUNNE BOOK FOR MINOTAUR BOOKS.
An imprint of St. Martin's Publishing Group.

www.thomasdunnebooks.com
www.minotaurbooks.com

Library of Congress Cataloging-in-Publication Data

Leonard, Peter A.
    Trust me / Peter Leonard.—1st ed.
        p. cm.
    ISBN-13: 978-0-312-37903-2
    ISBN-10: 0-312-37903-X
    1. Thieves—Fiction.   I. Title.
    PS3612.E5737T78 2009
    813'.6—dc22   2008041741

First Edition: April 2009

10   9   8   7   6   5   4   3   2   1

For my girls,
Julie and Kate

Acknowledgments

I want to thank:

Pete Wolverton. He knew I could give him more and kept challenging me until he got it all. That's what a good editor does.

Jeff Posternak, the perfect agent. He's always cool and calm behind the scenes and tries to keep me that way.

Robert Gal and his mother, Edith Gal, for their help on the Hungarian translation.

Joe Young, for his insightful point of view on relationships.

Jennifer Ness, an expert on blackjack, twirling, and life in Garden City.

Gregg Sutter, master researcher.

The Bodary twins, Julie and Jean, my advance readers.

Jane Jones, ace proofreader.

Kenneth J. Silver, superb production editor.

Trust Me

One

Lou Starr was in bed reading, covered to the waist by a sheet. He'd set the air at sixty-eight and heard the compressor kick on outside. He pushed up the glasses that were falling off the end of his nose and stared at the signature hole of a new Robert Trent Jones PGA golf course called Whispering Palms.

He fondled the medallion that was hanging from a gold chain around his neck, resting on a sweater of chest hair. Lou said, "Want to see the best-looking new hole in golf?" He tilted the magazine toward Karen on the other side of the king-size bed, two feet of mattress between them.

Karen didn't say anything. She was propped up on pillows, the bedsheet angling across her chest revealing the pale white skin of her shoulder and the round curve of a breast. She was watching a sitcom on a Sony flat screen that hung on the wall a few feet away.

"It's a six-hundred-yard par five," Lou said. "Longest one in golf." He grinned now, imagining himself on the tee looking down the fairway. He took a couple practice swings with his Fusion FT-3 driver and blasted the ball three hundred and twenty-five yards straight down the pike. Hey, Tiger, beat that.

Lou hit his second shot over a bunker and a water hazard—on in two. He lined up the putt and sent the ball forty feet over a swale—left to right—for an eagle. He grinned big and closed the magazine and placed it on the table next to the bed. He took off his reading glasses, put them on top of the magazine and turned off the light.

Lou slid over next to Karen, touched her shoulder with his index finger, tracing a line down her arm to her elbow. He was horny. She'd been putting him off for a couple of weeks. First it was her period. What could he say about that? Then her allergies kicked in. What allergies? She'd never mentioned them before. And the past few nights she'd been too tired. From what, Lou wanted to know? All she did was go to the mall while he worked his ass off. He was wondering what he'd gotten himself into. They'd been living together for eight months and he was sure there were monks who got laid more than he did. Well he was going to get some tonight. He'd demand it.

Lou moved his hand under the covers, stroked Karen's thigh, her hip, the smooth round point of her pelvis under the nightie.

Karen pushed his hand away. "Come on, Lou. Not now."

"Not now," Lou said, "when?"

She was watching *Pardon My French*, this stupid fucking sitcom.

Karen said, "Chuck's getting married."

She sounded like she knew him. "Well, we're engaged," Lou said, "in case you forgot. How about my right to a piece of ass every couple months whether I need it or not?" He slid away from her, rolled over on his side.

A few minutes later it was over. He could hear the announcer's voice say: "*Pardon My French* has been brought to you by Levitra. The more you know about ED, the more you'll want to know about Levitra."

Lou got a kick out of that, Levitra for all the losers who couldn't get it up. He was fifty-six and still had a hard-on like a steel post. He glanced at Karen—hoping she'd slip her nightie off and attack him—this good-looking woman who was more interested in TV than sex. What was wrong with this picture?

He watched her yawn and close her eyes. The switcher slipped out of her hand and fell on the bed. Her eyes flickered open. She yawned again, picked up the remote and turned off the TV. It was dark, the room was quiet except for the ticking of his clock.

He'd been asleep for some time—he was sure of it—when he heard the noise. It was loud too, like something breaking, a window maybe, he couldn't tell. He looked at the clock. It was 2:48. He turned toward Karen. She heard it too, her eyes were big, a nervous look on her face.

"What was that?" Karen said.

She sat up and opened the drawer of her bedside table, took out her Airweight .357 and turned toward him. He was bringing the .45 out of his drawer, racking it. They got up with their guns and moved around the bed and went through the doorway into the living room.

Bobby saw them come in the dark room, holding guns, barrels pointed up like TV cops. They didn't go together, Bobby was thinking. The guy was short and hairy like a little gorilla. The girl was something though—lean and pale with skinny arms and nice jugs he could see hanging under the thin fabric of her nightie. He knew their names, Lou and Karen.

Bobby made his move coming in behind them, pointing the .32, telling them, if they moved, he'd blow their fucking heads off. Delivering the line like he meant it, surprised by the sound of his voice in the quiet room. They bent down and placed their guns

on the carpet, and now Lloyd entered from the other side of the
room.

"Folks, step back here, have a seat, will you?" Bobby said it
friendly and polite, no reason to be rude now that he had their attention. He waved the gun motioning them toward the couch.

Lou said, "What the hell do you want?"

"Have a seat over here, we'll let you know," Bobby said.

Lloyd picked up the .357 and the .45. Bobby was wondering
why these suburbanites were armed in the first place, not to mention with large caliber handguns. Lou grabbed an afghan off the
couch wrapped it around Karen's shoulders and they both sat
down.

"Come with me," Bobby said to Karen. She didn't hesitate, got
up and headed toward the bedroom.

Lou said, "Hey . . . where you taking her?"

Lloyd sat in a chair across from the guy, pointing the .45 at him.

Lloyd said, "We catch you and the little lady getting after it?"

"What the hell business is it of yours?" He was mad letting
Lloyd know it.

"I'm making it my business," Lloyd said. "I got the gun. You
didn't wimp out maybe you'd be holding on me. But you froze like
an amateur." He glanced around the room, checking things out.
It was dark, but his eyes had adjusted and he could focus now.
The furniture looked like it should be on a porch, not in somebody's living room, but he liked it. Real comfortable too, bent
wood frames with khaki cushions.

Neither of them said anything for a while, sitting in silence
like strangers on a bus until Lloyd said, "Nice place you got here.
Is that a real one," pointing to the zebra skin rug on the floor.

"What do *you* think?"

Lloyd said, "Where'd you get it at?"

"I shot it," Lou Starr said.

Lloyd said, "You mean like on safari?"

"No, in the backyard."

"I hunt too," Lloyd said, "with a bow and arrow."

Lou Starr said, "Congratulations."

"What kind of gun you use?" Lloyd said.

"You don't give up, do you?"

"I was just wondering," Lloyd said, "that's all."

" A 30.06, okay? You happy?"

Lloyd wondered if the guy was always this grouchy. He was making a real effort to be friendly and it wasn't working.

In the dressing room, Bobby fixed his gaze on Karen. She was a knockout, red hair and pale creamy skin. He'd always had a weakness for girls like her.

"Do you think I'm going to overpower you?" she said.

"Huh?" He wasn't paying attention, his eyes staring where the afghan didn't cover her.

"The gun," Karen said. "You don't have to point it at me. I'm not going to try anything."

He was surprised she was so relaxed, like people broke in her house in the middle of the night on a regular basis.

"Do you mind if I put something on? This thing itches," Karen said. She didn't wait for permission; let the afghan slide off her shoulder onto the floor. She grabbed a robe off a hanger and slipped it on, tying the sash around her waist.

There was a framed sign hanging on the wall that read: "Everybody's a Star at Lou Starr's World Famous Parthenon." There was a photograph of a storefront and the word "Parthenon" in neon surrounded by a silver border of stars. He said, "What's that?"

"It's from Lou's restaurants," Karen said. "You get one when you eat there. Lou thinks it makes people feel special."

"He make you feel special?" Judging by the angry look on her face he would've guessed, no. "What the hell're those for?" He was staring at the wig stands, three of them on a shelf—two had salt-and-pepper hairpieces on them.

"They're Lou's."

"No kidding. I thought they were yours." He glanced at her and felt himself grin. He lifted one of the hairpieces off the stand and studied it. It looked like a furry little creature in his hands. He was going to try it on but didn't want to mess up his own hair. "Is it real?"

"Yeah," Karen said. "It's hair from a fourteen-year-old Chinese girl."

"Does he put it on, and get a yen for chop suey?" Bobby grinned big. He couldn't help it. He surprised himself sometimes.

"He has them custom-made in London," Karen said. "The same place Burt Reynolds gets his."

Bobby said, "Burt Reynolds wears a rug, come on?"

"Are you kidding," Karen said, "his hair looks like it was made by Karastan."

"What's a custom rug cost these days?" Bobby said.

"They start at $700 and go up from there."

"That's a lot of money to look like an idiot. Why's he have three?"

"They're all different lengths so it looks like his hair's grow-ing," Karen said.

"Where's the third one?" Bobby said, eyeing the blank wig stand.

"On his head," Karen said.

"Duh," Bobby said. How'd he miss that?

· · ·

Lloyd was staring at a framed picture on the end table next to him. The guy across from him was in a safari outfit and there was a dead animal at his feet. Lloyd turned the frame toward him so he could see it. "Look at you. What is that, a lion?" Lloyd put it back on the end table. "What's a lion weigh?"

"Three fifty, four hundred," Lou Starr said. "This one went four twenty-five."

He finally got the grouch's attention. "Four twenty-five, whoa hoss, that's a big cat, ain't it?" Lloyd grinned at him. "You were in Africa, right?"

"Botswana."

"That's been a dream of mine," Lloyd said. "Get some sahibs to carry all the shit, go out every day and hunt. Smoke any of that homegrown they got over there?"

He stared at Lloyd. Maybe he didn't know what homegrown was. Lloyd was just trying to be nice to the guy, making conversation, trying to pass the time and he was being a real dickhead. "Ever hunt whitetail?"

Lou Starr said, "Uh-huh."

He wasn't giving him much. "You prefer a tree stand or a blind?"

"Who the fuck cares?"

"Ever got yourself a trophy buck?" Lloyd said. "One that made book? I'm not talking about seeing it while you're up on a limb. I'm talking about nailing it, bringing it home."

Lou Starr looked across the living room to the bedroom, glanced at his watch. "That's it," he said, standing now.

Lloyd aimed the .45 at him. "Don't be a dumbass. Sit down."

He dropped back on the couch, covered his face in his hands. He had a huge diamond ring set in gold on his little finger. Lloyd hadn't noticed it before, too busy looking at other stuff. "I like your ring," Lloyd said. "Always wanted one of those."

"I got an idea," Lou Starr said grinning. "When you get out of prison, get yourself a job and start saving up."

Bobby stared at a hanger-rack-ful of Lou's guayabera shirts: white and blue and yellow, reminding him of the shirts barbers wore, same style with the open collar and little vents on the tails. But these had a decorative quality to them and he imagined a roomful of short compact Latin men in the same kind of shirts, dancing and drinking wine.

Bobby turned and looked at her. "What nationality is he?"

"Take a guess," Karen said.

"Something Mediterranean," he said. "Italian or Sardinian."

"I'll give you a hint," Karen said. "Lou's real name is Starvos Loutra."

She was sitting in a chair now, chiseled legs visible, sticking out of the bottom of the robe.

"He doesn't have a brother named Spartacus, does he?" He smiled thinking he was funny and she smiled back telling him she did too. "Beware of Greeks bearing gifts," Bobby said, "and don't bend over and pick up the soap. That exhausts my knowledge of Greek heritage."

"I'm impressed," Karen said. "I can see you're a real scholar."

Bobby said, "Where's the money at?"

"What're you talking about?" Karen said.

"The $9,600 Lou won at the casino."

Karen said, "It's locked in the safe at one of his restaurants."

"I'm not walking out of here empty-handed," Bobby said.

"Do you want to make some real money?" Karen said. "Two hundred fifty thousand, maybe more."

"What do you think I just fell off the back of a turnip truck?

Do I look that dumb?" She stared at him and he wondered what she was thinking. "Where's it at?"

"In a house in West Bloomfield," Karen said.

"Whose house?"

"We can get into all that," Karen said. "Does this sound like something you might be interested in?"

A quarter mill and a shot at her, hell yes he was interested. But he didn't trust her. How could he? You didn't break into someone's house in the middle of the night and expect to get propositioned. He fixed his gaze on her and said, "Are you scamming me?"

"No," Karen said. "I've been waiting for you."

Two

The guy from the dressing room, who looked like he belonged to a fraternity, tied them back to back on the bed, grinning and winking at her while he did it, like they were buds. Lou started twisting and turning as soon as he left the room, trying to untie the ropes that bound them at the ankles, wrists and shoulders. He was pulling at the knots and the rope cutting into her. "Lou," Karen said, "take it easy, will you? You're hurting me."

"What do you want me to do, lay here till Carol and Betty come to clean?"

"Let me help you," Karen said. "If we work together, it'll be easier."

"How do you know?" Lou said. "Are you into bondage now like your freak sister?"

"Lou, don't take this out on me, okay?" Karen said. "It isn't my fault."

"How'd they know I won money?"

"Maybe they saw you cashing out." Like it was a big mystery. Karen pressed the tip of a fingernail into the knot at her wrist, trying to loosen it.

"I didn't see anyone watching me," Lou said.

So if he didn't see anyone then no one could've seen him. He was in his Lou mood now. And when he was like this, you couldn't talk to him.

"I'm going to get those assholes," Lou said. "The ring's irreplaceable."

"It's insured, isn't it?" Karen thought it was a blessing in disguise. It might've been the ugliest ring she'd ever seen in her life.

"You're not listening," Lou said. "It's custom, one of a kind."

She thought it was odd that he didn't ask her what happened in the dressing room. Did the guy molest her or try to hurt her? All Lou cared about was the ring. He cared about it more than her, obviously. She slid a fingernail in the knot and felt it move. She slid the short end of the rope through the knot and freed their hands.

Lou said, "How'd you do that?"

"I've got nails."

Karen undid the rope around their shoulders and sat up and untied their feet. Lou got up and looked at her.

"I'm calling the police."

"It's three-thirty in the morning. Do you really think they're going to get your ring back tonight?" He gave her a dirty look and she got in bed and turned her back to him.

Karen woke up thinking about the scene in the dressing room. She pictured the expression on Fratboy's face. She could see he wanted to believe her, but he wasn't sure. He'd need time to get comfortable with the idea. He sure didn't look like the kind of guy who'd break into somebody's house in the middle of the night, wearing his J. Crew outfit: green button-down-collar shirt and khakis.

They agreed to meet the next morning in Eastern Market. Karen didn't think it made sense. Why drive all the way to downtown

Detroit? She'd suggested 220 Merrill in Birmingham, sit at the bar have a couple of drinks, see if there was interest from both parties. But Fratboy didn't like it. She could have the cops there, he said. Karen wanted to tell him she could have the cops at Eastern Market too, but the cops weren't part of the plan.

Karen took I-75 south to the Mack exit and saw the skyline of Detroit spread out in the distance. She took a left over the freeway and a right on Russell, and drove slowly through the bustling, congested streets of the market. Hi-Los were zigzagging, vendors were stocking their stalls: icing down fish, hanging sides of meat, filling bins with fruit and vegetables and flowers. Karen steered around trucks that were double-parked on Market Street, dodging workers that suddenly appeared in front of her, looking for R. Hirt, the wine and cheese place. She saw it at the end of the street, a red-brick building built in the twenties.

Karen wondered if he'd still be there. She was late because there was an accident, traffic had stopped in the four southbound lanes for twenty minutes, while a wrecker towed a jackknifed semi off the road. She parked in the R. Hirt lot, and got out of the Audi and looked around, but didn't see the fratboy or his sidekick, who reminded her of a Russian that played for the Red Wings. He was a stocky guy with frizzy blond hair and a goatee. She took a cigarette out of her purse, and lit it and smoked, watching the action at the market, crowded now at eleven in the morning.

Karen finished the cigarette and dropped it on the asphalt and stepped on it. She looked at her watch, it was 11:05. She'd give it a few more minutes and if he didn't show, she'd assume he wasn't interested. She watched a vendor pull a huge iced-down snapper out of a plastic tub, and fillet it on a wooden cutting board for a customer. She watched a butcher French and chine racks of lamb. She checked her watch and took a final look around the parking lot and opened her car door and got in. Her phone was ringing.

She reached for her purse, grabbed the phone and pressed it to her ear.

"Hey," Fratboy said, "where're you going?"

They went to a place called the Boar's Head, a small dark bar in the market area, and sat in the back, Karen across the table from Fratboy and Goatee, the only people in the place who weren't wearing long white coats with bloodstains on them. Four meat cutters at a table next to them were staring at Karen like she was a side of Angus prime.

Fratboy noticed them and turned in his chair. He got their attention and said, "Something we can do for you?"

The butchers all glanced over, but none of them said anything.

He said, "Then quit staring at us like a bunch of fucking morons."

Fratboy didn't look tough at all but he delivered the line with such confidence it sounded like he could take them all on. They met his gaze and looked away. Karen lit a cigarette, inhaled, and turned her head and blew out the smoke and said, "You're making this way more difficult than it has to be."

"That's the way Bobby is," Goatee said.

"We don't need to know anyone's name, all right," Fratboy said.

"You know mine," Karen said. She picked up her beer bottle and took a drink. "Maybe I should make up names for you if you want to be so secretive. You could be Chip," she said pointing at Bobby, and "You're Billy Bob," she said to Goatee.

"Billy Bob? That's a southern hick name," Goatee said.

Karen said, "What I'm trying to say is, if we don't trust each other, we might as well get up right now and go about our business."

Goatee said, "You're right. I'm Lloyd, Lloyd Diehl."

Karen noticed Lou's ring on his second finger, too big for his pinky. He kept looking at it, reminding her of a girl who'd just gotten engaged, looking at it and grinning.

"And *his* name's Robert Gal," he said pointing his beer bottle at the fratboy, "but goes by Bobby."

"That better?" Karen said. "Now that we've been properly introduced—"

Bobby cut her off. "Anything else you want to tell her?" he said to Lloyd.

"Bobby's really Canadian," Lloyd said, "but doesn't want anyone to know it. He's from Guelph, Ontario. Know where that's at?"

"I don't hear a Canadian accent," Karen said. "You know, aboot or eh?"

"He lost it," Lloyd said. "Sounds American, doesn't he?"

Karen said, "Is that your real name—Gal?"

"No, I made it up," Bobby said.

Lloyd said, "Yeah, it's his real name."

"What nationality are you?" Karen said.

"Hungarian," Bobby said, "I can run home, get my family tree if you're interested."

She couldn't have found two more perfect guys. Karen took out another cigarette and held it between her teeth until she lit it, and blew smoke across the table at Bobby. He fanned the cloud with his hand.

"If we're through talking about my family history," Bobby said, "maybe we could get down to business, discuss how we're going to steal the $250,000. Where'd you say it's at?"

Karen said, "In a house in West Bloomfield."

"Whose house we talking about?" Bobby said.

"A guy I know," Karen said.

Lloyd took a drink of beer and said, "What's he do, sell dope, guns?"

"He's a businessman," Karen said.

"What's your connection?" Bobby said.

Karen said, "I used to go out with him."

"Love is a many splendored thing," Bobby said. "What happened?"

"I gave him money to invest," Karen said. "We broke up and he kept it." That was basically what had happened although there was a little more to it. "Help me get my money back and you can split the rest."

Lloyd said, "How much are we talking?"

"At least $250,000," Karen said. "Probably more like half a million." She told them about the guy, a wealthy Chaldean who owned high-end gourmet markets, party stores and Coney Island hot dog places around Detroit. He also ran a bookmaking operation and had a dozen people on the payroll.

Bobby finished his beer and raised his arm, signaling the bartender for another one.

"He keeps all the money from his gambling operation in a safe in his house," Karen said. "You open two cabinet doors and there it is."

"I don't know," Bobby said. "Arabs are nuts, man. They hunt you down with some Old Testament code and say Allah's telling them to do it."

Karen wanted to tell him Allah and the Old Testament had nothing to do with each other. But she had a better way to ease his mind. "You don't have to worry about Allah. Chaldeans are Catholic Arabs."

Bobby said, "Does he have a wife and kids?"

She took a drag and blew out the smoke and said, "He's divorced and his kids are grown up and gone."

Lloyd said, "How many guys in the house with him?"

"Three, at least," Karen said, "sometimes more, and, they're armed." She took a sip of beer. "But we're not going to shoot any-body. We're going to go in and get the safe and get out. Nobody gets hurt." Then Karen told them she had a partner. (She didn't yet, but had someone in mind.) They needed four people to do the job. "A driver and three of us to go in the house."

Bobby said, "You're full of surprises, aren't you? Anything else you want to share with us?"

Karen said, "Sure, there are a few more details, I'll tell you about them as we get closer."

"You didn't say anything about splitting it four ways," Bobby said.

"I told you, you'd make some serious money—and you will, if we can all take it easy and agree on a plan."

Lloyd said, "Who's your partner?"

"You'll meet him soon enough," Karen said. "I'll call you in a few days."

"Can we trust you?" Bobby said.

Karen liked that—the two burglars worried about trust. She said, "Yeah, but can I trust you?"

Three

O'Clair read the number on a piece of paper. This was the address Johnny had given him, 612 Rosewood. He'd called him an hour earlier and asked if O'Clair would pick him up. O'Clair had said, "Where are you?"

"At a friend's," Johnny said.

That was code for: I met a girl and shacked up with her. O'Clair was going that way anyway so he said okay. He parked his Caddy on the street, leaned back against the seat, looking at the small single-story white house. Now the front door opened and Johnny Karmo appeared, buttoning his shirt. Johnny stopped like he was talking to someone, then moved back in the house, kissing a girl with long blond hair. He pulled himself away from her and started down the cement walk that led to the street. The girl went after him again, and he kissed her one final time.

Johnny got in the car and said, "I knew when I walked in the bar and saw her I'd take her home. I got this vibe."

O'Clair said, "You got this vibe, huh?"

Johnny gave him a look. "You want to tell it, or let me do it?"

O'Clair said, "I'm on the edge of my seat."

"I held her hand," Johnny said, "traced a line down her palm, like I could see her whole life in that line, and I said, 'You've been hurt, haven't you, baby? By a man.' Who the hell else was she going to be hurt by?"

"She could've been a lesbian," O'Clair said.

Johnny wasn't listening.

"Then I looked into her eyes and she said, 'How'd you know?' Christ they believe anything you tell them."

O'Clair noticed Johnny was losing his hair, going bald on top, dark hair combed over from the side trying to hide it, and dark spots under his eyes, as he sat back in the seat and let out a breath, Johnny, the palm-reading gigolo, looking old.

"She wore me out," Johnny said. "Twenty-two wanted to go all night."

O'Clair put it in gear and the Seville moved away from the curb, accelerating past parked cars. He saw Johnny take a gold wedding band out of his pants pocket and slip it on a nail-polished finger. Then he took a cell phone out of his shirt pocket, dialed and listened.

"Rosita, Johnny, do me a flavor . . . send a dozen to Darlene at Nino's Salon in Troy." He listened. "I don't know her last name." He paused. "Wait a second . . ." He glanced out the window. "Okay, ready? 'If I can't be with you these should.' You got it?" He paused again. "Okay." He turned off the cell phone, put it back in his shirt pocket and glanced at O'Clair. "I also use: 'When you look at them, think of me.'"

O'Clair thought Johnny the Chaldean romantic should be writing greeting cards with those corny lines. "If you spent as much time working as you do fucking around you'd be rich." O'Clair shook his head. "Where's your car at?"

"A parking lot in Auburn Hills," Johnny said.

"What were you doing way out there?"

Johnny said, "I've got to go places where people don't know me."

"That's right, you're married," O'Clair said. "I forget. What do you tell Ann-Marie when you don't come home at night?"

"I'm working," Johnny said. "She's used to it."

"I've got to make a stop first," O'Clair said.

Johnny looked at his watch. "I've got an appointment at nine."

"You're not going to make it," O'Clair said.

T. J. Dolliver stared at himself in the mirror, eyes puffy and blood-shot. He got maybe three hours sleep, his mind was racing and wouldn't stop. He didn't have the money and didn't know where he was going to get it. He looked at his watch. It was ten to eight. His wife, Renee, thank the Lord, was up north at her parents' summer home for a month.

T.J. lathered his face with shaving cream, turned on the water, just the hot, and picked up his razor. He heard a voice and looked out the bathroom window. His ditzy neighbor was walking her dog. The window was open and he could hear her through the screen. T.J. put the razor under his sideburn and moved it down his jaw feeling the tug of his beard, clearing a smooth path of skin. He moved the razor around his chin and cut himself and blood appeared, mixing with the shaving cream. He heard a car and glanced out the window as it passed by—an old Cadillac. Take it easy, he told himself, quit worrying.

He finished shaving and splashed water on his face and grabbed a towel. He dabbed the cuts—three of them—with little pieces of Kleenex. He looked out the window and thought he saw some-one on the front porch and he moved through the living room and stood at the front door, glancing out one of the narrow vertical windows that flanked it. The doorbell rang and rang again. The sound startled T.J. and he took off, moving through the house to the back door. He fumbled with the lock, swung the door open and stepped out on the deck. Something hit him in the chest and he was down on his back, gasping for breath, squinting up at the morning sun.

O'Clair stood over him. "T.J., where're you going?"

"Watering the plants," he said, getting his wind back.

"You're a little late," O'Clair said, scanning the deck, seeing wilted flowers and weeds in the planter boxes.

T.J. was wearing a black V-neck tee shirt, black pants and strange-looking black tie shoes with thick rubber soles that reminded O'Clair of the shoes nuns wore. He knew T.J. was married and was some kind of advertising executive. He made TV commercials and had twenty people working for him. Put on a black outfit, pretend like you knew what you were doing. O'Clair was in the wrong business.

He was a young guy too, didn't look older than thirty. Borrowed money, lost it gambling, borrowed more and that's where O'Clair entered the picture. He'd stopped by T.J.'s office to collect the original loan plus the juice. First, a snippy receptionist kept him waiting for twenty minutes and then T.J. appeared and started bullshitting him, talking to O'Clair the way he probably talked to his clients, calling him "my friend."

"Give me the fifteen grand I'll be on my way," O'Clair had said to T.J. when they were in his huge corner office that looked out over Troy. O'Clair liked the view. He could see subdivisions and the Somerset shopping mall and I-75 in the distance.

"Ever done any acting? You've got a great look, my friend." T.J.'s cell phone rang and he said, "It's New York, I have to take this."

New York calling him, he must've been important, or thought he

was. While T.J. talked, O'Clair looked around. There were stacks
of black boards with scenes on them, commercials, he assumed, and
a giant TV with a couch and two chairs, and a desk covered with
stacks of papers. On the other side of the room, O'Clair looked out
and saw the Silverdome where the Lions used to play. Nice office.
T.J. ended his conversation, put the phone down.

"Like commercials, my friend?" T.J. said moving toward the
TV. "Want to see our new campaign for the world's thinnest con-
dom? We're calling it Freedom, like screwing with nothing on."

"Listen to me," O'Clair said, "I'm not here to look at commercials, understand what I'm saying?"

T.J. paused and gave him a big grin. "The good news is I have
it. Bad news, I don't have it here. Can I get it to you later? Meet
you somewhere? Name the place."

O'Clair did, Joe Kool's on Sixteen Mile, and T.J. said, "No problem, my friend, I know where it is, I owe you one."

T.J. looked nervous now stretched out on a La-Z-Boy recliner in
his family room. O'Clair stood behind him holding the back of
the chair. Johnny was standing next to the chair, gripping a silver
aluminum bat that O'Clair had taken out of his trunk. Johnny
choked up high, holding the bat like he was ready to swing for the
fences. The bat was for show. O'Clair wasn't going to hurt T.J.,
'cause if he hurt him, T.J. wouldn't be able to work and repay his
debt. "He told me the good news was he had it," O'Clair said to
Johnny. "Agreed to meet me and never showed. Isn't that what
you said?"

"If you touch me," T.J. said, "I'm calling the cops."

"They can't help you." O'Clair was tired of T.J. jerking him
around. He picked up the remote off a table next to the La-Z-Boy,
pressed the power button and watched the big Mitsubishi pop on
transforming from wavy gray lines to crisp color. Jerry Springer

appeared in close-up, asking three seedy-looking guys with mullet haircuts why they had an affair with their mother-in-law.

"With their mother-in-laws," O'Clair said. "Where do they find these wackos?" He turned up the volume and looked at T. J. Dolliver. "Listen to me, my friend. I want you to put the money, $17,500, in my hand by five o'clock today. I don't care what you've got to do to get it. Take out a second mortgage, sell your car, sell your wife if you have to. Hear what I'm saying, my friend?"

T.J. said, "I only owe you fifteen."

"I'm charging you a late fee."

T.J. nodded, looking sad, eyes wet, face splotched with blood from the razor cuts. O'Clair believed he'd finally gotten through to him. He didn't tell T.J. what was going to happen if he didn't come up with the money. T.J. was the creative ad guy—let his imagination run wild.

O'Clair took Johnny to his car and went to Samir's. On the wall behind the table was a huge black and white photograph of Beirut shot from the Mediterranean side. O'Clair told Samir that he'd given T. J. Dolliver a little more time to come up with the money. Samir listened with a mouthful of burgul and mjadara, his snow white walrus mustache moving up and down as he chewed. Across from Samir was Ricky Yono, Samir's nephew in a black nylon warm-up with red and white stripes running down the arms and legs, and a pile of gold chains around his neck that reminded O'Clair of the black dude with the Mohawk.

Ricky didn't acknowledge O'Clair. He kept shoveling kibbee neyee into his mouth, practically inhaling it. Moozie was next to Ricky, flashing his silver front tooth while he ate. Moozie's real name was Mehassen. He was also a nephew of Samir's. He'd come from a village outside Beirut. Samir was trying to figure out what to do with him and had assigned him to Ricky for a couple weeks.

As Samir had said, Moozie didn't know shit about their business, but spoke English. That was a start. And he was a good kid and such, not a smartass like a lot of them his age.

"Hungry?" Samir pointed to the platter of burgul and mjadara with his fork. "Sit down, eat something."

"I'm good," O'Clair said.

"Ricky's going to take Moozie around tomorrow, teach him the business."

O'Clair said, "Who's going to teach Ricky?"

Samir laughed.

Ricky glared at him.

Moozie smiled showing his silver tooth and a mouthful of hummus and tahini.

Samir said, "What about this guy, Gall? Have you found out anything?"

His name was Bobby Gal, a car salesman who'd borrowed money and disappeared.

The Sales Manager at Tad Collins Buick-Lexus said he hadn't seen Bobby for a couple weeks and if O'Clair found him to tell him he was fired. One of the sales consultants, that's what they were called now, told O'Clair Bobby hung out at the Millionaires Club on Eight Mile and also the casinos.

"I'm working on it," O'Clair said answering Samir's question.

"Work harder," Ricky said, "mutt's six weeks late."

Ricky had it wrong as usual, but O'Clair didn't say anything. Ricky had bought a used Lexus from the guy and ended up loaning him twenty grand. Ricky let him slide the first time the vig was due. Now Bobby owed sixty grand and Samir had given the collection to O'Clair.

Samir said, "Anybody seen Johnny?"

O'Clair said, "He had an appointment."

"What does that mean?" Samir said.

"He's probably out hustling some babe," Ricky said.

O'Clair took a wad of bills out of his sport coat pocket and put it on the table next to Samir's plate. "Everybody but T.J."

"You're short," Samir said. "Ricky's short. What's going on?"

"I said I'd have it tomorrow," Ricky said on the defensive.

O'Clair had heard that Ricky was using his collections to gamble and he was in trouble. Samir picked up the money and moved across the room to a cabinet, a built-in, made out of pine with double doors. He opened the doors and there was a black floor safe with gold leaf and Samir's family name in Arabic on the front, Abou Al Fakir. The safe had been in Samir's family since the late 1800s, purchased at the Mosler factory in Hamilton, Ohio, by his grandfather. Samir went down on one knee to work the combination.

O'Clair turned to Ricky. "Hey, Rick, that's a nice outfit, you going to walk around a mall."

"Fuck you," Ricky said spitting bits of kibbee neyee out of his mouth.

He and Ricky had been bumping heads since O'Clair started working for Samir, and things had gone downhill from there.

Ricky didn't have the eight grand he was supposed to collect. He lost it to a sportsbook, an eight-team parlay, got every one wrong. What were the odds of that happening? He was broke and he owed Samir $8,000. That was bad, but what was worse, he'd borrowed $12,000 from CashFast, a payday loan place on Grand River near Eight Mile Road six weeks earlier. He'd done the same thing, used collection money to gamble, and lost it all.

Ricky had gone to Dearborn High with the owner of the place, a cocky asshole named Wadi Nasser. Wadi was about five five, wore Tommy Bahama shirts, smoked Montecristos and drove a Benz. Wadi said he didn't usually loan more than a couple grand at a time, but for Ricky he'd make an exception. Ricky had two weeks to pay back the principal and a $1,800 service charge. Was that okay? No, it wasn't okay, it was fucking robbery, but what choice did he have?

Two weeks later Ricky was in even worse shape and told Wadi to roll the loan over. Sure, no problem Wadi said. He seemed to get a kick out of Ricky having money problems. Now Ricky owed $13,800, with an interest charge of $2,070, and a total debt of $15,870. Ricky felt stupid, dumber than the people he collected from. He was paying Wadi more in interest than Samir charged his clients.

Ricky rolled the loan over two more times, and a month later he owed $35,707.50. Wadi grinned when Ricky stopped by the CashFast office and called him his best customer. Ricky missed the next payment and the next one. He was coming out of the Original Pancake House in Southfield after breakfast one morning, and noticed two Arabs getting out of an Escalade with twenty-four-inch rims. They were coming toward him. One was tall, six two maybe, with a bad complexion and a blank expression. The second guy was shorter and stockier. He had dark serious eyes and a sculpted beard that must've taken a long time to keep so neat and trim—skinny lines of hair that started at his temples and swept down curving along his jaw, meeting his mustache and goatee. He wore his sunglasses on his head, black hair, razor-cut like the beard. His shirt had a zipper that was open at the top, showing chest hair and gold chains.

"Mr. Nasser is concern about you," Beard said. He had a heavy accent. "He does not see you in a long time, want to know, are you okay?"

"Tell him he's got nothing to worry about," Ricky said. "Everything's fine. Wadi and I went to school together. We're old buds."

Beard said, "You know how much you owe?"

Sure, Ricky knew. $35,707.50.

"You know how much is going to be on Thursday of the next week?"

Beard's dark eyes stared into him, never looking away for even a second.

Ricky couldn't figure out what 15 percent of $35,707.50 was, but knew it was a lot. "You're Wadi's collection agency, huh?"

"Forty-one thousand sixty-three dollars and sixty-two cents," Beard said. "Roll it again and it will be—"

"I know," Ricky said, cutting him off. "I get it. You don't have to keep reminding me, okay?" Now they were pissing him off.

"You have collateral?" Beard said.

"You have collateral?" Ricky said, trying to sound like him, imitate his heavy Middle East accent.

Beard grinned now. "You give us something of value. We give to Mr. Nasser until you pay debt."

Ricky said, "Like what?"

"This is your automobile?" he said, looking at Ricky's Lexus.

"You're not taking my fucking car," Ricky said. He put his hands on his hips, flexed his biceps that were sticking out of a black Gold's Gym tank top. They wanted to get tough he'd give them all they could handle.

"Listen to me," Beard said. "It's not finish until you pay. You have to give Mr. Nasser something."

Mr. Nasser. Jesus. If he called Wadi Mr. Nasser again, Ricky was going to deck him. Wadi, the midget Chaldean rich kid. Ricky would always think of him as the loser from high school who didn't have a friend. Ricky considered his situation, heard what the Arab was telling him and took his watch off and handed it to Beard. "It's an 18 karat gold Rolex President worth fifteen grand." He loved it. Hated to give it up but he had to give him something. "Tell Wadi to hang on to it. I want it back." That's how he got out of that one, but now another payment was due and he didn't have the money.

Four

Karen had met Samir on the way to the ladies' room at the Blue Martini in Birmingham.

He said, "I'm Samir." He took her hand and kissed it. "Where do you want to have dinner?"

Karen said, "I'm with someone."

"Now you're with *me*." He said it like a guy used to getting what he wanted.

She liked his confidence, thinking he could stop someone, a stranger, and ask her out. She found him attractive, but she was also curious. Who was he? Karen went back to the table and told her date, a stockbroker named Jon Uffelman, that she was leaving. She'd heard enough about economic indicators, the devaluation of the dollar and the risk of deflation. Uffelman was talking to her like he was giving a seminar. It was their first and last date.

He said, "What're you . . . kidding? We just got here."

She stood up and said, "It wasn't going to work anyway," and walked across the room past the scene makers, up the stairs to the foyer. Samir was standing by the door ready to open it for her, Omar Sharif from *Doctor Zhivago*, dark hair going gray and a silver mustache.

A car was waiting, a white Mercedes, and a man in a suit was standing at the rear door holding it open. Karen got in and Samir got in next to her, close but he didn't crowd her. They had dinner at the Lark. Karen asked him how he could walk in and get a table at a restaurant that was booked for months in advance.

Samir said, "There must've been a cancellation."

He owned the big Mercedes and had a chauffeur, but he was cool. He made fun of himself. He was in the grocery business. He sold fruit and vegetables and owned a few stores around town, and then it hit her: he was the guy that owned a chain of gourmet markets called Samir's. Karen said, "You're that Samir?"

He said, "I'm a greengrocer, like my father."

That's what Karen liked about him. He was a down-to-earth rich guy with no ego. She liked his accent too, and his deep voice that sounded gentle.

He said, "What about you?"

He was staring at her tan legs, crossed and sticking out of a black miniskirt. "I model," Karen said.

"You mean fashion?"

"Sportswear and swimwear, and I do TV commercials."

"Where would I see you?" Samir said.

"I just did a Chevy spot," Karen said. "I'm driving a red Corvette convertible on the Pacific Coast Highway north of Malibu."

"That was you?"

"And a few weeks ago I did a swimwear spread for Lands End," Karen said. "Do you get the catalogue?"

"You think that's the way I dress?" He said it serious, but smiled.

She touched the sleeve of his sport coat. It was custom-made. She could tell by the buttonholes, they were real. One was unbuttoned, the way it was done. "You dress well for a guy who sells fruit and vegetables."

He smiled again.

"How did you get into modeling?"

Karen told him it was a long story that started the night her father was killed. "He was a manufacturer's rep. He sold injection-molded parts, door trim panels and center console assemblies to Chrysler and GM. How do you decide that's what you want to do with your life?"

"It's luck or timing or maybe bad luck," Samir said. "You do what your father did. Or you get a job, get married and get stuck in something. I sell fruit and vegetables. You think I planned it?"

"My dad was driving home after having dinner with a Chrysler purchasing guy," Karen said, "and was hit head-on by a drunk driver, killed instantly at forty-four. I remember him in the kitchen, tying his tie, getting ready, excited because he was sure he was getting a contract for the new X platform cars. With the commission we'd be able to move to a bigger house." She paused and sipped her wine that tasted like butterscotch. Samir's eyes were on her as if he couldn't look anywhere else. "It's strange because when I think about that night, I think of the movie *Grease*. I was watching it with my mom and sister, Virginia."

Samir said, "Travolta was skinny then with a pompadour."

"He reminded me of my dad, who was still a greaser from high school—slicked-back hair and a black leather jacket. He could've been an extra. Travolta was singing a duet with Olivia Newton-John when the Garden City police came to the door. I remember my mother was hysterical while they were belting out 'You're the One That I Want.'"

Samir met her gaze and reached for her hand.

"I'm not a big fan of musicals," Karen said.

"Me either."

She didn't tell him about the funeral home, her dad's life told in photographs displayed around the visitation room. Shots of a skinny teenager in a bathing suit, someone squirting water from a hose outside the frame. Her dad in a white tux on his wedding day, smiling, holding a drink, his bow tie hanging from one side of his collar. Her dad posing with his bowling buddies—four dudes decked out in their red King Louie shirts with black trim. In another one, her dad was holding up a center console assembly.

Karen had been a senior at Garden City High at the time. She'd planned to go to Michigan State and major in advertising. It looked like a fun business. She liked TV commercials, the funny offbeat beer spots like the Bud Light spot where the only word of dialogue is "dude." She had $1,700 in the bank, money earned working part-time at Meijer's Thrifty Acres in the toy department, wearing a red vest, making $7.25 an hour.

After her dad died Karen knew she'd have to postpone college for a while and get a job and help support her mom and sister, Virginia. But doing what? Friends had always told her she should model. She had a unique look and a great figure. Karen would stare at herself in the mirror, thinking she didn't look bad. Five seven, a hundred and fifteen, and she was in shape. She was a former twirler and started on the volleyball team.

Rumor had it that a girl in her English class, a tall quiet brunette named Stephanie, was modeling and making a lot of money. Maybe it was true. She was five ten and good-looking, and she drove a BMW. Stephanie, as it turned out, was surprisingly nice and helpful. She knew a photographer who agreed to take some shots of Karen for her comp sheet, and helped arrange interviews at talent agencies around town, and two weeks after graduation Karen was posing for Hudson's fall catalogue.

Samir fixed his kind dark eyes on her, sitting close, a table against the French doors, and touched her arm. They'd been together for maybe an hour and she was relaxed, comfortable with him, like they were old friends.

Over dinner—four courses—Samir told her he'd been married

for twenty-three years, divorced for five, the marriage arranged
by his father and a friend of his in the village where they lived
outside Beirut. He didn't even know the girl, who was only sixteen at the time, and he, twenty.

Karen said, "How can you marry someone you don't know?"

"It was custom, tradition," Samir said. "You didn't have a
choice."

"Was she good-looking?"

Samir took a sip of wine, holding it in his mouth as if he was
trying to decide.

"Very," Samir said. "I couldn't believe my good fortune. But
she didn't speak English and my Arabic was not so good."

"Maybe that was a bonus," Karen said.

Samir smiled at her and said, "She didn't know how to cook,
either, and that wasn't a bonus. I said to her one day, what do you
know how to do?"

"What did she say?"

"She looked at me and said, 'I know how to shop.'" He finished his wine, picked up the bottle, poured some in her glass first
and then his own.

"Girls are the same everywhere, huh?" Karen said.

Samir said, "Exactly what I thought."

"So what happened?"

"It didn't work," Samir said. "We had nothing in common."

"Twenty-three years," Karen said, "and you had nothing in common?"

"You go along and suddenly ten years pass by, and one day I
thought, I can't do this anymore."

"Do you have kids?" Karen said.

"Two. Both grown."

Karen said, "Where's your wife live?"

"Ex," Samir said and grinned. "She bought a condo in Naples."

Karen said, "Italy?"

"Florida," Samir said.

Karen said, "Do you ever see her?"

"No reason to," Samir said.

The waiter appeared with plates, rack of lamb Genghis Khan, and served them. Samir picked up his knife and fork, cut a piece of pink lamb and put it in his mouth. "You're not going to believe it."

Karen picked up a lamb chop and bit into it. He was right; it was delicious.

After dinner they went back to Birmingham and had a drink in the Rugby Grill at the Townsend Hotel. Samir said, why don't we get a room? Karen said she liked him but it was way too fast for her.

They started going out, seeing each other a few days a week, and then every day. There was a trip to Napa, and another one to France: Paris, Bordeaux and Burgundy—tasting the latest releases from the top vineyards. It was a new experience—traveling by private jet and chauffeured limo.

After that Karen moved into Samir's West Bloomfield compound. He asked her to quit modeling and be available. He took care of her and showered her with gifts. They talked about getting married. He was fifty-two and she was thirty-six. That was close enough, and they had a lot in common. He asked her to call him Smoothie, the affectionate name all his close friends used, but Karen couldn't do it.

She had three hundred grand in a mutual fund that wasn't doing well—money she'd saved working as a model for eighteen years and asked Samir what she should do. He offered to invest it for her. Thought he could double it in three years. She said, are you kidding? Karen sold the fund and gave Samir a check for $299,560, her life savings. How could she miss with him handling her money?

Six months later their relationship started to unravel. Samir wasn't the kind, patient listener he first appeared to be. He was surly and chauvinistic and wanted to know where she was every minute. He'd call her ten times a day to check up on her. The other problem was living in the house with Samir's people—all his hangers-on. She couldn't do it anymore and told him she was leaving and she wanted her money back.

He said, "I leave you, you don't leave me."

She said, "Watch me." He hit her in the face with his fist and she went down on the marble floor of the foyer.

He said, "Get out."

That's what she did. Got up and walked out the front door and got in her car. She looked at her face in the rearview mirror. Her left cheek was bruised and beginning to swell but she felt relieved. She'd known for at least a month that it wasn't going to work, but was too nervous, too afraid to make her move. Now she'd never have to go back there and pretend again.

She'd kept her condo, a rental in Birmingham, the one smart thing she'd done, figuring if things didn't work out she'd need a place to go, and went back there now. She'd left most of her clothes at Samir's. That didn't bother her, but what did was getting her money back. She had no proof she'd given it to him. No forms or receipts or anything. Not even a canceled check with his name on it. At the time, he said, what do you need a receipt for? You think I'm going to steal your money? She'd made the check out to cash like he suggested, which, in retrospect, was pretty dumb. She tried calling Samir, but never got him on the line. She wrote him a letter but never heard from him. Why not give her money back? He was rich. It wasn't going to change his life. But she'd insulted him and he was an old-fashioned guy, and you didn't do that.

She talked to Robert Schreiner, an attorney who lived down the street. Based on his knowledge of contracts—and he was no expert in the field—she was up to her ass in alligators and somebody had drained the swamp. But he agreed to give it a try, and Karen didn't have to pay him unless he got results, and if he did, Schreiner's fee was 20 percent.

"That's fifty grand," Karen said.

Schreiner said, "The standard fee is a third."

She studied him. He was wearing a tee shirt that said *Make Love Not Law Review* in bold type. She stared into his puffy eyes. He didn't give her much of a feeling of confidence. He needed a shower and some clean clothes for starters.

Schreiner said, "How much you got now?"

"What?" Karen said.

"You don't want to cut me in for 20 percent, but how much do you have now? Nothing."

He had a point.

"Come in have a toke," Schreiner said. "We'll discuss your legal travails."

What did she have to lose?

First Schreiner sent a registered letter on his Robert P. Schreiner Attorney at Law stationery, telling Samir he had a week to give Karen Delaney back her $299,560 or he'd file a complaint with the Oakland County Circuit Court. The way Schreiner told it, he went to work a few days later and there were three dark-haired guys in his office who looked like they were beamed from the streets of Fallujah. They surrounded him as he walked in. The one who did the talking wore a track suit and had a lot of chains, and looked like he worked at a party store. He told Schreiner if he filed a lawsuit or ever contacted Mr. Fakir again, they'd come back and break his legs. This was the warning.

Schreiner asked them who they thought they were talking to? He was an officer of the court and if they threatened him he'd have them arrested for breaking and entering and intent to do great bodily harm.

That's when the guy in the track suit stepped in and hit him in the side and took the wind out of him. Schreiner said he bent over, trying to draw a breath. He told Karen the whole story when he stopped over the next day, moving like he was in pain, showing her white tape the doctor wrapped around his fractured ribs.

Karen said, "Did you call the police?"

Schreiner shook his head. "I'm going to file your lawsuit next week."

"If you do, it's going to be your last." She admired Schreiner's tenacity, but there was no way she could go through with it. "Next time they're not going to break something, they're going to put you out of business." She wasn't going to let Schreiner get hurt or killed over the money. She'd have to figure out another way to get it back.

He said, "Fuck them. They can't get away with this."

She said, "I agree with you, but it's not worth it."

They became friends after that. They had dinner occasionally and smoked weed and watched movies on Schreiner's plasma TV.

Then she met Lou.

Five

Megan had come up with the idea of robbing gamblers of their winnings one day when she was handing $9,600 in crisp, just-off-the-press $100 bills to a guy named Lou Starr.

He'd said something dumb like, "Be still my heart, I think I'm in love," staring at her chest. She heard a lot of bad lines so that was nothing special. Most guys took their shot and moved on, but he wouldn't give up, this guy who looked fifty-five—older than her father—wearing a toupee, she was sure of it.

"Everybody bet the Yankees," he said.

Megan said, "Except you. How'd you know?"

"I have a system."

"Well it obviously works," Megan said. "I have to tell you though, you're responsible for paying your own taxes."

"I'm going to run right home, fill out a 1099 and send it to my Uncle." He gave her a big grin. "I'm Lou. Want to come upstairs, see the Presidential Suite? It's got a hot tub. We could have some fun."

"I've seen it," Megan said, wondering if Lou thought he was irresistible or something. Like she was going to go up and bang this little ape on her break.

The next time she saw him he was with a redhead, who even Megan had to admit was a knockout, the redhead standing next to the little guy, towering over him in four-inch heels. Megan wanted to say, hey Mr. Starr, do you still want to take me up to your room have some fun?

Lou Starr had taken his money and walked away, but the idea of robbing the winners stayed in her head. And the more she thought about it the more sense it made. People won money playing black-jack and craps and roulette. People won money betting the sports-book. They won and came to Megan to cash out and she handed them stacks of bills. It was amazing what people told her too, of-fering things about themselves: what they did, where they worked, where they lived, like Lou, who had a house on Walnut Lake in Bloomfield Hills.

Anybody who won more than $1,200, the casino was supposed to deduct the taxes. Megan had a chart that showed her how much to take out, and the gambler had to fill out a form. Everybody ex-cept the regulars. If Megan knew the guest was a regular she could waive the tax form.

Guests like Lou Starr, once she got to know them, could take home the full amount they won and pay their own taxes. So what would they do with the money? Put it in the bank? No way. They'd hide it somewhere in their house. It was fun money. They were going to spend it.

She pitched the idea to Bobby, the guy she was seeing.

He said, "Sweetie, that's genius." Then he hugged her and looked into her eyes and said, "Megan, honey, you've got it all: beauty, brains and balls."

They would work out the logistics later and come up with a plan. They'd start with Lou Starr and see how it went.

• • •

Megan and Bobby found the Starr residence, a ranch house right on the water. It was fun. They felt like spies, parking and watching the place. Bobby had even thought to bring binoculars. They snuck through a wooded area and went down to the lake behind the house. They used the tall reeds for cover, crouching at the water's edge. A line of little ducks swam by following their mother. Megan said, "Oh, look at all the little duckies. Aren't they cute." She told Bobby her mother loved ducks and had a house full of duck things: decoys and paintings and little duck knicknacs.

Bobby said, "That's really great. Thanks for telling me. I forget are we here on a nature hike or are we casing a fucking house?"

Bobby had no patience and would get pissed off at little things, but she liked him. He was real funny too. She watched Lou Starr and the redhead from the casino she now knew was Karen, his fiancée, through the binoculars. They were sitting on the deck behind the house talking. They looked like they were having an argument. Karen got up and went in the house. Lou turned and looked at her and said something.

Bobby decided they'd go in the next night, Bobby and a guy named Lloyd, he met in a bar. Lloyd had done time in the Oakland County Jail. Megan thought he was weird and creepy-looking. Bobby said it wasn't a personality contest, okay? He liked Lloyd, said he was real, no pretensions, an old-fashioned American. Best of all, Bobby said Lloyd took direction well, did what Bobby wanted him to do.

Megan asked Bobby what Lloyd did time for and Bobby said, assault, beat a guy up for cutting him off in traffic. Lloyd followed him to his house in Birmingham and broke his jaw. Megan said she wanted to go with them. Bobby said no way, Lou Starr knew who she was. It was way too risky.

That was the last she'd heard from him. They were supposed to meet at Bobby's the next morning, split the money three ways and plan the next one. So, where the hell was he? She'd left six messages on Bobby's machine and hadn't heard back from him. He could've been in jail for all she knew.

Megan had met Bobby at the Post Bar downtown one Friday night. The place packed as usual. Bobby introduced himself and they started talking and found out they had some things in common. Bobby liked to play blackjack, his most fun thing in the whole world, and Megan was a cashier at a casino.

"How do you like that for karma?" Bobby said. "This is wild. I'll bet you've cashed my chips, and here we are together."

Megan thought he was overdoing it a little.

After a few drinks, Bobby said, "Ever fed a piranha?"

"Not in the last few hours," Megan said.

"Want to?"

"Do you really have one," Megan said, "or are you giving me a line?"

"I really have one," Bobby said.

Thirty minutes later they were in Bobby's apartment, standing next to his fish tank.

Megan said, "What do you feed him?"

"They're not too particular," Bobby said.

"That's Larry," Bobby said, handing her a cosmo in a martini glass. He had one too. "I named him after my former boss. He has razor-sharp teeth too, and devours his enemies."

Megan was staring into the tropical fish tank and Bobby was behind her, pressing himself against her, pointing at an ugly little fish with a red belly.

"The red piranha is a *Pygocentrus nattereri*."

He dropped a Ball Park hot dog into the tank. It looked like a torpedo sinking in the blue-tinted water, moving past a sunken model ship, an old-time one with cannons and masts and sails.

"They've got 18 percent more lips and snouts this year, hot dogs do," Megan said. "According to an article I read in the *Free Press.*"

"That's gross," Bobby said. He sipped his cosmo.

It didn't seem to affect Larry's appetite. He was attacking the hot dog now, and the water was cloudy with fragments of meat.

Megan said, "You ever put mustard on them?"

"I'll have to try that," Bobby said.

"Why do you only have one fish in this big tank?"

"I used to have a pumpkinseed and a southern redbelly dace, a rainbow darter, a neon tetra and a bunch of other beautiful fish. Larry, the voracious carnivore, ate them all."

Megan sipped her cosmo. It was strong, like it was all booze. "Are you trying to get me drunk?"

Bobby wasn't listening now. He said, "You have beautiful eyes," staring at her. "Anybody ever tell you that?" He brushed her cheek with his finger. He had a dreamy look on his face.

Megan put her drink on the coffee table and pulled her sweater up and lifted it over her head and said, "Where's the bedroom at? I'm not driving all the way back downtown."

Bobby decided not to say anything to Megan about Samir. She didn't have anything to do with that job, so there was no reason to cut her in. He was at the apartment pool, checking out the action, young professionals letting loose after work on a Friday evening. Bobby lay back in a lounge chair, taking in the scene, talking to a couple of girls. They were drinking vodka and lemonade, watching a muscular guy in a Speedo, posing as he got out of the pool, flexing and sucking in his gut, trying to make it look natural.

The tall skinny girl's name was Nicole something, Bobby wasn't

listening that carefully and what the hell difference did it make?
She worked in after-sales marketing at Chrysler she told him. The
one with the jugs, Kirsten, sold fur coats at a store in Bloomfield
Hills. She was going to move to South Beach, her big plan, and was
getting retail experience selling mink and sable coats. It seemed
an odd choice for someone going to Miami Beach. Bobby wanted
to say if the fur job doesn't work out, what're you going to do, try
snowmobiles? Bobby finished his drink and poured himself another
one out of an orange plastic pitcher.

The muscular guy came over and the girls offered him one. His
name was Todd Bendler, a systems analyst at GM. Bobby shook
hands with him. He had an iron grip and tried to crush Bobby's fingers. Todd had a deep voice and was very serious when he talked
about his job.

"My team's responsible for the M cars, Monte Carlo and Malibu."

Bobby said, "What exactly does a systems analyst do?"

"Analyze data," Todd said.

"Sounds interesting," Bobby said. He winked at Nicole then
closed his eyes and dropped his chin like he was falling asleep.

Nicole smiled and put her hand over her mouth trying to hide
it. Todd started talking about GM's Customer Satisfaction Index
and Bobby got up from his lounge chair and said he had to go.

Back in his apartment, five o'clock, Bobby made himself a cos-
mopolitan and checked his messages. Another one from Megan,
sounding pissed off.

"I know you're there, pick up the fucking phone. If I don't
hear from you—"

Bobby punched erase, rolled a joint and went in the bedroom
to get dressed. A few minutes later he danced into the living room
with the joint in his mouth, drink in hand, listening to *The Black
Parade* by My Chemical Romance. He heard a knock on the door,

thought it might be Nicole, danced over and opened it. Megan came at him, glaring and grabbed the collar of his black Lacoste golf shirt.

"I've left six messages."

Bobby said, "You're kidding. Must be something wrong with the machine."

"I think there's something wrong with you," Megan said.

"What kind of talk is that? You're my honey girl." Bobby tried to say it with feeling, but he sounded like a soap opera actor. He wasn't ready for this, hadn't prepared. He put his arms around Megan, still holding the glass and the joint. She pushed him away, spilling the drink, Jesus, on the beige carpeting.

"I did my job," Megan said, still in his face. "Now I want my money. It was my idea in the first place."

Bobby said, "I have it. What's the problem?" He decided to give her some of his own money rather than try to explain what happened. He was going to be rich soon anyway.

Megan followed Bobby into the kitchen. He opened the refrigerator, took out an opaque plastic pitcher and pried off the top. There was a white number ten envelope inside. "It's kind of cold," Bobby said. "But it'll warm up once you get to the mall."

Megan took the money out, a stack of bills, all hundreds, and started counting.

Bobby said, "Can I get you a drink? How about a nice cosmo? Fix you right up."

Megan finished counting the money and looked at Bobby. "You've got to be kidding. This is only $1,500. Where's the rest of it at?"

Bobby gave her a puzzled look.

"The man cashed out with $9,600," Megan said. "I know for a fact because I handed it to him."

"Trust me, I only found $4,500 in the house, and you got a

third like we agreed." He said it straight and serious, trying to hold back the grin that was forming on his mouth.

"Come on," Megan said. "That's bullshit and you know it."

She opened the refrigerator and started dropping things on the floor: a plastic half gallon of milk that slid into the base of the island counter; a carton of eggs that hit and exploded sending yolk and chunks of shell all over the floor and wall.

Bobby said, "What the hell're you doing?"

"Looking for my money. You owe me $1,700 more."

He said, "Lloyd's got it."

Megan said, "You expect me to believe a control freak like you is going to let Lloyd keep your share of anything? Come on?"

Bobby was surprised. He'd never seen Megan act like this. She'd seemed different than most of the girls he'd gone out with. Not moody or bitchy or a pain in the ass. The only thing he didn't like were the fucking cats, but she was fun and seemed to get things and liked to drink and she had great tits that Bobby referred to as her fun bags. Everything was good until now. And now all this rage was coming out like he'd hit a nerve, pressed some button that flipped her out, made her lose it. He hoped the thing with the Greek's woman worked out because this sure wasn't. Bobby said, "Listen, I'll get your money and bring it to you."

Hearing that calmed her down. She picked up his cosmo off the counter and took a big drink. That seemed to help too.

Megan said, "My B—my bad . . . I just . . ."

Bobby wanted to finish her sentence: "Went fucking schizo."

Megan said, "I didn't hear from you. I was mad. I guess I over-reacted."

She moved to Bobby and put her arms around him, holding him close, not moving now, hugging him.

"You okay?" she said.

Bobby stood there frozen, staring down at the mess on the floor,

Megan clinging to him. She freaked and asked him if he was okay. Huh? Bobby said, "Sure." What else was he going to say?

"You don't sound like you mean it," Megan said.

"Everything's wonderful," Bobby said, "tip-top," putting a little more energy into it.

Six

Lou Starr was in Vegas at a restaurateurs convention, excited because he was staying at the Wynn. It was the nicest hotel he'd ever seen in his life. Karen should see it.

"Cost almost $3 billion to build," Lou said, with pride in his voice. "Makes the Bellagio look like a Super 8. They've got a championship eighteen-hole golf course. They've got a spa. They've got a casino. And you're not going to believe this, they've even got a Ferrari/Maserati dealership in the hotel."

Karen hadn't heard Lou that excited since he'd added all-you-can-eat moussaka to his menu.

"There's even a wedding chapel," Lou said. "We could come out here and elope, spend our honeymoon gambling, going to shows and screwing."

Karen wanted to tell him there wasn't going to be a wedding or a honeymoon in Vegas or any other place, but this wasn't the time. He'd been driving her crazy for months. Karen counted the things he did that annoyed her, and the list kept growing. Clearing the phlegm out of his throat. She'd hear him horking in the bathroom and say, "Come on, Lou, that's disgusting."

He'd say, "Want me to choke to death?"

Picking his toenails in bed was another one. Leaving hair on the floor of the shower like somebody skinned an animal in there. But the real deal breaker was his pushy, demanding attitude—telling her things he wanted her to do every day like she was the hired help. The list went on and they'd only been living together for eight months. Eight months going on eight years.

She'd met Lou on the rebound. It was a fix-up, a blind date. At the time she didn't have any great desire to go out with anyone, the breakup with Samir was still fresh in her mind. It had been three months since she'd walked out of that relationship and her good friend Stephanie said, when you fall off a horse you've got to get back on. Stephanie was dating a disc jockey named Michael Harris who had a friend named Lou Starr. Why not meet him? Stephanie said. What do you have to lose?

Her first impression of Lou: he was too short and too old. But he redeemed himself, taking her skeet shooting at the Metamora Gun Club on their first date.

He'd said, "Ever fire a gun?"

She'd said, "Does a BB gun count? My dad and I used to shoot empty Coke and Bud cans in the backyard when I was a kid."

Lou said, "A BB gun, huh? I'm impressed."

At the range, after telling her skeet was a Swedish word that meant "to shoot," Lou put a Krieghoff 20 gauge over-and-under in her hands and taught her the basic fundamentals: how to stand; how to tuck the gun inside her shoulder to minimize recoil; how to swing through; how to lead and point out; how to hold position and when to call pull.

Lou said, "Know how many muscles it takes to pull a trigger?"

She assumed it was a trick question and said, "One."

He said, "One? Try twenty-seven."

"Come on?" Karen said.

"It's a fact. Twenty-seven muscles in the upper and lower arm and hand to pull a trigger. And only four or five to let it go." He grinned to let her know he was just goofing around with her.

They shot from eight high and eight low stations. Lou was perfect. He hit every target and she only missed three out of thirty-two. She liked the balanced feel of the Krieghoff, bringing it up from below her waist, swinging it across her body, aiming two feet in front of the target and pulling the trigger—*Ka-boom*, watching the clay pigeon disappear in an explosion of dust.

"You're amazing, a natural. You sure you've never done this before?" he said, giving her a questioning look.

"Positive," Karen said.

"What'd you think?"

"It's a blast," Karen said and added, "No pun intended."

Lou smiled. "That's good. You always this clever?"

Karen said, "I guess you'll just have to wait and see." She was surprised how much she liked skeet shooting and Lou. It was her best first date ever.

Over dinner, elk steaks in the gun club dining room, they talked movies and music: his favorites were *Jurassic Park* and Led Zeppelin.

Karen's picks were *The Godfather* and Van Morrison.

They started going out after that and became an item. Karen had pretty much decided she didn't want to jump back into another relationship and before she knew it, she was involved in his life. Lou had a house on Walnut Lake filled with trophy heads, large and small, he had shot on his many hunting trips and safaris. The heads hung from the walls in the living room like some bizarre hunting museum, and it creeped her out.

When Lou asked her to move in she said, "I'd like to but I can't live here with all these animals staring at me." It seemed like something out of a Stephen King novel.

Lou said, "If they bother you, I'll get rid of them. You're more important."

Karen liked that, a man with his priorities in the right order.

They had fun together. He took her to the Santa Fe Wine and Chili Festival, to Mardi Gras in New Orleans and pheasant hunting in North Carolina. But the trip that really brought them close together was the safari in Kenya.

Lou said, "Want to go to Africa, hunt the big five?"

Karen said, "What're the big five?"

"Lions, leopards, buffaloes, elephants and rhinos," Lou said.

Karen said, "I don't want to shoot animals for sport, I just want to see them."

He surprised her a few days later with plane tickets to Nairobi. He said, "Ever see the great migration of the wildebeest?"

"It's been a while," Karen said. She had no idea what he was talking about.

"Want to?" Lou said. "It's a wildlife safari, no hunting."

That appealed to her. "Can you tell me a little bit more about it?"

"Every year a million and a half wildebeest and zebras come up from the Serengeti into the Mara looking for food. And right behind them are the predators: lions, leopards, cheetahs, jackals and hyenas. It's the cycle of life."

Karen said, "I know you're talking about Africa, but where?"

"The Masai Mara in southern Kenya—largest game reserve in the world, hundreds of square miles of grasslands and savannahs. You can't imagine how incredible it is. Wildebeest, a massive herd, from horizon to horizon."

Karen said, "I don't even know what a wildebeest is."

"It's a kind of antelope that looks like an ox and has horns like a cape buffalo, with a horse's tail."

"Are you making this up?" Karen said.

"No," Lou said. "That's what it looks like."

"The migration of the wildebeest, huh? I have to tell you it doesn't sound all that great."

But it was.

From Nairobi they flew in an Air Kenya prop plane forty-five minutes and landed at the Musiara Airstrip, with its collection of Quonset huts made out of corrugated steel, in the middle of nowhere. A tall thin dark-skinned guide named Jomo, who had the whitest teeth she'd ever seen, was waiting in a Land Rover and took them to the camp. On the way Lou spoke to him in a language she'd never heard. Karen said, "What is that?"

"Swahili," Lou said. "And Sheng, a mix of Swahili, English, and Maa. I'm telling him where we live."

"Where'd you learn Swahili?" Karen was impressed.

"I picked it up over the years. I've been here a few times."

The camp was like something out of a Hemingway novel—a small village of white tents. Theirs had twin beds and a toilet and shower but no electricity. At night they lit kerosene lamps and it was romantic. Lou showed her where they were on the map, a dot in the Mara Triangle in southern Kenya. He showed her the Serengeti Plains in northern Tanzania where the great migration started and ended. They took a hot air balloon ride, looking down at the giant herd of wildebeest. They took a boat ride down the Mara River, watching crocs and rhinos sunbathing on the banks. They had breakfast and lunch outside, watching the action. There was always something interesting—lions or elephants or wildebeest or zebras or Masai tribesmen herding cattle. It was like a non-stop wildlife film. Lou would point out the different animals, many Karen had never heard of.

"There's a topi," he would say. Or, "I don't believe it. Ever seen an orbi? There's one right there."

Karen said, "What's that," pointing at a big tan-colored animal with long horns that angled back.

"An eland," Lou said. "What you're eating."

"I thought it was beef," Karen said.

Lou said, "No, it's antelope."

"It's good," Karen said.

Lou told her lions were colorblind and when they saw a herd of zebra it looked like one big mass of stripes. The lion had trouble picking out an individual zebra to attack. He told her about the Masai, the tall good-looking tribesmen she would see in the distance, carrying spears and wearing red shoulder cloaks called shukas.

"They believe the rain god Enkai gave them all of the cows to tend," Lou said.

He told her the Masai lived in huts made out of cow dung and grass that baked and hardened in the sun. He told her the women shaved their heads.

Karen said, "Maybe they've got the right idea. It would save a lot of time. They don't have to worry about the current style or washing and blow-drying their hair every day."

Lou said, "Why don't you try it. I think you'd look cute."

After dinner they'd take their port or cognac and sit outside, staring out at the plains, and the distinctive plumes of acacia trees in the distance, the sun going down—red sky fading. Lou was next to her, the rakish big game hunter who spoke Sawhili and wore tailored safari outfits.

In retrospect, Karen thought the tranquil bliss of the safari had clouded her judgment, thinking this was what life was going to be like with Lou. He proposed in Mombasa a few days later. They were at a resort on the Indian Ocean, drinking champagne when he popped the question and Karen said yes.

A few weeks later Lou said he wanted to elope. Let's just do it, let's get married. I can't wait any longer. Karen put him off then and kept putting him off and finally realized she'd never be able to go through with it.

Living with Lou for eight months had been a distraction, but as things began to fall apart she thought more about the $300,000 she'd given Samir to invest and had never seen again. She wanted it back and decided she was going to get it. How exactly she wasn't sure until Bobby and Lloyd broke in that night and got her thinking, gave her an idea.

Karen went looking for Wade Robey Tuesday afternoon, three days after Bobby and Lloyd broke in. She heard he hung out at a biker bar in Royal Oak, and there he was, sitting at the bar, drinking beer with an occasional shot of peach schnapps, smoking Marlboros like he was on death row. Karen watched him for a while, sitting at a table, drinking vodka tonics. She knew he'd be there. He'd been out of Jackson prison for three months after doing five years for armed robbery. He was looking for a gig too. Karen had found all that out from Fantasy, the sister of a friend she'd modeled with. Fantasy was a skinny blond stripper whose real name was Bobbi Jo Shipp. Fan had gone out with Wade before he went up. Fan said he was kind of dumb and he'd do anything. That fit the job description of the person Karen was looking for.

Wade Robey wore black boots and jeans and a black Guns N' Roses T-shirt. She moved to the bar and sat down next to him when a seat was available and introduced herself. "Hi, I'm Karen, how you doing?" She offered her hand. "I understand you're looking for work."

Wade stared at her not sure what was going on. "Who the fuck're you?"

"I'm a friend of Fantasy's," Karen said.

Now he offered his hand—a big limp fish. Wade said he was

pissed at Fan 'cause she'd taken up with a black dude while he was away and had his kid. Karen studied the tattoos that covered his arms. He had a skull and crossbones and a swastika and Heil Hitler on one arm, and an eagle holding a snake in its talons on the other. She saw the blue-green snake wrapped around his forearm first and didn't know what it was until she saw the eagle on his biceps, putting the illustration in perspective. Karen told him she had a tattoo.

Wade said, "Of what?"

"A gremlin," Karen said.

Wade said, "Where's it at?"

"I'd show it to you, but I'd have to take off my pants. It's right here." She pointed to a spot where her leg met her hip.

"It's okay with me," Wade said.

Karen said, "Huh?"

"You want to take your pants off." Wade grinned big this time, showed his teeth that were nicotine-stained and crooked. "I was just kidding."

He was a real comedian. He had five years to think up zingers like that at the state prison in Jackson. Karen glanced down at Heil Hitler in wavy blue ink on his forearm. "Fan didn't tell me you were with the movement."

"What movement's that?

"White supremacists."

"Oh, the tats," Wade said. "They're mostly for show. Keep the porch monkeys from trying to fuck with me in stir. You got to join a gang or you don't have a prayer."

Karen told him about the safe and the money and Wade said it sounded pretty good. He was a fairly mellow guy, not at all what she thought he'd be like, judging by the way he looked. Karen said they'd talk again soon, put a plan into motion, but she already had the plan.

Wade said he was GTG.

Karen said, "What?"

"Good to go."

Things were falling into place. She had commitments from Bobby and Lloyd, and now Wade.

There was just one more thing she had to do.

Seven

T. J. Dolliver got there early and ordered a Ketel One martini up, extra dry, Dean Martin style, with a lot of olives, five ounces of icy vodka to settle his nerves. He was sitting at the bar at Joe Kool's, watching the door for O'Clair. Get the crazy Irishman off his back and never borrow money again. He had to go to his father-in-law for a loan and explain how he'd gotten himself in trouble and then agree to counseling, talk to a psychologist about his gambling problem. He also had to pay his father-in-law, the cheap bastard, back the loan plus 10 percent, the going rate for sons-in-law who fuck up.

T.J. finished the martini and ordered another one. He felt good, a nice relaxing buzz settling over him. He'd somehow managed to get through it all without his wife, Renee, finding out. Count your blessings, he said to himself.

He looked over at the door now and saw O'Clair come in and his body tensed. O'Clair came right at him, eyes glued to him the whole way. Looking at him and then past him at the half dozen drinkers stretched out along the length of the bar. T.J. took another sip of vodka.

"A prompt man is a lonely man," O'Clair said.

"Huh?" T.J. wasn't expecting that.

The bartender came toward them and asked O'Clair if he wanted something and he shook his head. Now O'Clair stared at T.J., his face was blank.

"Got the money, my friend?" O'Clair said, using T.J.'s line, putting it in his face.

T.J. felt a rush of nerves like he was back in his house stretched out on the La-Z-Boy with O'Clair and the other guy. "Right here," he said, patting the front of his sport coat.

"Give it to me outside."

T.J. picked up his martini and finished it and felt the cold liquid burn his throat.

They walked out and T.J. followed him across the parking lot to the back of the building. He was thinking about what O'Clair said when he walked in: a prompt man is a lonely man. It was true. The shylock was a philosopher. T.J. reached into his sport coat pocket and took out the envelope and handed it to him. "That's all of it, seventeen five."

O'Clair took the envelope and hit him in the stomach and T.J. felt his insides explode. He dropped to his knees, holding his gut, bent over and threw up the two martinis and six olives. T.J. sucked air and heard him walking away now, relieved, the heavy sound of his shoes on the asphalt parking lot.

The girl on stage whose name was Misty took off the pleated schoolgirl skirt at the start of the second song, and was spinning around the silver pole in a G-string with a crazy expression of liberation on her face. O'Clair watched from the bar. If he saw Bobby he'd wait till Bobby walked out and follow him. He'd locked the money he collected from T.J. in the glove box of the

Seville. He'd drop it by Samir's later, make his 15 percent, plus the twenty-five hundred T.J. overpaid.

Misty was crawling around the perimeter of the horseshoe runway in her G-string, collecting bills from drunks and fools. The G-string looked like some kind of carnival outfit with all the bills sticking out of it. O'Clair drank Early Times and water and scanned the crowd. He asked the bartender if he knew a guy named Bobby Gal.

The bartender said, "The country western singer?"

"No," O'Clair said, "the car salesman."

The bartender shook his head.

The house disc jockey said, "Give it up for Misty Rain."

O'Clair got up after Misty finished her set and moved down the bar past three guys in golf shirts, drinking Lite beer. They were trying to impress a young stripper who was wearing a G-string and high heels.

"Gaskets are my life," one of the men, a balding salesman in a pink golf shirt said, "and it's a damn good one."

The stripper didn't seem too impressed, like she entertained gasket salesmen all the time. O'Clair moved toward the bouncer. He was a big guy, with a beer gut, six three, must have gone two sixty. O'Clair stood next to him and felt small. Guy wore a leather vest over a Stevie Ray Vaughan tee shirt, ball cap on backwards, plastic tightener let out all the way. O'Clair watched him give people a hard time, ruling over his little area of authority. O'Clair said, "Seen Bobby Gal around?"

The bouncer said, "Who?"

"Bobby Gal, car salesman comes in here," O'Clair said.

"Preppy smartass, son of a bitch?"

That sounded about right.

"Never heard of him," the bouncer said.

O'Clair knew where he'd hit him first, step in, nail him in the solar plexus, see how funny he was then. "You know, with that wonderful sense of humor you've got, you should be on stage telling jokes not standing here giving paying customers a lot of shit." The wop bouncer stared at O'Clair for a couple of seconds, but didn't say anything, his brain working overtime.

"That's what I want to do," he said. "How'd you know? I've got a routine and everything," excited, trying to be friendly but still had the tough guy edge.

O'Clair tried to imagine this clown doing stand-up, coming across like a raunchier version of Andrew Dice Clay. If you didn't laugh, he'd jump down off the stage and kick your ass. O'Clair said, "What's your stage name?"

The bouncer said, "Justin the Bouncer. What do you think?"

Justin the Bouncer, was he kidding? O'Clair said, "I'll be looking for you on Letterman."

He said, "Want to hear my opening joke?"

"Another time," O'Clair said. "I got to find the car salesman."

"He lives with Colette. She's off today."

"Got an address?"

O'Clair woke her up, he was sure of it, one in the afternoon. He knocked for five minutes before the door finally opened and he saw Colette standing there in shorts and a tank top, a cigarette hanging down from the corner of her mouth, eyes puffy, voice gravelly as she talked about Bobby, stopping to inhale a Newport 100, blowing smoke through the screen door, coughing. She sounded sick, the coughs coming up from the depths of her lungs. She came out on the second story porch and sat on the railing, scratching her head where blond hair turned dark running along the part. She lived in the upper flat of a building behind an adult bookstore and a massage parlor. He could see cars zipping by in the distance on Eight Mile Road.

"Bobby was a regular at the club," Colette said. That's where she got to know him. "And when he wasn't at the club he was downtown, playing blackjack."

Colette said Bobby was the only guy she'd dated in ten years who wasn't a drummer and should've known better. It was a bad omen. O'Clair asked her why she was attracted to drummers?

"They've got the beat," she said. "There's something primal about them."

She'd lived with Corky, the drummer of a speed metal band called Ramrod, before Bobby moved in. Corky was an asshole too, but at least he had coke all the time. Woke up, had a speedball for breakfast. Bobby, on the other hand, was a mooch from the word go. Had alligator arms, couldn't reach his wallet. Never paid for a thing the whole time he went out with her.

O'Clair said, "You know where he is?"

"No," Colette said, "and I don't want to."

"If you were trying to find him, where would you look?"

"I'd call his cell phone."

Of course, O'Clair was thinking.

"248-555-5035," Colette said.

O'Clair left Colette and went to his car and called the number she gave him on his cell phone, and was surprised when he heard Bobby's voice say hello.

"Hey Bob," O'Clair said, "how's it hanging?"

"Who's this?"

"Guy you owe sixty grand. What're you—" That's as far as he got before Bobby hung up. Of course, he hung up. What did O'Clair think he was going to do, invite him out to lunch?

O'Clair called Ameritech, asked for Stu Karp in security. He and Stu had worked Green Street, an East Side precinct together, part of the same squad. He contacted Stu from time to time when he needed phone records or subscription information. O'Clair gave Stu Bobby's number and asked him to do a tower check, see if he could find out where Bobby was at when he made or received his last phone call. Stu told O'Clair to relax, give him a little time and he'd get back to him.

Ten minutes later Stu called and said he's in downtown Detroit. What's at 3rd Street and Bagley?

"The MGM casino," O'Clair said.

"Then that's where I'd go if I was looking for him," Stu said. "I hear it's got a new Wolfgang Puck restaurant."

"No kidding," O'Clair said, wondering who Wolfgang Puck was. He drove downtown and parked at MGM valet. He walked through the casino, checking tables. It was a big room with restaurants at the far end. He saw the Wolfgang Puck Grille, the Saltwater and the Bourbon Steak. None of the names meant anything to him. Colette said blackjack was Bobby's game. O'Clair walked past tables and looked around but didn't see anyone that fit Bobby's description. He walked over to the slots and cruised past rows of video poker games, and slot machines with bright flashing lights and the lure of huge instant jackpots.

O'Clair went back through the casino a second time, and saw the high-limit room and went in and there was Bobby holding court at a blackjack table. He took the picture Colette had given him out of his pocket just to make sure. Yeah, it was the same guy, no mistake about it. O'Clair watched him throw down drinks and strike up conversations with people around him. He bet a lot of money and people noticed him. How could you not?

"Who's going to win the next hand? Bobby is."

He bet $500 and won.

"I told you," Bobby said.

It was a high stakes table in the high stakes room. He was pissing off the other gamblers. But a crowd had formed behind him and the people liked him; he was entertaining.

"Who's going to win the next hand?" Bobby looked around, making eye contact with people in the gallery. "I can't hear you. Who's going to win the next hand?"

And now the crowd responded: "Bobby is."

"That's better," Bobby said. He finished his drink and held the glass up, shaking the ice cubes. "Bobby needs another one, cosmo on the rocks."

A waitress in a black vest showing a lot of cleavage pushed through the crowd and handed Bobby a fresh drink and took his empty glass.

"Thanks, hon," Bobby said. "Keep them coming."

The drink was red and looked like something a kid would order, a Roy Rogers or a Shirley Temple. Bobby took a sip and slid a stack of chips toward the dealer. He split a pair of tens and busted. O'Clair could see the guy next to Bobby grin, probably thinking this loudmouth was all show, he didn't know what he was doing. Bobby's chips were stacked in front of him and reminded O'Clair of the skyline of a city. He started with Chicago and now he had Detroit. Bobby's mood changed. He stopped talking, concentrating but lost three more hands, then a fourth.

"Come on, you idiot," he said to himself. "Get your goddamn head out of your ass."

The dealer told him to watch his language. Now the pit boss came over and asked Bobby if there was a problem.

"I just lost ten grand," Bobby said. "You ask if there's a problem. What're you a moron?"

He moved toward Bobby and Bobby said I'm out of here. He passed his chips to the dealer and colored out. O'Clair tracked him as he moved across the casino to the cashier cages. Watched him cash in his chips and get a stack of bills that he divided in two and stuffed in the front pockets of his khakis.

He followed Bobby to an elevator, but didn't get on in time. He watched it go up to the second level and come back down and O'Clair got in and rode up to the poker floor. He saw Bobby standing near a table. Bobby watched a couple hands and moved to another table and watched a couple more. O'Clair took his eye off Bobby for a few seconds, staring at a good-looking cocktail waitress in a low-cut dress. When he looked back Bobby was gone. O'Clair scanned the room and saw him heading for the elevators.

O'Clair moved fast and got there as the doors were closing and pushed his way in. It was packed with gamblers. Bobby moved in next to two blondes with big hair and blue eye shadow. They were wearing tube tops, showing their taters. The elevator started to go down.

Bobby said, "Know what's white and ten inches long?"

The girls gave him dirty looks.

He said, "Nothing," answering his own question.

A couple guys with sideburns and ball caps on backwards laughed.

"Thanks a lot . . . ladies and gentlemen, I'll be here all week," Bobby said.

Now the blondes cracked a smile

Bobby said, "What're you doing later?"

The girls looked at each other and said, "Nothing. What do you got in mind?"

"Ever fed a piranha?"

Bobby glanced at him and O'Clair said, "Where's the money?" O'Clair reached over and pressed the emergency button and the elevator jerked to a stop between floors.

"You talking to me?" Bobby said. "What're you drunk, had a few too many?"

"The sixty grand," O'Clair said, "you borrowed from Ricky."

"Who's Ricky?" Bobby looked at the girls, winked and said, "He should go home sleep it off."

"I'll take what you won," O'Clair said, "and anything you got on you. See where we stand." The elevator was buzzing. People looked nervous. He pushed the button and they started to go down. The elevator stopped on the main floor and the doors opened. O'Clair grabbed Bobby by the collar of his yellow golf shirt that had a little green alligator on the front and pulled him out of the elevator.

"Get your hands off me," Bobby said. "Help," Bobby yelled. "He's trying to rob me."

Three beefy security guards, muscles bulging under blue blazers, came running toward them and surrounded O'Clair. They were all bigger than him and looked capable. They had fake smiles on their faces, trying to appear friendly but ready for action. The gamblers moved past them coming out of the elevator, looking at him, probably thinking he got what he deserved.

Bobby said, "He watched me cash out and followed me."

"Sir, you're going to have to come with us," the first security guard said to O'Clair. He was Italian and reminded O'Clair of De Niro, but a bigger version, De Niro on steroids. It didn't make any sense to argue. He was going with them whether he wanted to or not. They escorted O'Clair to a room that reminded him of an interrogation room at a police station. He sat at a long table across from two of the security guys, nobody saying anything. What was he going to do, tell these meatheads he was collecting the vig from a mark who was four weeks late? Would they understand that?

Eight

The door opened and Frank Moran came in wearing an expensive-looking black sport coat and tie. He looked at O'Clair, and said, "Are you out of your mind? Next time wait till he walks outside. You can't hold up our customers in the casino. It's bad for business." Now he grinned.

O'Clair said, "Frank, how you doing?"

"Not bad," Moran said.

"Seen Sparkle lately?" O'Clair said.

"Funny you should say that," Moran said. "I was just thinking about her the other day."

Frank Moran was a former robbery-homicide investigator O'Clair had worked a case with ten years earlier. The body of a woman was found in a motel Dumpster on the Ferndale side of Eight Mile Road, just outside the Detroit city limits. She'd been strangled with a piece of electrical cord. Two more bodies—strangled the same way—had been found a mile and a half away in Detroit near Palmer Park. O'Clair worked the case for the Detroit police department, Moran for the Ferndale PD. They had a rough description of the killer and a plausible motive. The women were

known prostitutes and the killer had an appetite for crack co-
caine.

O'Clair and Moran hung out around Palmer Park for a couple
of weeks, giving money to, and making friends with, every transves-
tite, homosexual, pimp, prostitute and freak they came in contact
with. They broke the case when the killer attacked a streetwalker
named Sparkle Jones. Sparkle fought him off and got away and
called the police. O'Clair and Moran questioned her at Henry Ford
Hospital where she was admitted for stab wounds in both hands and
her right shoulder. Sparkle gave them a description of her assailant
and his probable motive.

"He was a tall, skinny, cracked-out homeless motherfucker
lookin' for money for his next fix."

O'Clair said, "Sparkle, that's a good name. Did you make it up?"

"No sir, it's my given name, Sparkle Tiffany Jones. Was a
sparkle in my mom's eye when she have me."

O'Clair remembered, glanced at Moran, both of them trying
not to smile or laugh.

Moran took him up to his office that was open and spacious and
had a big desk. "What do you think of the place?"

"I like it," O'Clair said. "You've done well for yourself." Thinking he'd come a long way from his days as a robbery-homicide
detective in Ferndale.

"It's the largest casino in the state—ninety table games. You
can play craps, roulette, baccarat, two-way monte, Spanish 21, you
name it. We've got 4,500 of the latest slots and video poker games,
Detroit's premier poker room, a four-hundred-room hotel with
nine rooftop VIP suites and the only full-service spa in southeast
Michigan. There's even a dance club, Oak. I know how you like to
shake your booty." He smiled now.

There was excitement in his voice. He was fifty but looked ten years younger—his hair was full and didn't look like it had a speck of gray.

Moran said, "Still working for the Chaldean?"

"Got to do what you've got to do," O'Clair said. It sounded lame, and at the moment he felt like a loser, seeing Moran doing so well.

"Who's Robert Gal?" Moran said. "Wait, let me guess. He borrowed money and can't pay it back."

"How do you know his name?"

"He's downstairs," Moran said. "I wanted to detain him, see what was going on till I talked to you."

"He's up to sixty grand," O'Clair said.

"They never learn, do they?" Moran said. "Well he cashed out with $7,500. That's a start. Come in the other room let's see what we can find out." Moran took him in the surveillance room. There was a wall of monitors showing different parts of the casino and a team of security techs sitting at a long desk under the monitors, zooming and tilting and panning the hidden cameras. O'Clair saw Bobby mouthing off at a blackjack table in one of the screens, Bobby standing in front of a cashier's cage in another one, and Bobby flirting with a cute little blond cashier in the third one.

"What're you doing after your shift?" Bobby said to the blonde.

"Sir, we're not allowed to fraternize with casino guests," she said giving him the company line.

"Is that what you think I want to do," Bobby said, "fraternize?" He winked and the girl smiled.

"Who is she?" O'Clair said.

"Megan Freels, "Moran said. "Been with us since we opened. Good worker, reliable, dependable."

To O'Clair it seemed like there was something there, something going on between them.

One of the techs glanced at Frank and said, "Mr. Moran, I found this too."

There were shots of Bobby from previous visits, Bobby playing blackjack and craps and roulette.

"He's something of a regular," Moran said. "Been here seven times in two months."

"When are you going to let him go?" O'Clair said.

Moran said, "You tell me."

He hung back on the expressway, following Bobby, but giving him plenty of room. It was ten to four and the highway already packed with shift workers on their way home. Bobby got off at Eight Mile, the road that separated Detroit from the suburbs, and pulled into a gas station. There was a party store next door. It had bars over the windows and a big neon LOTTO sign. Bobby got out went inside. O'Clair parked in the alley behind the place and waited for him.

K-nine was walking past the Robin Hood Bar. Dude with a bow, string pulled back ready to shoot an arrow on the back door, green paint faded now. He saw the old Seville parked up ahead at the gas station. K-nine considered it a blessing from God the way his feets hurt from walking. He'd just been thinking about jackin' something, ride downtown to the Ethnic Festival, rip off some Grosse Point chickenhead wore those outfits all pink and green and yellow, look like tropical birds come to the inner city, sample exotic African favorites like spare ribs.

Pac and Skinny were trailing behind him carrying quarts of Mickey's, niggas going at it about who was the baddest rapper on the street, Lil Wayne or 50 Cent.

Pac Man said, "Wayne's the man. You hear his new one *Tha Carter III*? Sixteen cuts, they all good. Not one of 'em bootsy."

Skinny Pimp said, "Fifty's the bigga nigga. Boy got some knock. Check out 'Fat Bitch.' That motherfucker's bumpin'."

Pac said, "Who done 'Perfect Bitch'? Know that one?"

"Ain't no such thing," Skinny said.

"You missin' it, dawg," Pac said. "She not real. Perfect bitch got Janet's titties, booty of Tyra—like that."

"Should call it 'Impossible Dream Bitch,'" Skinny said.

There was a big white dude standing next to the Seville parked in the alley, leaning against it now. What the fuck he doin'? Chickenhead motherfucker look lost or something.

O'Clair saw a black dude with cornrows coming toward him and two more dudes behind him. One wore a sweatshirt with a hood, reminding O'Clair of a guy he'd fought twenty years before in Golden Gloves. It was the city championship, light heavyweight division. The third one dressed like a farmer in blue overalls. Both wore ball caps on backwards, bling swinging from their necks. They had green beer bottles in their hands, big ones, quarts or GIQs.

O'Clair was more concerned about Cornrow, who was closing in on him, only twenty feet away now. He wore long shorts low on his skinny hips showing three inches of plaid boxer above his waist, his white tank tucked into the shorts. There was a tattoo just below his right shoulder that appeared to be a miniature version of himself, his face but without the rows. He had something on his mind as he walked up to O'Clair, measuring him. Cornrow was O'Clair's height, about six feet maybe a little taller. He was muscular but lean. O'Clair didn't think he was coming to ask him for directions or a donation to his church.

Cornrow said, "Yo, Cap'n, we goin' take the boat. Give me the motherfuckin' keys."

O'Clair said, "You talkin' to me?"

Farmer and Sweatshirt moved up next to Cornrow, standing in a half circle in front of O'Clair now, the Seville behind him.

"You see any other chickenhead motherfucker standing here?" Cornrow said.

O'Clair said, "You must have me confused with someone else."

Cornrow grinned, flashing two rows of teeth, the front two displaying a diamond pattern. "Think so, huh? Who we got you confuse with?"

"Somebody that's going to let you take my car."

All three of them grinned now. Cornrow made the first move—came at O'Clair and O'Clair went to the body—nailed him in the gut. Cornrow grunted and bent over, holding his side like he'd been hit with a sledgehammer, and O'Clair threw a sweeping right hand and broke his jaw. Cornrow went down, and O'Clair juked and weaved and stepped in and hit Farmer, flattening his nose against his face, crushing it. He dropped and didn't move.

Now O'Clair turned ready for Sweatshirt, and a beer bottle crashed into his forehead and shattered. O'Clair took a step back against the Seville, dazed, leaning on the driver's door, blood running from a gash in his forehead into his left eye.

Bobby came out of the party store, scratching ink off an instant lottery card with a dime. He had a bottle of iced tea wedged in his armpit. He heard glass break. He glanced up and saw the big white guy from the casino, blood on his face, beating the shit out of a black guy in a hooded sweatshirt. Two more black guys were on the concrete parking lot.

He finished scratching the card, a game called Joker's Wild, and dropped it on the oil-stained asphalt littered with Day-Glo wrappers. Bobby unscrewed the top off the iced tea, took a drink and got in his car, thinking he'd better get the hell out of there while he could.

It took six stitches to close the cut on his forehead. O'Clair had gone to Providence Hospital Emergency. The waiting room was full of people that were bleeding and moaning. The admitting nurse took one look at him and put him in a wheelchair headed for Triage.

O'Clair peeled back the bandage and studied it in the rearview mirror, felt the red swollen skin and the prickly ends of the nylon stitches, while he talked to Stu Karp and found out Bobby's cell phone bills went to a PO box in Troy. O'Clair said, you got an address?

Nine

Karen said, "These are the two guys I was telling you about." And then to Bobby and Lloyd she said, "This is Wade."

Bobby said, "Wade, huh? I've never met anybody named Wade."

Wade had pale skin and long dark greasy hair. He glanced at Bobby, studying him, his face blank, expressionless.

"What's that got to do with the price of beer?" Wade said.

Bobby grinned and said, "What the hell does that mean?"

"Whatever you want it to," Wade said.

Bobby looked at Karen and winked. They were in Memphis Smoke, a big open restaurant and blues bar in Royal Oak. It was crowded with drinkers, wall to wall at the bar, and all the tables were taken with people eating platters of ribs and pulled pork sandwiches and washing it all down with cold beer. "The Very Thought of You" by Albert King was coming from the sound system. Bobby and Lloyd sat across from Karen and Wade.

"Tell me, Wade," Bobby said, "what do you bring to the party?"

Bobby was grinning now, holding the grin like his face was made out of plastic.

Wade didn't show any emotion at all. He just stared at Bobby and said, "What I bring is aimed at your acorns, bro."

Karen heard the click of a pistol being cocked under the table. She glanced at Wade and said, "Take it easy."

"Fuck with me again, I'm going to blow them off," Wade said, his gaze fixed on Bobby. "How's that sound?"

Bobby nodded now, losing the grin. He looked afraid.

"When'd you get out?" Lloyd said.

Wade said, "Of what?"

"Wherever you got those tats?" Lloyd said.

Wade put his hard guy stare on Lloyd.

"What were you in for?" Lloyd said.

Wade kept the stare going. "What's it to you?"

"I did two and a half at Stillwater," Lloyd said.

Wade said, "What's that, a juvie home?"

"Juvie home?" Lloyd said. "It's the oldest prison in Minnesota's what it is. The prosecutor wanted to give me ten years for car jacking on account of there was a dog in the car. You believe that?"

Wade said, "What kind a dog?"

"A Golden," Lloyd said.

"I had a Golden once, named Popeye," Wade said. "Used to ride on the back of my Fat Boy. Swear to God."

"You have a Fat Boy?" Lloyd said.

"Damn straight."

Karen sat there patient, listening. She said, "If you want to talk about Goldens and Fat Boys, I'll come back and meet you another time."

They all looked at her, surprised, but nobody said anything. The cute, bubbly waitress, who'd introduced herself as Stacey, came by with their food and served it.

Lloyd said, "Wait five minutes, bring me another beer."

Bobby took a bite of his pulled pork sandwich. "I assume we'll cut the phone line," he said, talking with his mouth full.

"He's got a security alarm," Karen said. "If you cut the phone line, the police will come." Karen took some of her red beans and drank some beer. "I'll give you the code."

Bobby said, "Okay, you've got the code, but that's after we get in. How we planning to do that? Ring the doorbell?"

"With a torch," Wade said.

Bobby said, "A torch?"

"Acetylene," Wade said, "melt the lock in a minute."

He took a bite of catfish. The plate was close to him edging off the table. His big tattooed arm was positioned in front of it as if someone was going to reach over and steal his food.

It was Karen's idea to go in dressed as cops. They'd wear blue windbreakers with the word POLICE on the back in reflective yellow type you could see across a dark room. Windbreakers and blue caps that also said POLICE. Go in selling themselves as cops looking for drugs and guns. "It's a diversion. Something to surprise them and give us the advantage."

"What about masks?" Wade said.

Bobby said, "We dress up like cops, we don't need masks. It's either or. Think about it. If we're cops, why would we be wearing masks?"

Wade mulled that over awhile. "Maybe so they don't recognize us," he said. "That ever occur to you?"

Bobby said, "How they going to recognize us with hats on in the dark?"

Wade paused, thinking again. "Where you going to get police jackets at? Run over to Wal-Mart?"

"No, I'm going to go online," Karen said, "and find a uniform supply place." She'd already googled and found americawear.com, The American Law Enforcement uniforms supplier, and ordered jackets and caps for Bobby, Lloyd and Wade. She told them she couldn't go in the house. They'd recognize her in a second. It was Thursday night. They'd hit the Sunday after next. Samir stays home to watch *Desperate Housewives* and *Grey's Anatomy*, and goes to bed. How's that sound?

Bobby and Wade nodded. Lloyd seemed lost in thought, in his own world. He was eating ribs and guzzling mugs of Rolling Rock, his glass stained with reddish brown fingerprints. He was looking around not really paying attention to the conversation. Stacey the waitress returned and picked up the empty drink glasses and plates. They stopped talking, waiting for her to leave. All but Lloyd, who looked up at her, hands covered with barbecue sauce.

He said, "I've been watching, you're one quick little thing."

The waitress smiled and said, "Thank you, sir." She seemed embarrassed by the compliment.

Karen thought Lloyd was trying to pick her up.

"I'll bet you're the fastest one here," Lloyd said, "aren't you?"

"One of them," the waitress said.

"Well if you're so goddamn fast . . ." Lloyd got up, farted and said, ". . . catch that and paint it blue."

She turned, walked past the table, and Karen heard her say "Asshole" under her breath.

Lloyd took a step and bumped the table with his hip. "Don't let her take my beer," he said, "I've got to go shake hands with the unemployed." Lloyd walked out of the scene.

Bobby said, "After a few too many Lloyd turns into Floyd, then Avoid."

Karen said, "What's the matter, does he have a drinking problem?"

Getting on his feet, Bobby said, "Not unless they run out of beer." He grinned and moved away from the table, stopped and said, "She comes back, get me another one."

Wade looked at Karen. "I don't know about those two. You sure they know what they're doing? Sure we can count on them?"

"Trust me," Karen said.

Ten

O'Clair pulled into the strip mall parking lot and backed into a space in the last row so he'd have a clear view of a store called Mail Boxes. According to Stu Karp, that's where Bobby had a PO box. O'Clair had said, "Why didn't you tell me that the other day?"

"You didn't ask," Stu said.

Behind the strip mall was an alley, but no place to park. O'Clair had checked it out. O'Clair figured if Bobby stopped by to pick up his mail, he'd pull in the lot. He wouldn't be expecting anyone to be waiting for him on Saturday morning. He'd park and go in.

There was a Blockbuster, a Little Caesars, a Starbucks, a dry cleaners and a CVS Pharmacy. O'Clair got there early, seven cars in the lot, the sun was rising over the strip mall roof, blinding him. He scanned the cars, didn't see a red Mustang Cobra with side pipes and eighteen-inch rims. He put the visor down and adjusted his position, leaning back so the sun was off his face. People were coming out of Starbucks with their designer coffee like junkies getting their fix. He watched a suburban mom in an exercise outfit put her cup on the roof of her Land Rover while she searched for her keys, got in, started the engine and drove off with her coffee still on the roof. Didn't remember it until she was almost pulling out of the lot. She stopped, got out, grabbed it and drove away.

His forehead itched from the stitches. He stared at his face in the rearview mirror. The skin around the Band-Aid was bruised and turning black and blue. He ripped the Band-Aid off and threw it out the window. Now he felt the prickly ends of the stitches and it pissed him off the way things had gone. If it hadn't been for the gangbangers, he'd be counting his money right now. He got 15 percent of what he collected. More than anyone else because he got results. Bobby owed sixty grand, so he'd make nine, or more depending on when he found him, the vig multiplying by a point and a half each week Bobby didn't pay his debt.

If Bobby had the money, Samir told O'Clair to make an example of him. Bobby made him look bad, and Samir couldn't afford to look bad. Not in his line of work. If Bobby didn't have the money, they'd take him to a warehouse Samir owned downtown and try to impress upon him the seriousness of the situation.

O'Clair had worked for Samir since he was released from the Michigan State Prison in Jackson after doing a little less than two years for using a firearm to commit a violent crime. A federal grand jury had indicted O'Clair, then a Detroit cop, for shaking down drug suspects for illegal searches. O'Clair thought it was un-fucking-believable. How could he be accused of violating the rights of someone breaking the law? O'Clair roughed up a heroin dealer named Skunk—'cause he had a little stripe of gray hair in his black Afro—took his dope and his money. Yeah? Isn't that what he was paid to do? His commanding officer had said, "Yeah, but you're not supposed to keep it."

The judge, a black dude with a chip on his shoulder, told O'Clair he was a disgrace to the men and women of the Detroit Police Department and gave him nineteen months.

O'Clair's attorney, Mike Solner, said he was the victim of a federal consent decree signed by the U.S. Justice Department and the Detroit police, to help stop violating the civil rights of citizens mistreated by city cops.

O'Clair said, "Huh? Want to run that by me again?"

Solner said O'Clair's record didn't help, the fact that he'd shot two people in three years and there had been two lawsuits against him, one dropped, one settled, the city of Detroit paying $400,000 in damages.

He dug a stained, bent Styrofoam cup out from the crease where the front seats met and poured coffee from a thermos into it. He took a sip and put the cup on the dash. Steam curled up, fogging a circle of windshield. He unwrapped a salami sandwich and took a bite, chewing as he watched the parking lot begin to fill up with SUVs. They were taking over—big, hard to park, bad on gas and preferred by women, the worst drivers in the world. He didn't get it.

O'Clair was watching all these good-looking suburban women come out of Starbucks and he tried to remember the last time he'd gotten laid, had to really think about it. What was her name? Cindy, yeah, that was it. She said she worked for a publishing company in the telecommunications department. What she really did, she called people at night after their long hard day and tried to sell them magazine subscriptions. That pain-in-the-ass call you got when you were having your supper.

Cindy had said, "You wouldn't believe how rude people can be. What I'm selling benefits them, enriches their lives, and they're giving me a hard time because I'm interrupting their precious evening."

After they'd gone out a few times, she started asking questions about money, probing into O'Clair's life. They were sitting at the

bar at Mr. B's in Royal Oak, O'Clair drinking Jim Beam and water and Cindy sipping a 7 & 7.

"Do you own your house?" Cindy wanted to know. "Belong to
a country club? Invest in the stock market?"

The questions all related to money. O'Clair said, "You want to
know how much money I have?" He swigged his bourbon. "I have
enough to buy you the 7 & 7 you're drinking and maybe another
one, you stop asking questions that aren't any of your fucking business."

She thought they had a future together, did he? O'Clair wondered if maybe she was hard of hearing, looked at her, said, no,
finished his drink and walked out of the bar.

He'd never had very good luck with women. Married a dental
hygienist named Joan right out of prison. She was Armenian, full-
body with a bush so dense she could've shaved it and knit a sweater.
At dinner, Joan would tell him about people's teeth, using words
like plaque and gingivitis. O'Clair'd be eating his stuffed peppers
as she'd describe how bacteria caused tooth decay, periodontal
problems and halitosis.

"If only their home care was better. You know you should floss
more yourself, mister, once a day, at least."

"I'm trying to eat my dinner," O'Clair said. "Can we talk about
something else?"

One of Joan's sisters—who was the size of an East African
rhino—had just had her stomach stapled so she wouldn't eat herself to death. "Mary's lost eighty pounds," Joan said. "And the poor
thing's having terrible gas."

That's how she changed the subject.

O'Clair had met Joan in the dentist's office. She cleaned his teeth
one evening, the last appointment of the day. She'd joked around
with him, the only two people in the office, and banged him in the

dental chair after she finished flossing him. She took off her blue scrubs and climbed on top. It was O'Clair's best trip to the dentist ever. If getting laid was part of the deal, Jesus, more guys would have their teeth cleaned. They'd be lining up.

Things went downhill fast after their wedding in the Armenian church with the gold dome near Northland. A friend of O'Clair's asked him when he knew the marriage was in trouble and O'Clair said, the day I proposed. Joan moved out after three months, and he hadn't seen or talked to her since.

At noon O'Clair got out of the Caddy and walked behind the drugstore and took a leak next to a green Dumpster and almost gave a stock boy a heart attack as he came out the back door and saw a big middle-age dude with his pecker out taking a wiz. O'Clair said hello to him and the kid ran to the door and disappeared inside.

O'Clair walked down to the pizza place and ordered a meatball sub and a Coke. The kid behind the counter said five minutes, and gave him a cup. He filled it with Coke and went out the back door and looked down the alley. There was a delivery truck parked and a guy in a brown uniform unloading boxes. Beyond the truck, Jesus Christ, was a red Mustang parked next to Mail Boxes, and Bobby was coming out, shuffling through his mail.

O'Clair dropped the Coke and ran through Little Caesars, knocked a balding dad in a golf outfit on his ass. He heard the kid behind the counter yell, Sir, your sub's ready.

He ran across the parking lot, going as fast as he could with his knee, the pain slowing him down. He got in the Caddy, fired it up and punched the accelerator as a white GMC Yukon backed out of a space in front of him. O'Clair laid on the horn. The driver's door flew open. O'Clair floored it, swerved around the Yukon, ripping the door clean off. He saw the driver in the rearview mirror, running after him. He swerved around a woman with a shopping cart, turned right and then left out of the parking lot. No sign of the Mustang. He went right on a side street, gunned it, and saw a glimpse of red sheet metal turning on to Rochester Road.

O'Clair caught up to him just before Sixteen Mile, passing a Wendy's, a Taco Bell, a Bob Evans, picturing the food at each place, knowing what he'd get and getting hungry. He followed Bobby to Somerset, stayed with him as he cut through the mall parking lot, O'Clair worried now that Bobby was going shopping. But he wasn't; he was going to the Somerset Apartment complex that must've been a mile long. O'Clair hung with him through a maze of streets until Bobby finally turned into a driveway and pulled into a carport.

O'Clair parked on the street and watched Bobby go into a tan-brick apartment building. The place looked pretty good to O'Clair. Somerset. It was called Sin City when it first opened, all the single professionals shacking up, a party on every balcony. It still looked that way, good-looking babes everywhere. You'd have to be a paraplegic not to score here.

There was a golf course that ran through the middle of the complex. All Bobby had to do was walk out his back door and tee off. There was a pool too. He could see girls in lounge chairs through the bars in the fence. It was a nice setup. O'Clair should get out of his dingy bungalow in Ferndale and move here.

He scanned the directory. There he was: R. Gal in apartment 22B.

The door to the building had a cheap lock with a lot of give. O'Clair picked it and went in. He saw the staircase and went up to the second floor and followed apartment numbers as he moved down the hall and saw Bobby in the doorway of his place talking to a dark-haired girl in a bathing suit.

O'Clair went back to the Caddy, sat in the driver's seat, started the car, and checked the rearview mirror. An SUV was approaching. He let it pass and made a U-turn, creeping by Bobby's building. He'd come back later. The hard part was done. If Bobby still had the money, it would be in the apartment—under the mattress or behind the toilet or in the ceiling—some of the classic places people used, thinking they were being clever.

Eleven

Karen was sitting behind the wheel of a Chrysler minivan Bobby and Lloyd had stolen off the used car lot at Jim Fresard Pontiac in Royal Oak. She was about to take her ex-boyfriend's safe, trusting three guys she barely knew. She felt a jolt of nerves, the full impact weighing on her now. She adjusted the electric seat to get comfortable while she watched the house. She was parked between Samir's and his neighbor's to the south, and had a clear view of the front door and the circular drive flanked by giant gold lions. The lions, Samir had once told her, were a symbol of the power and wealth of the Fakir family.

In a few minutes, she'd pull up to the front door and pick up the safe. But going through with it was a lot more difficult than planning it. For the first time she wasn't in control. Before Bobby, Lloyd and Wade got out of the van Karen had said, Don't say anything unless you have to. Don't make it personal, and whatever you do, don't shoot anyone. She didn't think Samir would involve the police. He'd take care of things himself, in his own way, unless someone was shot. Then he wouldn't have a choice. Karen saw headlights in the rearview mirror. She ducked down as a car approached, slowing as it passed her, a VW Jetta, and parked in front of Samir's house. She could see two people in the front seat, their heads coming together, probably kids making out. This was going to be a problem. She'd have to get rid of them and do it fast.

In the kitchen, Ricky said, "You'd like some of that wouldn't you? That's the centerfold. You're lookin' at Playmate of the Month." Moozie didn't seem to understand; he just wanted to see more pictures. The magazine was open on the kitchen table. Moozie was sitting across from him, staring at the airbrushed girl who had nothing on except fur boots and a fur hat. Ricky said, "Check her out, the pride of Juneau, Alaska." He glanced at Moozie, whose eyes were glued to the page. "Her turn-ons—you ready for this?—men who sweat. You got that covered. Riding her Jet Ski and honest people. Her turn-offs—oh, shit—dirty fingernails, bad breath and hair in the shower. Sorry, Mooz, you just struck out." Ricky grinned having some fun with his cousin from Beirut. He opened the centerfold all the way and gave the magazine to Moozie. "Here, you want to look at it. Just don't slobber on the pages, okay?"

They ate out of Styrofoam boxes, too late for dinner with Samir. Moozie hadn't touched his, feasting instead on the sculpted close-up of the girl's cootch. It looked strange, Ricky thought, that ugly little thing with folds of skin that men sold their souls for. "You don't want that, I'll take it," Ricky said, half finished with his meal, eyeing the one in front of Moozie.

Moozie opened the white box now and picked up a piece of grilled, marinated chicken with his fingers, taking his time. He put the chicken in his mouth chewing the meat, licking his fingertips, eyes still glued to the centerfold.

Ricky spilled tomato sauce on his yellow warm-up, rubbed it with a napkin and made it worse. It was Ricky's favorite outfit: pale yellow with black stripes down the sleeves and pants. He thought it reeked of class. He was going to teach Moozie how to dress.

His cousin looked like he crawled into a Salvation Army drop box, grabbed some things that didn't match and put them on in the dark.

They were going at it, all right, mashing and pawing at each other, but there was something strange. It was two guys with their arms around each other, making out, two suburban teenagers in khaki shorts and T-shirts. Karen stood next to the car, looking in the open driver's window, and said, "I'm with Neighborhood Watch. I'm not going to tell your parents. Just get out of here and don't come back." It must've sounded believable. The two guys stopped kissing and looked at Karen. Neither of them said a word. The Jetta started and accelerated, tires spinning, kicking up stones and dirt. Karen watched as they took off down the street.

In the living room, Samir sat on a white leather couch with Minde, one of the Automotion dancers he'd seen performing at halftime at a Pistons game, and arranged to meet. Minde was an auto parts model hoping to turn that into acting.

"I act when I perform," she'd said to Samir on their first date at the Phoenicia, a restaurant in Birmingham. "I become different people expressing different feelings. I might be Helen of Troy one night, or Joan of Arc. Great heroines of the past."

Samir didn't care who the hell she was as long as she would go to bed with him later, and she did, Minde with her long dancer's legs bending into positions he'd never seen before. She was something, all right, until she opened her mouth and started talking and never stopped.

They were watching Samir's favorite program, *Desperate Housewives*, on a fifty-inch flat screen. There was a close-up of Eva Longoria in a dramatic scene, her face filling the screen.

Minde said, "Smoothie," cuddling next to him, "do you think she's prettier than me?"

He wasn't listening, he couldn't take his eyes away from the TV.

"Smoothie, I'm talkin' to you."

Eva was making out with the gardener.

"You're not even listening," Minde said, "are you?"

"I'm watching the show," Samir said. "If you don't mind."

Minde said, "Who's better-looking her or me?"

Samir rubbed his jaw as though he was considering between them and said, "Her."

"Who's got the better bod?"

"Her." He winked at Minde and smiled.

"You son of a bitch. I hope you like sleeping alone."

Samir said, "You have the best body I ever seen and it's real. No silicone." It wasn't true, but he said it to shut her up.

Minde said, "You really think so?" She snuggled up next to him and put her arm over his shoulder.

He'd trade Minde in for a night with Eva Longoria in two seconds. Minde, like most women, was a pain in the ass. Always needed attention like right now, leaning against him, crowding him—four feet of couch next to her. Samir fixed his attention back on the TV. He was pulling on his mustache. He could feel her eyes on him, staring at him.

"Smoothie, you shouldn't do that all the time. It's a bad habit."

Why did she care if he pulled on his mustache? A twenty-two-year-old girl talking to him like he was a kid. Samir said, "Go get me something to drink, a glass of juice."

Minde stared at him the way his mother used to. "You could say please, you know." She got up off the couch sniffing the air. "I smell something burning."

Samir glanced at the fireplace that hadn't been cleaned since last winter. "It's the fireplace. Nothing to worry about."

Minde moved around the couch behind Samir, stopped, bent over and kissed his bald spot. He turned looking up at her. "What're you doing?" She could really be annoying.

"I love that little spot, it's so soft," Minde said.

Samir edged sideways on the couch, watching her over his shoulder not sure what she was going to do next. "I'm dying of thirst here," he said.

Minde stared at him and smiled. "Oh, you big baby . . ." She danced out of the room, moving to some beat in her head. Always dancing, stretching, where'd she get the energy?

There was a *whoosh* of gas and then a pop as the fire ignited, turning into a long multicolored flame that was yellow on the bottom, turning red and then blue at the tip. Wade turned a dial on the base of the torch, adjusting the flame, shortening it into a thin blue dagger. He wore thick goggles that made him look like a crazed aviator in the dim light. The torch was hooked up to a big industrial tank on wheels. You could weld a skyscraper together with this rig, Wade had said earlier.

Bobby thought it was overkill until Wade melted Samir's front door lock in a few seconds and Bobby pushed the door open and went in. The foyer was dark. He could hear a TV on in the living room thirty feet away. Bobby found the alarm pad right where Karen said it would be, punched in the code, everything going according to plan.

Minde stepped into the darkness of the foyer. A staircase with a gold banister curved up to the second floor. She sniffed the air. Something was definitely burning. "Smoothie, I'm telling you your house is on fire. You better come here."

"Will you get me my juice," Samir yelled.

He sounded mad. Her eyes adjusted to the darkness and she

noticed the front door was open slightly, and there was smoke and this strange smell. Then she saw the cop coming out of the closet. What was going on?

He said, "Ma'am, there was a burglary next door, please stay calm. Did you see or hear anything unusual?" He had a gun in his hand and he was wearing a police jacket and a hat.

Bobby didn't know who was more surprised, him or the girl. The line about the burglary next door had come to him in a flash of inspiration. Sometimes he even surprised himself. He saw Wade come up behind her and put his hand over her mouth and pull her backwards. Somehow she twisted out of Wade's grip and kicked him in the balls with a nifty kung fu move. The blonde assumed the classic karate fighting pose now. Bobby had seen enough chop socky pictures to know she was the real thing. Karen hadn't mentioned a girl karate expert on the payroll. Wade was bent over in pain. Bobby aimed his .32 at her and said, "You're under arrest."

"Bullshit," she said. "You're not cops."

"It really doesn't matter now," Bobby said. "Does it?"

From the living room Samir said, "What the hell is going on out there?"

"Smoothie, they're trying to rob you."

Bobby kept the gun on her, giving her space, watching those feet. Out of the corner of his eye, he saw Wade straighten up, step in and hit her in the face, cold-cocked her, and she went down hard on the marble floor.

"Bitch almost put me out of business," Wade said.

Bobby rushed in the living room and met Samir coming across the white shag. Bobby pointed the .32 at him, but he wasn't looking at Bobby. He had his eyes glued to Wade, who appeared with a Remington 870 tactical response shotgun. Looked like the same one Arnold used in *Terminator*. Wade had said it's the weapon designed to get people's attention without firing a shot. He was right. Samir stopped in his tracks.

"Police," Wade said. "Get the fuck down," taking charge.

Samir seemed stunned, he stood there frozen just staring until Wade racked the slide and got his attention. He got down on his stomach on the pure white carpeting, eyes searching for Wade, who moved behind him out of sight.

"Think you can handle it from here?" Wade said to Bobby. He was pissed. "Or do I have to do everything?"

"Whoever you are," Samir said, looking up from the floor, "you better hope I don't find you."

Wade stepped over to him and jammed the barrel end of the shotgun against his cheek. "You threatenin' me, Abdul?" Wade kicked him in the ribs and Samir grunted. Wade kicked him in the face and rocked his head.

Karen came in the room and said, "What are you doing?" She stepped between Wade and Samir, aiming her Smith & Wesson .357 Airweight at Wade's chest. "I told you and we agreed, no one was supposed to get hurt."

"He asked for it," Wade said, on the defensive.

Samir was moaning and his face was a mess, bruised, swelling up and bleeding from Wade's steel-tipped biker boots. Karen got on her knees and rolled Samir on his back and put a pillow from the couch under his head. He was out, unconscious. He needed a doctor. She'd have to call EMS.

Karen was watching Bobby roll the safe out of Samir's office when she heard the shotgun blast and it startled her it was so loud. She ran down the hall to the kitchen, and looked in the doorway and all she saw was blood, spatters of it on the white walls and white tile floor and even on the ceiling. More blood was covering the crumpled figure of a man on the floor, she now recognized as Yalda, the cook, his white shirt splotched with red. Wade was standing there with the shotgun, a crazed look on his face, aiming at Ricky and a young guy she didn't recognize. They were lying on the floor, and their hands and feet were duct-taped together.

Bobby came in behind her and squeezed through the doorway into the kitchen. "We've got to get out of here," he said to Wade.

Wade glanced at him and said, "They know what I look like." He aimed the shotgun at Ricky on the floor.

"Be cool," Bobby said. "I need your help in the other room."

Wade lowered the shotgun and Bobby and Lloyd escorted him into the foyer where the safe was. It was a tense moment, she could see Wade, the psycho, shooting everyone, including them.

"What did I say? Jesus, what's the one thing I told you not to do?" Karen said, adrenaline still pumping. She was glancing over her shoulder at Wade in the back seat behind Bobby. They were moving down Samir's driveway, heading for the street.

Wade said, "What the fuck do you know about it?"

"I know the police are going to be involved now, you dipstick." She was trying to get her money back and now she was involved in a murder, two, if Samir didn't make it.

"I didn't have a choice." Wade glanced at Lloyd. "Tell her."

"He pulled a gun," Lloyd said.

"What's done is done," Bobby said. "Don't worry about something you can't do anything about."

"Thanks for the inspiring words," Karen said. "I'll try to remember that when the police come looking for me."

They'd taken off the police hats and jackets and stuffed them in a plastic bag that Lloyd threw out the window. What kind of bonehead move was that? Karen lit a cigarette. She took a right on Coolidge. The safe shifted and rolled with a *bang*, crashing against the opposite side of the minivan. She glanced in the rearview mirror at Lloyd. "I thought you had that thing tied down." She looked through the windshield, eyes back on the road, trying to calm down. It wasn't supposed to happen like this. Nobody was supposed to get hurt.

Twelve

O'Clair smelled kitty litter and sneezed as he walked in the apartment.

Megan said, "God bless you."

O'Clair hated cats. He was also allergic to them. In a few minutes his eyes would start to itch and his nose would run. A strawberry blond cat appeared, rubbing against his leg. He could hear music coming from another room, nothing familiar, some kind of rock tune.

"That's Snickers. He's saying hello. Aren't you, boy?" Megan bent over when she talked to the cat, getting closer to it. "He's a short-haired Exotic, and about the nicest little guy in the whole world. Yes, him is." Megan straightened up, her gaze still on the cat. "This is Detective . . . what'd you say your name was?"

"Conlin," O'Clair said, picturing the square jaw and flattop haircut of his first sergeant. He flashed a silver badge at her, a real one he'd taken from a detective he didn't like before he was kicked out of the department, figuring it might come in handy and it had. The little blonde surprised him by asking what it was made out of.

O'Clair said, "What?"

She said, "You know, is it metal or plastic?"

"Metal." What kind of question was that?

He'd gotten a list of incoming calls to Bobby's apartment from a cop he'd had a fling with, who was now a detective on the Violent Crimes Task Force. Her name was Pam Bond. Six out of his last ten calls were from Megan Freels, the cashier who worked at the MGM and lived at the Lafayette Apartments downtown. The other calls were from a phone number in Montreal. O'Clair tried it and a voice answered speaking French and he hung up.

"The detective's here to ask us some questions," Megan said. And then to O'Clair, "Come on in and sit down."

She led him into a good-size living room with a hardwood floor and a great view of downtown Detroit, and the city of Windsor, Ontario, across the river. Megan went to the stereo turned the music down. She was a hot little number.

O'Clair said, "Who's that?"

"Guided by Voices," Megan said.

O'Clair said, "Where're they from?" He'd never heard of them.

"I think, Ohio," Megan said. "The lead singer was a schoolteacher. He drinks like twenty beers during a show. Best live band I've ever seen, but they broke up."

He rubbed his right eye. He could feel it swelling up and itching like crazy.

"Do you have something in your eye? I've got drops if you need them."

"It's all right," O'Clair said, but it wasn't. He didn't have much time.

"I hope you're not allergic to Snickers." Megan sat in a worn leather chair with her back to the wall.

O'Clair took the couch. "Nice view," he said. "Detroit doesn't look so bad from this angle. How long have you lived here?"

"I moved in when I got the casino job. So I guess about a year and a half."

Snickers walked across the floor in front of O'Clair and jumped into Megan's lap. Her eyes lit up. "Well, look who wants some attention." Megan stroked the cat and hugged it.

O'Clair noticed it had a strange pug face like somebody had squished it. He wasn't going to ask any questions about why the cat's face was that way, and hoped he didn't have to hear any cat stories. "I'm looking for a suspect named Robert Gal, goes by Bobby."

"What's it have to do with me?"

"He's a regular at the MGM. I'm hoping you can ID him." O'Clair got up and handed the photograph of Bobby to Megan. She stared at it without any kind of reaction. Why was she pretending she didn't know him?

"I'll say this, he does look familiar. I've probably seen him. Maybe even cashed him out."

O'Clair knew Bobby wasn't in the apartment at that particular time. His car wasn't in the parking lot. He wanted to scare her, give her something to think about. But if she was afraid, she didn't show it. She was cool as could be.

Megan took another look at the photograph. "Can I keep this? I'll ask the girls at work, see if anybody knows him." She stared at the photograph one more time. "He's kind of cute."

A white cat with black spots on its head wandered into the room. Megan said, "Look who just woke up from her nap."

The cat yawned.

"Is her still tired? Is my girl teepee house?" Megan said in a singsong voice.

The cat jumped up on the couch and curled up next to O'Clair, burrowing in close.

"You've got yourself a friend, Detective. Her name's Judy, and she's a cuddler and a teeper, aren't you girl?"

Megan, O'Clair noticed, had a goofy look on her face when

she talked to the cats. Her tone of voice was also different, like somebody talking to a baby.

"Judy's a Van."

Jesus, there she goes.

"Vans are Exotics—usually with white fur, spots of color on their head and a colored tail."

O'Clair was in fucking agony.

"Not to be confused with Harlequins."

His eyes were on fire.

"They're a lot like Persians except for the coat."

O'Clair sneezed.

"God bless you." Megan held up Snickers. "I think the poor detective's allergic to you guys." She put the cat on the floor.

O'Clair had to get out of there. He stood up. The white cat stared at him and purred.

"What should I do if I see him?" Megan said.

O'Clair said, "What?"

"If I see him," Megan said, "you know, the guy?"

"Call me." He had a small notepad in his pocket. He wrote his number down and handed it to her.

O'Clair didn't know if she was fucking with him or not. All that cat talk, she might have been putting him on. Her reaction when he mentioned Bobby was strange too. He planned to come back for another visit if his eyes ever recovered.

Megan knew if they found Bobby it was all over. He'd give her up in a second to save his own ass. Blame the whole thing on her. She had to talk to him. He'd taken off and she hadn't seen him in a few hours. He was going to get her money.

What if they checked her phone records and saw all the calls she made to him. She was getting nervous, paranoid. Why was she even being questioned? There had to be a lot more to it than what she'd been told.

Aside from cashing him out, Megan was careful never to talk to Bobby at the casino. Never to be seen with him. Wait a minute, did this have something to do with Lou Starr? How could it? There was nothing to connect her. So what did they have? Nothing was her guess. Megan was coming out of her funk now. Fuck 'em. They didn't have shit. She turned up the music and heard the start of "Glad Girls."

"Hey, hey, glad girls, I only want to get you high."

O'Clair thought Megan would panic and make a move, run to Bobby and tell him the police were looking for him. He waited in the parking lot for thirty minutes and when she didn't come out he drove to Bobby's and knocked on the door. Nobody answered. He picked the lock, went in and said, "Anybody home?" Silence. There was a lamp on in the living room. Bobby had nice-looking furniture, leather couches, an overstuffed leather chair with an ottoman, plasma TV, tropical fish tank; Bobby Gal was living pretty good. The tank must've been five feet long and there was only one fish in it, an ugly little thing floating on its side near the surface of the water. It looked dead. He poked it with his index finger and the little son of a bitch spun around and tore off a piece of his flesh in a split second. There was a cloud of blood in the water and O'Clair was bleeding like crazy.

He went in the kitchen and wrapped his finger—the tip was bit off and gone—in a paper towel that turned red as soon as it touched his raw flesh. He folded a paper towel three times around the end of his finger that stung like a son of a bitch, and wrapped the whole thing in duct tape he found in a drawer.

What kind of fish was it? O'Clair would've guessed a baby barracuda or a shark, but it just looked like a normal dumb fish.

He went back in the living room and looked in an old rolltop desk that was against a wall at the far end of the room. He found a bent photograph wedged in one of the narrow compartments. O'Clair stared at it. It was Bobby, no question, squinting, a big grin like he had a buzz on, holding a cocktail, posing with his arm around Megan, the little blonde he'd just visited.

He put the photo in his pocket. There were a couple of bills and an orange flyer announcing a Friday Night Mixer in the desk. These swinging Somerset people really knew how to have fun. The answering machine showed six messages, but no tape. He already knew who the calls were from.

O'Clair checked the bedroom. Pulled the mattress off the box spring, slashed it open with a knife from the kitchen, a serrated blade that sliced through the soft fabric, making a big X from corner to corner, exposing the guts, but no money. The bedding was in a pile on the floor. He picked up each layer, sheet, blanket, sheet, and shook it, but didn't find anything.

He went through a chest of drawers, pulled out clothes, socks, underwear, khakis, Levi's and then rows of golf shirts. Bobby had four times more clothes than O'Clair. He was neater too—all his stuff was folded in perfect piles, perfect rows. Maybe he was a fag. Who else would spend time folding his clothes like that? Even his underwear was folded in neat piles.

O'Clair looked in the closet. On the floor he noticed a pair of brown and white saddle shoes. He wondered how a grown man could wear shoes like that even to play golf. This guy Bobby had to be light in his loafers. He picked up Bobby's two-tone golf bag that said "Taylor Made" on it, and dumped the clubs out on the living room floor. He grabbed a 3-iron, took a swing, dropped the club and went through the golf bag, checked every pocket and compartment. Nothing except golf shit: tees and balls and a couple of gloves, a scorecard, a warm can of Bud.

He went back in the bedroom closet and pulled out all the coats, checked the pockets and threw everything on the bedroom floor. He looked in the closet one more time, checked the shirts that were lined up on hangers. He found a folded piece of yellow paper in the pocket of a green long-sleeve button-down. It was a receipt from a warehouse in Clawson. The name on it said "Lloyd Henry Diehl," with an address in Southfield. He'd stop by the warehouse in the morning check it out.

O'Clair hit the jackpot in the kitchen. He found $5,700 in a Green Giant Baby Sweet Peas box in the freezer. Found $1,800 more in a metal Johnson & Johnson Band-Aid box with a hinged top in the cupboard next to a bottle of aspirin. God people were dumb.

O'Clair figured the money, $7,500, was a bonus for all he'd had to put up with trying to find this clown. There was a bottle of Canadian Club in a kitchen cupboard. He made himself a drink and took it into the living room to get comfortable and wait for Bobby to come home, when his cell phone rang. It was Ricky all excited, saying Samir had been robbed and Yalda was dead. What?

O'Clair drank the whiskey, put the glass on the coffee table and went over to the fish tank and looked at the fish. It was still floating on its side close to the surface of the water. He reached behind the tank and pulled it toward him, the tank teetering on its metal stand before going over. The glass panels shattered as it hit the floor and water rushed out, flooding the living room, running into the kitchen, the bathroom. He didn't see the fish but figured it didn't have too long, riding the wave and then flopping around trying to find water. His finger still hurt like hell and he wondered if you could get any kind of disease from a fish.

Twenty minutes later O'Clair was parked in front of Samir's, watching the action. Four West Bloomfield police cars and two

EMS vans were parked in the driveway, lights flashing, and an un-marked Crown Vic was parked on the lawn. It took him back—crime scenes flashing in his head. Dead bodies that had been shot, strangled, stabbed, beaten—and cops standing around drinking coffee, talking, waiting for the homicide detectives, the medical examiner, trying not to contaminate the evidence.

He got out of the car and went up to the house. Two para-medics wheeled a gurney out the front door. Samir was on his back, his face bruised and swollen, and there was an IV swinging from an attachment over his head. Now Minde came out of the house crying, hysterical, her face red and puffy on one side. The para-medics picked up the gurney, slid Samir in the back of the EMS van.

Minde said, "I have to go and take care of him."

One of the paramedics helped her in and closed the doors. O'Clair was surprised, thought she was in it strictly for the money. She could've gone back to her apartment, had a couple drinks and watched TV. But she insisted on going with him. You could never be sure with women.

He moved toward the house. There was an acetylene tank, a big one on the front porch. At first he thought it was an oxygen tank the paramedics had brought, but now he knew what it was. The paint was chipped and it was dented like it had been used on construction sites. They'd wheeled it up to the front door and melted the lock. The molding around the front door was scorched black and smelled like there'd been a fire, that smell that got in your nose, you couldn't get rid of. The door itself was burned black on one end, and there was a hole where the lock had been.

In the foyer, a hardass West Bloomfield uniform asked O'Clair who he was and what he was doing there.

From the living room Ricky said, "It's okay, he works for us."

Ricky was on the white couch, talking to a detective.

"Give me a few minutes," he said to O'Clair, trying to sound like he was in charge.

There was a bloodstain on the white carpeting, looking strangely out of place in the perfect room. O'Clair had never wanted to go in there, afraid he'd mess it up, track something on the carpeting. Why'd everything have to be white? Samir's living room, his kitchen, even his cars. And yet the man himself dressed in black. O'Clair couldn't remember him wearing anything else. He thought of Samir as the Chaldean Johnny Cash. He moved into the man's office. The cabinet doors were open and the safe was gone. Who'd have the balls to come in here and do that?

Thirteen

Karen was leaning against the side of the minivan, smoking a cigarette, still tense from the events at Samir's. She couldn't stop thinking about Yalda, who she'd always liked, and Samir, who she didn't, but now worried about. This had been her worst fear, something going wrong, and someone getting hurt, or worse. She'd called 911 on Samir's phone, from Samir's office, and hung up.

Now she was in the warehouse, staring at the safe in the middle of the bare concrete floor. It was a Mosler, with gold Arabic writing on it, and weighed six hundred pounds. She had watched Bobby, Lloyd and Wade struggle to lift it in the back of the van, and then struggle again taking it out when they arrived at the warehouse.

Bobby had his back to her. He turned and grinned and said, "Next time I rob a Chaldean bookmaker with a safe I'm going to rent a Hi-Lo."

Wade was on one knee in front of the safe, turning the combination dial. He looked like he was praying, and Karen thought it was an odd contrast for an ex-con.

Bobby looked over at her again and said, "Well, without further ado," swinging his arm toward her, palm open in a theatrical gesture.

"Do you want me to do a trick or something?" Karen said.

"Just open the safe," Bobby said.

Karen said, "What're you talking about?"

"I hope you're kidding," Bobby said.

"I never said I could open the safe." She'd implied it for sure but never actually said she could do it.

"I don't fucking believe this," Wade said. He took a step toward Karen. "You just get it out of there, I'll take care of everything else." He turned toward Lloyd and Bobby. "Remember her saying that?"

"I don't know," Lloyd said.

"You don't know," Wade said.

"Cut her some slack, " Bobby said. "We'll figure something out."

"I'm going to cut more than that," Wade said, "we don't get this thing open."

There was a big construction toolbox made out of wood in the corner of the room. Wade walked over to it and came back to the safe with a sledgehammer and a crow bar.

Bobby said, "Yeah, that's going to do a lot of good."

He winked at Lloyd, pointed his index finger at his temple and rotated it, indicating that Wade had a screw loose.

Wade said to Bobby, "Want me to come over there use it on you?"

Bobby didn't answer. Wade raised the sledgehammer and swung at the door of the safe, the head of the sledge pinging off the heavy steel. He swung again and again with no apparent damage—sweat popping on his face, finally too tired to continue.

Come on," Bobby said. "You're close. Couple more swings you'll have it."

He grinned, having some fun, probably figuring Wade didn't have the strength to go after him.

"Get me the tools," Lloyd said. "I'll open her."

"We're not leaving this safe full of money here with one of you," Bobby said. "Have it mysteriously disappear while we're gone. No offense."

"No offense, huh?" Karen took a drag, dropped her cigarette on the concrete floor and stepped on it. "Maybe we should all go. Stick together till we divide up the money." She made eye contact with each one of them showing she had nothing to hide.

Wade said to Karen, "How do we know he's not planning to have someone come by when we leave? He rented the place."

"He said we could trust him," Karen said.

"And you believe that horseshit?" Wade said.

"You got a better idea," Bobby said, "let's hear it."

"Or you can try the sledgehammer again," Karen said.

Wade threw the sledge and it skidded across the concrete floor. "Don't put this on me. You're the one fucked up."

Sparks were flying and blue smoke drifted up from the safe as Lloyd guided the saw across the top. The blade was brick red and it was made out of some kind of carbon fiber that ripped a seam right through the heavy steel. Lloyd had picked it out when they were at Home Depot, arriving before the place even opened, waiting in the parking lot in the minivan. Robbing Samir was turning into a major production.

Under a sign that said "Power Tools," Lloyd found what he was looking for and held up a shrink-wrapped package.

"This little honey cuts through steel like buttah," he said.

He bought four carbon fiber blades just in case, and a high-performance Milwaukee circular saw. Standing in Home Depot first thing in the morning with Bobby, Lloyd and Wade was strange. With the boots and Def Leppard tee shirt, Wade could've been a construction worker. But the rest of them were dressed too nice, even Lloyd, GQ-ing it in khakis and a white open-collar shirt that looked like it was made out of linen. Wade decided since they were there, he'd buy himself some new spark plugs for his Fat Boy. Karen asked him if there was anything else he needed, some plumbing supplies maybe, or gardening equipment?

Wade said, "What the hell for?"

He was still wound up tight from the night before. She was too after trying to sleep sitting up in the back seat of the minivan, Bobby next to her, Lloyd and Wade in front.

When they got back to the warehouse, Bobby said to Wade, "There it is and you were worried about someone stealing it."

Now a layer of red dust and metal shavings covered the top of the safe. Lloyd worked methodically, cutting a line through the heavy gauge steel. The noise was deafening. It was giving Karen a headache. He cut two lines one way and two the other way, form-ing a square. He wore safety goggles that were coated with red dust. Karen wondered how he could see. Every couple minutes, Bobby stepped in with a can and squirted cutting oil into the kerf. Lloyd had used the word. He said it was a groove made by a cut-ting tool. Karen had never heard it before.

Wade said, "Be careful don't get the money wet."

Lloyd finished the job and put the saw on the floor and took off his goggles.

Bobby patted him on the back. "Is he beautiful? Man knows how to get jiggy with a saw."

Wade came over to inspect Lloyd's work. There were four in-tersecting cut lines on top of the safe. Wade touched the one Lloyd had just finished and burned his finger.

"Fuck," Wade said, shaking his finger, then sticking it in his mouth to cool it down.

"Careful, it's hot," Lloyd said.

Wade glared at him.

Lloyd picked up the sledgehammer and swung it over his head and put his weight into it, bringing it down on top of the safe. The solid thud sound was gone. There was like an echo now. Lloyd dropped the sledge and picked up the crowbar, wedging it into one of the kerfs, levering back and forth. The cut-out square on top of the safe wiggled. Lloyd drove the sharp edge of the crowbar into another seam. He pulled back and the cut-out piece rose up and then fell into the safe with a metallic *clang*. The safe was empty.

Wade locked his gaze on Karen. "What the fuck is this?"

"Don't look at me," Karen said.

Wade flashed a lunatic grin. "Well I guess we'll all go home and try again some other time, eh?" Wade drew a Colt Python from under his Def Leppard tee shirt and leveled it on Bobby. "Where's the money, slick?"

"Ask her," Bobby said, looking at Karen. "You must think we're dumb and dumber. We leave the safe here, go to Home Depot and somebody comes by, cleans it out."

"I don't know what you're talking about," Karen said. She was nervous now, thinking Wade was going to lose it and start firing like he did at Samir's.

Wade aimed the Colt at Bobby and cocked the hammer back. "Where's the money? You got three seconds."

"I'm telling you, it wasn't me, I don't have it," Bobby said, pointing at Karen. "She took it."

Wade aimed the Colt at her now.

"Think about it," Karen said. "He rented the warehouse. I didn't even know where we were going."

Lloyd and Wade stood on opposite sides of the safe. Lloyd held the crowbar at arm's length down his right leg.

Wade aimed his pistol at Bobby. "I believe *her*. Now where's the money at?"

"If what she's saying is true," Bobby said, "how'd I know the combination? I never even met the man." He gave Lloyd a quick glance. "I assumed someone would try to screw someone over. I figured it would be you, Wade, just out of the joint, overcome by greed, going for the whole score."

Wade moved toward Bobby, aiming the Colt, and Lloyd stepped around the safe with the crowbar and swung it, making contact with the back of Wade's head. He staggered and went down, dropping the gun. Karen made a move for it but Lloyd got there first and hooked it with the crowbar and sent it sliding across the floor.

Bobby walked over and picked up Wade's Colt Python and moved back toward Karen and Lloyd. He said, "Where's the money?"

"I don't know," Karen said. "There were a lot of people who knew Samir had a safe in his house."

"Strange," Bobby said. "You never mentioned any of this before. It was a slam dunk, I believe was the verbiage you used."

"It never crossed my mind," Karen said. "Why would it?"

"Now that it has," Bobby said, "who do you think did it? Which one was the renegade?"

Karen said, "I have no idea."

"You dated the man, knew the whole gang," Bobby said.

Lloyd said to Bobby, "Can I talk to you for a minute."

"Step into my office." Bobby swung his arm out indicating the open area of floor where the toolbox was. "Would you excuse us?" he said to Karen.

Bobby and Lloyd walked over to the far end of the room, but Bobby kept his eyes on Karen the whole time.

Lloyd said, "What the fuck's going on here? You going to let her scam you again?"

Again? Bobby wasn't sure what Lloyd was referring to but let it go. "No, I'm trying to let her think she's scamming me. It would work a hell of a lot better if we weren't standing here having a conversation."

"You want to find out where the money's at? Give me a few minutes alone with her," Lloyd said.

"That's one way to do it," Bobby said. "Or we can make her think we're all in this together. We all got screwed, and follow her to the money. I like the element of surprise myself."

"You love to give orders, don't you?" Lloyd said. "Tell people what to do."

Where'd that come from? Lloyd was starting to worry him. "I'm expressing my opinion," Bobby said. "That's all. I'm not giving anybody orders. I'm trying to get the money back the best way I know how. You want to try the hardass approach, go ahead."

Lloyd gave him a blank look. "All right," he said, backing down, "we'll try it your way."

"You sure?" Bobby said, "I don't want to give you orders, tell you what to do."

Karen backed the minivan out of the warehouse and took one last look at Samir's safe in the middle of the floor. When she was all the way out, squinting in the bright morning sunlight, Bobby pressed a button inside the warehouse and the garage door started to go down.

Karen didn't think she'd ever get out of there. Time had never gone so slowly, the last twelve hours creeping along. It was torture. Karen figured Wade would freak and he did. She didn't know what Bobby would do, or Lloyd. He gave Wade a run for his money in the psycho department.

Bobby's plan was to have Karen drive the minivan to the parking lot behind Sears at the Oakland Mall, park and walk away. Bobby and Lloyd would pick her up. Let some shopper find poor Wade on the floor behind the front seat, cooking in the hot sun.

Karen had her own plan: she was going to get away from Bobby and Lloyd, get the money and get out of town. She didn't feel anything close to sympathy for them. They were thieves; they got what they deserved.

She could see the red Mustang in the rearview mirror, cutting in and out of traffic a few car lengths back. She saw the entrance to I-75 up ahead and pressed down on the accelerator. She passed a Ford Taurus going maybe thirty, and took a hard right at the last second from the left lane. Wade's body slid across the floor, and banged into one side of the van and then the other as she turned the wheel and corrected her course, merging on I-75. The Mustang was nowhere in sight. Karen let out a breath.

"Make it look like she's losing us," Bobby said. He let Lloyd drive so he could keep an eye on the minivan.

"I don't have to," Lloyd said. "She is."

As they were coming up on the left in the outside lane, the van swerved right, fishtailing up the expressway entrance ramp then gunning it, heading south on I-75.

"All you had to do was hang back give her a little room," Bobby said.

Lloyd downshifted and turned the wheel hard, making a U-turn over the double yellow, tires squealing, horns honking, cars bearing down on them. Bobby put his hands up bracing himself for a crash.

Lloyd said, "What's the matter, afraid?"

For the first time since Lloyd met him, Bobby didn't say anything.

"You said follow her. That's what I'm doing." Lloyd shot around a slow car and floored it, going left through a gap in oncoming traffic, speeding up the expressway ramp.

"If we'd a done it my way," Lloyd said, "we'd be splitting the money right now. But you wanted to create an element of surprise. Well surprise, she's gone."

Fourteen

Samir was in intensive care, flat on his back in bed, and Ricky couldn't believe how lucky he was. The heart-rate monitor was beeping behind him, and the respirator made a weird pulsing sound. Samir had IVs in both his arms, and there was a plastic oxygen tube that snaked across his chest and disappeared in his nose. Ricky couldn't believe this incredible turn of events. He was happier than he'd ever been in his life. Samir was near death and he was in charge, the one calling the shots. He wanted to yell, he wanted to scream.

O'Clair walked in the room, ignoring him, eyes fixed on Samir.

"He's in a coma," Ricky said back in concerned mode. "May never wake up and if he does, who knows if he'll ever be the same."

"Is that your medical opinion?" O'Clair said. "Or is that what the doctor says?"

"Doctor don't know shit. Mentions things he calls scenarios, what could happen. Covering his ass," Ricky said. "I wanted you to see what they did to him." The side of Samir's face was bruised and swollen. O'Clair put his hand on Samir's wrist and felt his pulse. "I'm running things till he comes back," Ricky said trying out his new role of authority.

"This ought to be good," O'Clair said.

"Hey, fuck you."

"I'll bet you know who did it," O'Clair said.

Ricky said, "What're you talking about?"

"Somebody you do business with," O'Clair said. "Or did. Maybe somebody who works for Samir. It could be you."

"You got a lot of fucking nerve coming in here, saying that to me." Ricky's right hand made a fist. God he wanted to hit him. Step in and drill him. Thinking about it calmed him a little. "Maybe it was you," Ricky said.

"Relax," O'Clair said.

"You relax." Ricky could feel the adrenaline pumping.

"I'm making a point. Whoever it was knew his routine." O'Clair paused. "Knew when to hit, who'd be in the house, where the safe was. It wasn't random, if that's what you're thinking. They happened to be in the neighborhood, picked the house with the lions out front." O'Clair rubbed his knee. "The neighbors see anything? Three guys dressed like cops rolling a welder's tank up to the front of the house."

Ricky said, "How do I know?"

"You talk to them," O'Clair said.

Ricky paused, remembering he'd heard a girl's voice when he was on the kitchen floor, and it definitely wasn't Minde. He decided to keep it to himself, not say anything to O'Clair about it. Ricky didn't trust him, not when it came to a safe full of money.

The door opened and Dr. Kirshenbaum walked in the room. He had silver hair combed back, glasses balanced on the end of his nose, and an angry look on his face.

"Who said you could come in here?" he said to O'Clair. "This patient's in critical condition."

"That's what you're going to be," O'Clair said, "you say one more word."

The doctor turned and walked out.

O'Clair said, "He the one giving you the scenarios, can't make up his mind?"

"Yeah," Ricky said, "that's Dr. Kirshenbaum. You better get out of here before security comes,"

O'Clair moved for the door.

Ricky said, "Hey, tough guy, you find Bobby yet?"

He didn't answer, just opened the door and walked out of the room.

When O'Clair told Ricky he could've been the one who robbed Samir it was as if O'Clair was reading his mind. No, Ricky didn't have anything to do with it, but he sure had thought about it—in debt up to his eyeballs, staring at that safe full of money every day. Ricky was still in the hole fifty grand to Wadi Nasser and the Iraqis were hounding him, driving him crazy.

Thinking about them gave Ricky an idea. Why not use the Iraqis to find Samir's safe? Proposition them. Christ, offer them a piece of the action. "Whatever Wadi's paying you I'll double it," Ricky could hear himself saying. But even if they were interested, where would he tell them to look? If he didn't know who stole the safe, how would they? Samir had enemies. There were plenty of people who might have a motive. But how many would have the nerve and ability to pull it off.

Maybe O'Clair had something to do with it? But if he did, why would he be hanging around? Johnny was another possibility. Ricky knew he had money problems, who didn't, but where the hell was he at? Ricky had been calling Johnny since the robbery. No answer. It was like he'd disappeared, vanished.

O'Clair left the hospital thinking about Ricky. He reminded him of the hothead son with the big dick in *The Godfather*. Sonny—that was his name—Sonny in a warm-up suit. He drove to Samir's and parked in the circular drive. There were strips of yellow police tape across the front door. He got out of the car and went around to the back. More tape crisscrossed the kitchen door. He turned the handle. It was locked. He punched in one of the panes, and unlocked the door.

There was blood everywhere on one side of the room, and holes in the wall from the shotgun, big ones, right through to the studs. He pictured Yalda, who didn't take shit from anyone, standing up to the robbers.

O'Clair went to the house across the street and told a woman with curlers in her hair he was with the West Bloomfield police, investigating the homicide of Yalda Naseem, who'd been murdered the night before, right across the street. The woman looked forty and had a mustache and reminded O'Clair of a guy he'd played football with at Bishop Gallagher. She was real sorry to hear about the poor man who was killed, and hoped Samir would be okay. He was a good neighbor. He didn't make noise and kept his yard nice. No, she hadn't seen anyone, although there was a minivan parked out front for about twenty minutes, a dark-colored one she'd never seen before.

O'Clair went to five other houses. Nobody saw or heard anything or even asked to see his ID. So far all he had was a minivan. Down the street, a teenager was washing a car in the driveway. At first, he thought it was a girl 'cause of the long hair and skinny arms and the way the kid moved. O'Clair walked up and said, "Hey, how you doing?"

The kid didn't say anything, just stared at him, holding a big pink sponge dripping soap bubbles.

"I'm investigating the murder last night of one of your neighbors down the street, Yalda Naseem," O'Clair said. "Did you see anything?"

"No," the kid said. His voice was too deep to be a girl and he had a bulging Adam's apple. He turned away from O'Clair and started washing the driver's side of the car O'Clair now recognized as a Volkswagen Jetta. "You know there's a reward for information . . ."

The kid stopped washing the car now and turned toward O'Clair. "How much?"

"Five thousand dollars," O'Clair said, giving the little sissy something to think about.

The kid said, "When do you get the money?"

"First, you've got to tell me what you saw," O'Clair said.

The kid dropped his sponge in the brown plastic bucket.

"There was a girl in the minivan parked in front. She said she was with Neighborhood Watch, whatever that is."

O'Clair said, "What'd she look like?"

"She had red hair."

O'Clair took off heading for his car, moving as fast as he could without running. His leg hurt, but he didn't care.

The kid yelled, "Aren't you going to take my name? Hey . . ."

When the sissy said the girl in the van had red hair, Karen's face appeared in his head. Karen, who else? When she was hanging out with Samir, she was Karen Delaney. He never did find out what happened, but one day Karen was gone and Minde, the Automotion dancer, had taken her place. O'Clair'd heard Karen was living with a Greek who owned a chain of restaurants, guy named Lou Starr.

On the way to Karen's, O'Clair stopped by the warehouse in Clawson. He parked and walked in the reception room and waited for the guy behind the counter to get off the phone. The guy wore a decorative western shirt with pearl buttons and piping around the pockets, and a lot of turquoise jewelry: a ring, bracelet and a necklace. The guy's nametag said: "Randy." He was talking and enjoying himself. It sounded like a personal call and he didn't seem to be in any hurry to get off. On the wall behind him was a sign advertising additional services. Ask about special pricing on packaging, assembly and trucking.

O'Clair moved to the end of the counter where there was a hinged section and lifted it and went behind where Randy was.

He stopped talking now and said, "Whoa, what do think you're doing? This is for authorized personnel only."

O'Clair grabbed the phone out of his hand and hung it up. "First rule of business, never keep a customer waiting."

"Chief," Randy said, "you're not allowed back here, period in a sentence."

O'Clair handed him the receipt he found at Robert Gal's apartment. "See if it's still being rented."

"It is," Randy said. "There's a three-month minimum. See here? Date's June 10."

O'Clair said, "Remember who rented it?"

"Was two of them as I recall," Randy said.

O'Clair took a photograph out of his pocket and held it up.

"Oh yeah, he was definitely one of them."

O'Clair said, "What about the second guy?"

"Stocky fella with a goatee," Randy said.

O'Clair said, "I'm going to need you to open the warehouse."

"I can't do that, chief. See, that would be against the law."

"Randy, you seem like a bright guy," O'Clair said, "so let me tell you what your options are so there's no mistake, okay? You can give me the key, stay here mind your business and everything'll be fine. Or you can continue to fuck with me and take your chances. Tell me how you want to do it."

O'Clair hit the light switch on the wall. Above him the huge mercury vapor lights hissed and came on, warming up, taking a few minutes to get bright then casting the huge room in yellow-green light. The walls were white, the floor was industrial gray with a clear epoxy that gave it a shine. There were muddy tire tracks just inside the entrance, the marks heavier where a vehicle was parked for some period of time, the outline of the tread visible on the concrete floor.

O'Clair studied the scene. Samir's safe was in the middle of the warehouse floor, it was black with ornate gold accents, and said "Abou Al Fakir," Samir's family name in gold Arabic characters. Samir told O'Clair how his grandfather had bought the safe at the Mosler factory and had it shipped to Beirut. He brought it back when he moved to Dearborn in the fifties. O'Clair remembered Samir telling it like it was an important event in American history.

The top of the safe had been cut open. There was a contractor-grade circular saw on the floor along with an extension chord, a crowbar, three chewed-up blades, and a pair of dust-covered safety glasses. They knew what they were doing. All around the safe and floor was red dust. He could see footprints—some clearly visible, others obscured. There was a lot of blood too, a few feet from the safe. Somebody had gone down and was dragged to a car or van. He followed the footprints and streaks of blood back to where the car had been parked. Okay, Bobby and his crew stole the safe that much seemed clear. What he didn't get, what didn't make a lot of sense was the connection between Bobby and Karen. How'd they know each other?

Fifteen

Karen closed the door. She could hear the shower on in the bath-room. That's what she wanted to do, take a shower and sleep for a couple days. On a table between the two queen-size beds was a brown plastic ice bucket with a bottle of champagne in it. The bot-tle had an orange Day-Glo sticker on it. All that money, he was drinking ten-dollar champagne.

One bed was made and the other one was a mess like some-body had been sleeping in it for a week. She heard the shower turn off and a couple minutes later Johnny appeared, coming out of the bathroom with a small white towel around his waist and another one over his shoulder, hair slicked back and wet. He had a gut. She hadn't really noticed before. He saw her looking at him and sucked it in.

"Jesus, when'd you get here?" Johnny said. "You don't come in, say hello? I was starting to wonder."

Karen didn't say anything. She was tired, exhausted, completely out of it.

"Maybe something happened. Ricky's been calling me nonstop. Jesus, I've been going out of my mind," Johnny said.

Karen said, "Did you talk to him?"

"No, I didn't. And now I won't have to—ever again." He stepped over and put his arms around her.

Karen pushed him away. "You're all wet."

"Everything go okay?" Johnny said. "You look a little tense."

"Do you know why? Because I am." She pictured Wade's loony face and said, "Spend fourteen hours in a hot warehouse with an armed psycho and you would be too." She could feel herself getting angry, thinking about Johnny lying around, watching TV, drinking champagne while she was getting the job done. And *he* thought *she* looked tense.

"Let's celebrate." Johnny poured champagne into two plastic flutes and handed one to Karen. "This'll take the edge off."

She took a sip and wiped the bubbles off her upper lip. "They've got a lot of nerve calling this champagne," Karen said. "Where's the vodka? I want a real drink."

"Don't you want to know how much we got?" He moved to the closet, slid the door open and rolled a big black suitcase out and put it on the bed next to her. She watched him unzip it and turn it over, dumping banded packs of money out on the brown comforter. It was strange after all she'd been through, seeing the money didn't excite her. She didn't feel anything; she was numb.

"Guess how much?" Johnny said.

"Five million," Karen said.

Johnny grinned. "Come on. We've got a million six hundred and fifty-four thousand dollars. I counted it three times. Karen, if that doesn't make you happy, nothing will."

It didn't.

Johnny finished his champagne and poured himself another one, drinking it like it was Dom Perignon. She glanced down at the money and thought about Yalda, who was dead because of her. She looked up at Johnny. "Get me some vodka, will you? Something good, Pearl or Belvedere."

"First tell me where you want to go?"

"I'll think about it while you're gone," Karen said.

Johnny slipped on a pair of black pants, lost his balance and almost fell over.

"You all right?" Karen said. He seemed loaded.

"Fine," Johnny said. "Now that you're here."

He finished the outfit with a tight-fitting Zegna polo that probably cost $200. He straightened his hair and slipped on a pair of white loafers. "Don't move, I'll be right back." He stopped at the door and said, "Can I trust you here with all this money?"

Now it was his. She said, "I trusted you, didn't I?"

The thing that amazed Karen was how easy it had been talking Johnny into it. Lou the Great White Hunter always said lions attacked the weakest member of the herd. That's what Karen did, picked Johnny out, lagging behind everyone, and went after him. He had weaknesses all right. He was dealt a full deck of them, Karen thought. Take your pick. He had a gambling problem, he was in debt up to his thinning hair, and he was a sex maniac. Johnny had showed some interest in her when she was seeing Samir. He never hit on her, but was always giving her compliments. He'd tell her how pretty she was, and how good she looked in a bathing suit—Samir had a pool in the backyard—and how lucky Samir was to be going out with her. He liked her then and she figured he probably still did. It was confirmed after the first drink, sitting at the bar at the Capital Grill on a Monday afternoon, two days after Bobby and Lloyd had broken in. Karen knew Johnny hung out there occasionally and pretended to run into him.

"Karen Delaney," Johnny said. "Wow, what're you doing here?"

He kissed her on the mouth. No tongue, but there was feeling behind it.

"You look good," Karen said, "are you working out?"

"I've been known to hit the gym," Johnny said.

She noticed he was still getting his nails done, and he had a tan that was so perfect it looked like it came out of a tube.

"You know I always had a thing for you," Johnny said, putting his hand on her thigh like he was testing her to see how far he could go.

"Come on," Karen said, "with all the girls you had around."

"I'm serious," Johnny said. "I used to think about you all the time, couldn't get you out of my head."

"I always liked you too," Karen said, feigning interest.

That was how it started. Thirty minutes later they were in the back seat of Johnny's BMW in the Somerset Collection parking lot, making out, Johnny putting the full court press on her. Karen handled the situation without embarrassing Johnny and made him think she was interested, telling him how much better it would be if they waited, how the anticipation would build, and it would be incredible. And if we do it here, Karen said, we're going to get arrested.

Johnny nodded. Sure, no problem, he understood.

Three days later they met in a cheap motel room—as opposed to the luxury suite they were currently occupying at the Red Roof Inn. It was Johnny's pick, Johnny another big spender, following in the footsteps of Lou Starr, the Grand Master of big spenders. Johnny wanted to get right to it. He was unbuttoning his shirt before the door closed. Karen handed him a vodka on the rocks and gave him her pitch: "Do you want to make a lot of money, enough to quit working for Samir and retire?" It was a variation of the line she'd used on Bobby and he was a brain surgeon compared to Johnny.

"What do I have to do?"

"That's the beauty of it," Karen said. "You don't have to do anything." She laid out the plan and he listened, not saying a word until she finished.

"Hell, no," Johnny said, making a face. "You think I'm going to rob my own uncle?"

"First of all," Karen said, "I'm not robbing him. He stole money from me and I'm getting it back."

"Come on," Ricky said. "Samir's rich. Why would he steal from you?"

Karen told him what happened. "I'm going to get my money back," she said. "Whether you help me or not." That was all it took. That little technicality seemed to clear the way for Johnny, absolving him of any guilt or responsibility. She was going to do it anyway, Karen could hear him saying, rationalizing his involvement.

The third time they met, again at a Red Roof Inn (he must've had stock in the place). They were lying on the bed. He kissed her and started unbuttoning her blouse, a look of excitement in his eyes. Karen said, "Let's wait till we're in a nice hotel. I don't want to take my clothes off in this dump and catch something. You know how much E. coli is on a motel room bedspread? I read an article on the subject and you wouldn't believe it. Just hold me."

And he did. Johnny the stud, cuddling with his clothes on, like they were in seventh grade. After that she called the shots and Johnny went along with it. What happened to macho Johnny Karmo? He was in love and told her so—making excuses at first.

"I don't know what's wrong with me," Johnny said. "This's never happened before. I've never met anyone like you."

And then he just accepted it. Landing Johnny had taken less than a week.

Karen told him all he had to do was park down the street from Samir's and follow them to the warehouse, although, at the time, Karen didn't know where they were going. All Bobby would tell her was the warehouse was in Clawson. On the way over she could see the headlights of Johnny's BMW in the rearview mirror, thinking he was following too close, hoping nobody would notice. Nobody did.

Then all Johnny had to do was wait in the warehouse parking lot. "No matter how long it takes," Karen had said, "don't try to come in the place. Be patient, and let it play out. They're going to freak out when I can't open the safe." And sure enough, they did. And sure enough, they didn't trust each other at all after that. And sure enough, they all ended up going to Home Depot together and Johnny went in the warehouse while they were gone and opened the safe and took the money. Karen had unlocked the steel entrance door as soon as Bobby and Lloyd were outside.

Karen loaded the money back in the suitcase. She picked it up and was surprised how heavy it was. She rolled it to the door and opened it and stepped out on the balcony. She saw police cars with their lights flashing, and an EMS truck and a mob of people in the restaurant parking lot next door, surrounding the purple van. She didn't think they'd find Wade that fast. She was nervous now, thinking the police would come over and start knocking on doors, asking if anyone had seen who was driving the minivan.

Lloyd was flat-footing it, had the Mustang up over a hundred—one ten, one fifteen, one twenty in the two-mile stretch to the next exit, passing cars like they were parked. Lloyd was showing an aggressive side Bobby hadn't seen before. It reminded him of a ride at Cedar Point where you think you're going to die. Lloyd was swerving around cars and people were honking at the maniac in the red Mustang, and Bobby now regretted letting Lloyd pilot his ride.

They didn't see the purple minivan and there was no place to get off the expressway unless Karen used that turnaround they passed for *Authorized Vehicles Only*. He doubted she'd do that with a dead man in the back.

Lloyd said, fuck, and pounded the steering wheel. He drove to the next exit, got off and took the ramp at about seventy, tires squealing, the back of the Mustang sliding out.

Bobby said, "Why'd you get off here?"

"You got a better idea?"

He didn't.

They went up Stephenson Highway, checking the parking lots of the mirrored glass office buildings, and, believe it nor not, there it was—the purple minivan—in visitor parking in front of a building with a sign that said "Telecom Devices." They pulled up, got out, checked inside, no sign of Wade. They got back in the Mustang and Lloyd gunned it, burning rubber.

"Still think we're all in this together?" Lloyd said, "You really screwed up, you know it?"

Lloyd was a world-class blamer. Make a mistake and he'd be there to remind you. "You can keep bringing it up, if it makes you feel better," Bobby said. "Or be a man, let it slide." Lloyd gave him a hard look.

"Be a man? Is that what you just said to me?" He hit the brakes and pulled over in the emergency lane, cars were flying by so close it made Bobby nervous.

"I should pull you out of this car," Lloyd said, "kick your smart-ass Canadian butt."

"Or you could put it in fucking gear and try to find her," Bobby said. Lloyd was really getting on his nerves.

Sixteen

Johnny didn't tell her how much trouble he'd had trying to open the safe. He had the correct combination he was sure of that. He'd copied it right out of Samir's address book: 42 R, 5 L, 15 R. He'd followed that exact sequence and it wouldn't open. What was he doing wrong? He tried it again and again, getting more pissed off each time it wouldn't open. He was nervous, thinking it was taking too long and they were going to come back and catch him. But on the seventh try, it worked and the door opened.

He was thinking about Karen. She'd come out of nowhere, knocked him on his ass. He was in love, really in love for the first time in his life. He hadn't banged another chick since him and her had run into each other that day at the Capital Grill. If that didn't prove he'd fallen for her nothing did. He sat in the BMW, thinking about their new life together. No more collecting money, no more putting up with Samir. He figured he could take the money they had and double it easy on the gaming tables of the world. He pictured himself in a white tux, playing roulette at a casino in Monte Carlo, and in a Hawaiian shirt, playing blackjack on Paradise Island in the Bahamas. It was going to be fun. They could go anywhere, do anything they wanted.

Leaving Ann-Marie wouldn't be a problem. After fifteen years of misery he'd never think of her again. He could hear her voice in his head, a nonstop monologue: you're never here; you know that's your third drink; do I have to do everything?; don't wear that tie; you're really getting heavy; your hair's falling out; we never have any money.

The bonus, he wouldn't have to see Nana, his mother-in-law, either, and have to listen to her advice about life, Nana, the expert on everything, who'd spent thirty years working in a party store. He'd miss the kids, for sure, Johnny Junior and little Ashley. That was the only thing he didn't like. But life was a trade-off, wasn't it?

Johnny heard sirens and saw something going on in the Mountain Jack's parking lot, and then he saw Karen come out of the room, rolling the suitcase along the balcony and he felt sick to his stomach. He got out of the car and waited behind the stairs. He could hear the suitcase coming down, bumping the edge of each step, taking forever. When Karen got to the bottom, he stepped out and surprised her.

"Jesus," she said. "Where've you been? We've got to get out of here."

"You weren't going to leave without me," Johnny said, "were you?"

"I heard sirens and got nervous," Karen said.

He studied her face to see if she was lying, but couldn't tell. "You think they're coming for you?" Johnny gripped the handle of the suitcase. He glanced at all the action in the Mountain Jack's parking lot and said, "Everything's cool, baby. Somebody probably had a heart attack, or got a chicken bone stuck in their throat, that's all."

Johnny lifted the suitcase and started up the stairs, so much for their new life together.

• • •

Karen didn't know if she should say something else or just let it go. She assumed Johnny believed her because he wanted to. Now she had to come up with another excuse to get away from him. Maybe she'd just wait till he drank more champagne and fell asleep. He stood the bag up on its wheels and closed the door. She was going to ask him where the vodka was when he turned and hit her and then she flew over the bed and landed on the floor, dazed, the shoulder bag twisted around her neck, choking her.

After that, it was like waking up out of a deep sleep. Karen was woozy, not fully conscious. She watched him come around the bed, towering over her. He stepped toward her and kicked her as she was trying to sit up and the pain exploded in her ribs, knocking the wind out of her. Her first instinct was to get air in her lungs. Then she put her hands up, trying to protect herself as he came at her and kicked her again. Her shoulder stung where he made contact. She fell back on the floor, the thin carpeting not giving her much of a cushion.

When she looked up he had a gun in his hand, a small semiautomatic. He racked it and aimed it at her, hesitated, moved to the bed and picked up a pillow. He was going to kill her there was no doubt in her mind. Karen panicked, reached her hand in her purse, trying to find the Mag. She felt the barrel and moved her hand down and wrapped her fingers around the grip as Johnny moved toward her again. The gun was stuck. She couldn't get it out and held up the purse, a Kate Spade knockoff, and pulled the trigger and the gun *roared*.

The round hit him in the stomach and went through him, punching a hole in the wall. He dropped the pillow and stepped back and sat on the bed, a look of surprise on his face, glancing down at the little red spot on his white designer polo. He still had the gun in his hand. He tried to raise his arm up and aim it at her, but didn't have the strength, and he fell back on the bed and didn't move.

Karen's ears were ringing from the gunshot. She sat up on her knees, her legs bent underneath her. She was still dizzy and leaned on the bed and pulled herself up and sat on the edge. Her vision was clearing, taking in the scene. Johnny was flat on his back—dead, eyes open staring at the ceiling.

Karen felt sick and got up and went in the bathroom and threw up in the toilet. She went to the sink and rinsed out her mouth and checked herself in the bathroom mirror. Her face hurt. Her left cheekbone was red and puffy. She went back in the bedroom and wrapped a washcloth around a handful of ice cubes from the bucket and pressed it to her face. She went to the window, hoping she wasn't going to see police cars pulling up, and cracked open the curtains. There was a red Mustang creeping though the parking lot below. Karen felt her heart race.

She opened the motel room door and watched Bobby and Lloyd cruise to the end of the building and turn right. She picked up her bag and left the room and went down the stairs, walked past the first floor rooms to the breezeway where the vending machines were, and crossed through to the opposite side of the building. The red Mustang was stopped behind her Audi. Bobby was out of the car looking through the driver's side window. She'd parked the Audi there yesterday because there were no spaces in front. Inconvenient at the time—now it was a stroke of luck.

Karen ran back upstairs, heart racing, nerves jangled, and fished the keys out of Johnny's pocket. She covered him with the bedspread and wheeled the suitcase out of the room.

Lloyd pulled into the Mountain Jack's parking lot and Bobby saw the flashing lights. Saw the minivan surrounded by cop cars, an EMS van, a fire truck, and a reporter from the Channel 7 Action News team, a good-looking black girl with a solemn expression, talking on camera. It reminded Bobby of a movie scene, people standing behind yellow police tape, gawking, trying to find out what was happening. Two paramedics lifted Wade out of the minivan onto a gurney.

"We better check the restaurant," Lloyd said.

Bobby said, "You think she stopped to have a piece of prime rib, do you?"

"You're the fucking know-it-all. Why're you asking me?"

Lloyd was developing a real attitude problem. Bobby said, "I think we've got a better chance of finding her at the motel if she's still around."

"Don't let me stop you," Lloyd said.

There was a Red Roof Inn next door. Maybe she went over and made a phone call, or got a room, and if they were real lucky, she'd checked in with her own name. They weren't. There was no guest by the name of Karen Delaney or Karen anything. The hick behind the reception desk, whose name was Gregg with three g's, couldn't remember seeing an attractive woman with red hair around the property. Property? Referring to it like it was a resort. Bobby got a kick out of that.

"You'd remember her," Bobby said.

They cruised through the parking lot hoping to spot Karen, but what they saw behind building number three was almost as good, a silver Audi A4 with black interior, the Audi looking out of place among all the trucks and SUVs. Bobby flashed back to Eastern Market, and saw Karen getting out of a car just like it. Lloyd said he was going to start knocking on doors. He'd check every goddamn room if he had to. He wasn't leaving till he found the money. Bobby had a better idea. You want to get people out of their rooms? Create an emergency.

Karen brought the suitcase down the stairs and saw Johnny's BMW parked across the driveway. She'd get her car later.

"Hey, miss, your brother's looking for you."

She heard the voice, a southern accent, and saw this sleazy-looking guy coming toward her. He was talking to *her*. She slipped her hand in the shoulder bag and gripped the Mag and said, "I don't have a brother."

"Well he's here looking for you. I'm Gregg with the motel."

She moved toward the BMW and he went with her.

"You were supposed to meet him."

She wondered if this Gregg with the motel was all there. "Listen to me," Karen said, "he's not my brother, we're not related." She approached the BMW and opened the trunk and Gregg helped her load the suitcase in it. Then the alarm went off and God was it loud, like the sound of a car alarm but twenty times louder. Gregg turned and looked around and said, "If you'll excuse me, I've got to check this out."

He took off heading for the office and people started coming out of their rooms now, trying to figure out what was going on. There was a guy with a towel wrapped around his waist and shaving cream on his face. Was there really a fire? Karen didn't see any smoke or anything. She turned and saw Bobby coming through the breezeway, locking his gaze on her as she got in Johnny's car. Things were happening fast. She heard sirens and people were scrambling all over the place. Karen slid the Mag out of her purse and put it on the seat next to her. She put it in reverse and backed up as Bobby ran to the BMW, standing in front of it, blocking her. She knew he couldn't do anything with all the people around.

Karen accelerated and the BMW took off and Bobby jumped out of the way. He tried to keep up with her, he ran next to the car, yelling something at her until she punched it and saw him fade in the rearview mirror.

Seventeen

O'Clair ordered lamb and rice and Roditis that was served up to the brim in a little juice glass. He sat in a booth and ate, watching the room with its fake Greek decor—plaster columns and plastic olive vines and black and white photographs of Greek monuments framed on the walls. The lunch crowd was about gone at 1:30 in the afternoon. People had eaten and headed back to work. O'Clair studied Lou Starr, watching him greet people as they came in the door, wondering why a guy who owned twenty-five restaurants didn't hire someone with a little more personality to do it.

"Welcome to the Parthenon," Lou said in a flat voice that had no enthusiasm. The voice saying I don't care if you eat here or not. He didn't have a Greek name. He looked Greek though, stocky, bull of a man, with a surly hardass edge. Nothing like Anthony Quinn in *Zorba the Greek*, who made being Greek look like a lot of fun, dancing and drinking wine.

O'Clair cut a piece of lamb off the shank. He piled some rice and tomato sauce on his fork and shoveled it in his mouth. The lamb was dry and hardly had any taste. He washed it down with a swig of wine.

Lou Starr said something to the hostess and disappeared down a hallway. O'Clair had seen it when he came in. There was an office and restrooms. O'Clair thought Lou should let somebody else greet customers and concentrate on making the food better. He'd have given it one star if he were a restaurant critic, one out of four. He got up and paid his bill.

The cashier said, "How was everything, sir?"

"The lamb was dry and the rice tasted like it was made yesterday, other than that it was okay," O'Clair said.

The cashier, a chunky bottle blonde about forty, in a beige uniform that had *Lou Starr's World Famous Parthenon* embossed on her chest, stared at him, wondering if he was trying to be funny. "Thanks for visiting us," she said. "Remember, everyone's a star at Lou Starr's Parthenon."

"Is that right," O'Clair said. "I don't feel like a star. I feel like someone who just had a second-rate meal." She tried to hand him a black and white photo of the restaurant exterior. He shook his head and moved past her, trying to dig a piece of lamb out of his teeth with his fingernail that wasn't long enough. He tried sucking the meat out now as he went down the hall toward the restrooms. He should've grabbed a toothpick.

Lou Starr was sitting at his desk, adding up the day's receipts. Business had been off for a while, the check average was slipping at all his restaurants, which he blamed on a combination of things, the stock market, the slowing economy, people weren't dining out as much, they were hanging on to their money. He felt the presence of someone and glanced up at a guy filling the doorway. It was amazing how many people stopped here thinking it was the restroom. Lou wanted to say, Hey, you see any toilets? No? Then it's not the men's. He'd been thinking it for a while and finally put it into words. *The consumer was a fuckin' idiot.* Lou said, "It's down the hall, door on the right." He didn't want him going in the ladies' by mistake, give some broad a heart attack, get sued by that loud-mouth attorney, Fieger.

The guy came in the room and pointed to one of the animal heads, hunting trophies he had covering the wall. He was big, six feet, two twenty. "What's that?"

"A dik-dik," Lou said, "it's a kind of antelope."

"How about this one?" the guy said.

"Rocky Mountain ram. That one made book, Boone and Crockett."

No reaction. He didn't know what Lou was talking about. He wasn't a hunter.

"They really bang horns when they fight?"

Lou said, "I saw two rams go at it forty minutes without stop-ping."

"Why do you have all these heads in here?"

"My fiancée, ex now, didn't want them in the house," Lou said. "They made her nervous." The guy surprised him, caught him off guard. "Before you start your spiel," Lou said, "I've already got a cigarette machine. You may have noticed it when you came in the door. I don't need another one. So you're wasting your time." He sure looked like a salesman.

"What're you talking about?"

Or was he a cop? Maybe he had the guy all wrong. "Is this about the robbery? Have you found them yet?" The guy made him un-comfortable, sitting on the edge of the desk like it was his office.

"Where's Karen?"

Lou said, "How the hell should I know?"

He came around the desk, on Lou's side now.

"Let's try it again," he said. "Where is she?"

"I don't know," Lou said. "We were engaged to be married, she just moved out. Left a note on the refrigerator. That's what I get after living with her for eight months and spending a fortune on her—a goddamn note."

"Did Karen ever mention a guy named Robert Gal? Goes by Bobby."

Lou shook his head.

"Bobby Gal, that doesn't ring a bell?"

"No," Lou said.

"She has family in the area, right?" O'Clair remembered that from her days living with Samir.

"Her mother, a born-again, lives in Garden City," Lou said. "And her sister lives in Ferndale and works at this freak show store called Noir Leather."

"Where is it?"

"Royal Oak."

"What's her name?"

"Virginia."

Eighteen

Karen was submerged up to her neck in the hot bubbly water, trying to relax, but couldn't stop thinking about Johnny. She pictured him dead on the brown motel bedspread, the front of his white polo soaked with blood, eyes open, staring at her. She couldn't look at him any longer and grabbed the end of the bedspread and pulled it up and over him, thinking what a shock it would be when the maid came in the next morning and found him. Karen didn't want to leave him like that but what choice did she have? This wasn't a Hitchcock film where you rolled the victim up in a rug and dragged him down the stairs to a car in the middle of the night, and put him in the trunk.

Karen knew the police would be all over the motel, talking to people in the rooms and checking the plates of every car in the parking lot. Why hadn't she thought of that before? Because she didn't imagine shooting Johnny or expect Bobby and Lloyd to show up. Her simple plan was unraveling, spinning out of control. She'd brought the phone in from the bedroom and called her sister.

"Hello," Virginia said.

"Is Fly around?" Karen said. "I need him to help me with something."

"I thought you didn't like him."

She didn't, but he seemed like the perfect guy for what she had in mind. "I've got a job for him."

"What's going on?" Virginia said.

Karen said, "I need him to pick up my car."

"Where's it at?"

"A motel. Is he there?" Karen said. "Let me talk to him."

"You're not cheating on Lou, are you?"

Karen said, "Why would you say that?"

"He's called a couple times looking for you," Virginia said. "I thought something was up."

"What did he say?"

"This is Lou, have you seen your sister? Something friendly like that," Virginia said. "I can't remember why you're with him. Is it his good looks, or his winning personality?"

Karen didn't say anything.

"What's going on?" Her sister dying to know.

Karen said, "I don't want to get into it right now, okay?"

"Where're you at?" Virginia said.

"In a hotel," Karen said. "Where's Fly?"

"What do you want him to do?"

"Pick up my car and take it to your place, and put it in the garage."

"He can't, it's got too much stuff in it. Fly's a pack rat. He's got newspapers dating back to the sixties. He thinks they're going to be worth something someday. And there's all his tools and albums. He's got like five thousand records: the original Grateful Dead, Canned Heat, Hendrix, Led Zeppelin, Cream, the Stones. Some are worth like fifty bucks."

"All right, but I don't want you involved," Karen said. "It might be dangerous."

"But you don't care if something happens to Fly?"

She could hear Virginia breathing through her nose. "He can take care of himself," Karen said, "and I'll pay him."

"How much?"

Karen said, "Two hundred."

"Where's it at?" Virginia said.

Now she was chewing something. Karen said, "What is that?"

"A carrot."

"You don't eat when you're talking to someone on the phone." Karen could hear it crunching.

"Does Lou know?" Virginia said.

Karen held the phone away from her ear till Virginia stopped chewing and said, "I'd say he's got a pretty good idea."

"You're being awfully secretive," Virginia said. "Just tell me what's going on, will you?"

"Lou and I are through," Karen said

"I knew it. And let me say congratulations. It's about time."

Karen told her where she was staying and to have Fly come and get the car key. She hung up and reached over the side of the tub and put the phone on the rug. Now she lay back in the hot water up to her chin, the surface covered with soap bubbles—luxurious imported bath oil from a spa in Switzerland it said on the bottle.

After leaving the Red Roof Inn Karen had driven to a hotel in Bloomfield Hills. She left Johnny's car in the lot and took a cab to the Townsend Hotel in downtown Birmingham. She checked in and walked to a Border's and bought a guidebook on Chicago, her next destination, and went back to her room.

Virginia showed up two hours later. She walked in the room and said, "Wow," glancing around. "What's this place cost a night?"

"Four fifty," Karen said.

"Four fifty? What'd you do, win the lottery?" She walked

through the living room into the bedroom, turned back and looked at Karen. "It's got two TVs?"

"Three. There's one in the bathroom too."

Virginia picked a half-eaten croissant from the room service tray and took a bite, talking while she chewed. "Now I know why they looked at me funny when I came in the lobby. I could never afford this place."

"Do you think maybe it's your hair and outfit?" Her hair was purple and she had a silver stud pierced under her lower lip, and she was wearing a dog collar.

Virginia grinned. "That's entirely possible." She walked in the bathroom. "Look at this tub, you could put, like five people in it." She came out and went back to the room service tray and popped the heel of the croissant in her mouth. "This place is unbelievable."

"They've even got a boardroom," Karen said. "You can plan your next stockholders meeting."

"Perfect," Virginia said and smiled, showing her tongue stud. "I've been looking for a full service facility."

Karen liked the fact that her sister never took anything too seriously.

"I've got to go. Fly's in the car waiting," Virginia said. "Are you going to give me the key?"

"I don't want you involved," Karen said.

"How's he going to drive two cars? I'm just going to drop him off and leave."

Karen handed her two $100 bills. "Tell Fly to call me when he's got the car, okay?"

"I don't care what you say," Bobby said. "She's coming back for it."

"I'll give it a little more time," Lloyd said. "But she don't show by dark I'm out of here."

They'd been sitting in the Mustang in the back of the motel parking lot since Bobby had seen Karen six hours earlier. He'd fallen asleep, gotten out three times to piss. They'd had the car running for a couple hours, putting on the air and listening to the radio and Bobby watched the gas gauge go from full to just over half.

They listened to a seven song AC/DC superset, Lloyd playing air guitar all the way through "She's Got the Jack," "Highway to Hell," "Thunderstruck" and "Back in Black." Bobby was amused, he wasn't used to seeing Lloyd so animated or enthusiastic about anything. He was a low-key Minnesotan, which was probably re-dundant.

Lloyd cut a loud fart and said, "Hear that, I think a moose is loose."

He glanced at Bobby and grinned. It smelled so bad Bobby had to get out of the car for fifteen minutes. Lloyd just sat there, looking out at Bobby, laughing. Jesus Christ. Bobby looked at his watch. It was 7:30 P.M. and still light out. He got back in the car ready to call it a day. He couldn't take any more of Lloyd, the guy biting his fingernails and farting. Bobby had his hand on the key ready to start the Mustang when he saw a little red car drive in the motel lot and park next to the Audi. A guy in a wifebeater got out of the red car and opened the driver's door of the Audi with a key. Okay. Now, finally, they were getting somewhere.

Lloyd looked like he was asleep. Bobby tapped him on the shoulder and Lloyd opened his eyes. He saw the Audi backing out and said, "What the fuck?"

"Exactly," Bobby said. He reached over, turned the key and heard the high-performance engine rumble to life. He shifted into first and followed the Tempo and the Audi out of the motel lot, going right on Rochester Road, hanging back, giving them room, but not too much. They took another right on Fifteen Mile and caravanned all the way to downtown Birmingham.

Bobby watched the Audi drive in a parking garage. He parked in a metered space on Pierce Street, next to a big red-brick hotel, and waited. A few minutes later Wifebeater came out of the parking garage, crossed the street in front of Bobby's car, walked to the end of the block and took a right. Bobby followed and watched him go in the hotel, nice-looking place called the Townsend. He'd bet everything he had that's where Karen was at that very moment, chilling, thinking about all the things she was going to buy for herself with her newfound wealth. Bobby enjoyed the situation now that he had superior position. He drove past the hotel entrance, saw bellhops in green uniforms, helping a couple with their luggage. He saw the red Tempo parked on the street, a girl with purple hair behind the wheel.

Lloyd said, "If she's in there let's go get her."

There was Lloyd jumping the gun again. "Know what room she's in?"

Lloyd gave him a dirty look. "What do you think?"

"I don't think you do," Bobby said. "And I don't think she registered in her own name, and even if she did, you think the hotel people are going to tell us? Oh, you looking for Karen Delaney? She's up in room 225. Why don't you go up and surprise her."

Lloyd said, "Don't use that high-and-mighty tone or I might have to reach over and break your fucking nose, okay?"

"You want to go in look around, be my guest. I'm going to wait till she comes out. What do you think of that?"

Nineteen

Karen saw Johnny flip the bedspread off him. He looked at her and grinned and got up. He chased her out of the motel room and down the stairs to the parking lot. She ran along the side of the building to the breezeway, and that's where Johnny cornered her, in the alcove by the janitor's room. His shirt was completely soaked with blood and his face was pale white. He aimed his gun at her and said, "Why'd you shoot me?"

Karen said, "I was afraid for my life. I . . ." That's when Bobby appeared aiming Lou's .45 and blew Johnny off his feet. Bobby looked at her and said, "Where's the money?" She opened her eyes and looked around the room. She was in a junior suite at the Townsend Hotel, sweating and afraid. It was a dream but it was as vivid as any dream she'd ever had. You didn't kill someone—even in self-defense—without repercussions.

Karen got up and went in the bathroom and brushed her teeth. She came back in the bedroom and turned on the TV. A line moving across the bottom of the screen said, *Channel 7 Action News Exclusive*. Now the camera panned a motel courtyard as a reporter's voice said, "A forty-year-old white male was found shot to death this morning at a local motel."

The camera framed the reporter, a middle-aged journeyman who looked vaguely familiar. He was standing on the second floor balcony of the motel. The room they'd found Johnny in was behind him. He said, "Fifty yards from where I'm standing, Troy police discovered another shooting victim in the back seat of a stolen minivan less than twenty-four hours ago. Are the two deaths related? Police are investigating."

Karen pushed the power button on the remote and turned the TV off. She started to get paranoid, picturing police dusting for prints and finding hers all over the van and the room. She saw herself in orange jail fatigues, her wrists cuffed to a belly chain, besieged by reporters as she made her way into court escorted by her attorney, Mr. Robert P. Schreiner.

She'd had the presence of mind to wipe off the minivan steering wheel, but what else had she left her prints on? She'd opened the motel room door and touched both sides of the door handle, and touched the ice bucket and the bedspread. Could they get fingerprints from a bedspread?

Karen had planned it all so carefully, every detail, and nothing had gone right. Two people were dead, and she was the prime suspect. Maybe not at the moment, but it could happen at any time. There was plenty of evidence if they looked in the right place. Samir stole her money and she was just trying to get it back. Wouldn't a jury sympathize with that?

She tried to calm down, analyzing the situation. So what if they found her fingerprints? She'd never been arrested. The police wouldn't have her prints on file. But a lot of people had seen her at the motel and could ID her, like the hillbilly manager who helped her put the suitcase in Johnny's car. Add it all up and it didn't look good.

But on the positive side, Karen had gotten her car back so there was nothing connecting her to Johnny. Fly had parked the

Audi where she told him to on the fourth floor of the parking garage, the extreme west side. Karen had watched to see if anyone followed him. Nobody had. She could look across Pierce Street from her hotel room window and see her car.

She'd picked up a backpack at Moosejaw and stuffed $500,000 in it. She'd put the rest of the money in two safe deposit boxes at a bank a couple blocks away. Her plan was to drive to Chicago, see her friend Stephanie, then head south to Miami and get on a cruise ship to the Bahamas, and deposit her money in a Bahamian bank—no questions asked. Then she'd fly to Nice and disappear in the coastal towns along the Mediterranean.

Karen had applied for a passport a couple weeks earlier. She had it sent to her mother's in Garden City, figuring she'd be on the run. She called her mom from the hotel to find out if it had arrived. No mail had come for her except for a Garden City High School 15 Year Reunion flyer.

"You're going, aren't you?" her mother said.

Karen said, "When is it?"

"The day after Thanksgiving."

"Mom, I've taken a modeling job in Europe. I have to leave as soon as my passport comes."

"Weren't you going to tell me?"

"I didn't know all the details until today," Karen said.

"Oh, dear," her mother said. "I'm so proud of you."

Karen wondered how proud her mother would be if she found out about all that had happened, hoping her picture didn't appear on the evening news and give her seventy-one-year-old mom a heart attack.

Karen called the passport office in Chicago and was told her passport had been processed and was going to be sent the next day. Finally. She decided to leave the hotel as soon as it was dark and find another place to stay. She had to keep moving. But where?

O'Clair was asleep when he got the call from Ann-Marie Karmo telling him Johnny had been killed. Troy police had knocked on her door at eight o'clock in the morning to give her the bad news, but few details. She wanted to know what happened and asked O'Clair if he'd look into it for her. What was strange, she didn't sound sad or upset, maybe it was a relief after all Johnny had put her through.

Now O'Clair was on the second floor balcony of the Red Roof Inn, looking across the parking lot at the building where they'd found Johnny. It was entertaining to watch the local cops secure the crime scene, taking O'Clair back to his own days on the force.

He stood there like one of the renters who'd gathered on either side of him, coming out of their rooms to see the action. Guys with shaving cream on their faces, cigarettes in their mouths; couple of girls in tank tops, girls drinking beer, smoking cigarettes—up all night, or just getting up—their idea of breakfast—breakfast of champions. It was strange seeing people partying so early in the morning.

At the far end of the building he saw a black maid in a China doll wig come out of a room and wheel her cart toward him. The wig was shiny black and had bangs that came down to her eyebrows. O'Clair moved toward her, blocking her way and said, "How're you doing?" Her skin was the color of dark chocolate and she had high cheekbones and dark eyes that wouldn't look at him. "You know what happened," O'Clair said. "Don't you?" Now she glanced at him.

"You with the police?"

He stared at her, picturing himself in his dark blue Detroit police uniform, his attitude and expression saying, I can make a lot of trouble for you.

"I didn't find him," she said in a slow voice with an island accent that sounded Jamaican. "Was Loretta. She like to faint, going in that room, blood all over, man dead under the bedcovers."

O'Clair said, "What else can you tell me?" He could see her hesitate like she didn't want to talk to him, like she had something to hide. "I'm not with the police."

"That right," she said. "Who you with?"

He could see beads of sweat on her upper lip.

"Man was a friend of mine," O'Clair said. "You saw who did it, didn't you?"

She looked over the railing where the police were. Sweat rolled down her face and she wiped it with the back of her hand.

"I was over in building A, across the lot from where they find the dead man at," she said. "I seen the red hair girl go in there. Come out later on, rolling a suitcase, looking around like she sneaking out."

"What else?" O'Clair said.

"Saw the red hair girl get in a black car, drive off, almost run this dude over. Seem like he know her."

O'Clair said, "What do you mean?" He wiped sweat off his forehead with the sleeve of his tan sport coat.

"Talking to her, like they friends, or was."

"What kind of car?" O'Clair said.

"BMW," the maid said.

O'Clair said, "What'd the guy look like?"

"White dude," the maid said.

"How old?"

"Can't say for sure."

O'Clair took the photo of Bobby out of his pocket and showed it to her. "This him?"

She glanced at it and said, "Could be."

"What do you mean?" O'Clair said. "It's either him or it isn't."

"I don't know. I got work to do," she said, and wheeled her cart past him.

He watched the action outside Johnny's room, local cops going through the motions, and wondered about Johnny. Was he mixed up in it too? Johnny knew Samir's habits, his routine. Knew who'd be in the house and the best time to hit. But O'Clair also knew Johnny and didn't think Johnny would have the nerve to do it.

O'Clair and Johnny had worked together on occasion over the years, helping each other out whenever two guys were needed. He tried to guess how many houses they'd broken into in the middle of the night, surprising the mark who was avoiding them, past due on payment, the vig having multiplied out of control.

In another life, they might've been burglars. They knew a few things about breaking into houses that was for sure. If O'Clair was giving advice to young collectors, he would've said: get yourself a crowbar. With a crowbar you could break into a house, any house in a couple minutes. Okay, a pocketknife too, a good one with a sturdy blade. And don't worry about security alarms because most people forget to turn them on.

What they'd do, O'Clair and Johnny would go into the mark's bedroom, wake the guy up sleeping next to his wife. O'Clair would say, Hey Jerry, or whatever his name was, get up, we need to talk to you. Scare the shit out of him. That was the point; make him feel vulnerable and afraid. The guy would get out of bed in his underwear, praying his wife wouldn't hear them.

One time they broke into a house and sat in the guy's family room and watched the end of a bowl game that was running late— Michigan State against Fresno State. The mark heard the TV, got up, came in rubbing his eyes.

O'Clair had said, "Hang on a second," waiting for the Spartans to score the winning touchdown.

"I'm calling the police," the mark, whose name was Rob Snipes, had said. "What do you think you're doing?"

O'Clair said, "What's the matter, don't you like football?"

Or O'Clair would wake the mark up, bring him in the living room and say, "Want Johnny to go in there keep the little lady company?"

Guy'd start begging. And O'Clair'd say: "You better quit fucking around, hand over the money."

If he got the impression a mark was holding out on him, they'd take his car or his wife's car. No guy wanted to get his wife involved. He'd never hear the end of it.

O'Clair left the motel and drove to the Palace in Auburn Hills to see Minde, the Automotion dancer, surprised the girls were practicing their routines on the Pistons' basketball court. There was a guy on a ladder replacing one of the nets, and maintenance guys in burgundy golf shirts, cleaning the VIP seats. O'Clair and Minde sat on the Pistons' bench, the dancers bending and stretching on the basketball floor—twelve girls with lean hard bodies in all kinds of different outfits—getting ready to practice some new routines for an exhibition game that night.

"He was unconscious when I found him," Minde said. "I was going to call 911, but the police were already pulling in the driveway. How'd they find out so fast?"

Good question. The police told Ricky someone had called 911 from the house. But who? It wasn't Ricky or Moozie or Minde, so who was it? He noticed Minde's face was bruised. It looked like she tried to hide it with makeup.

"My friends thought Smoothie hit me. He has a temper but he'd never do that. It was one of them dressed like cops who did it."

O'Clair said, "Where was Ricky when all this was happening?"

"On the kitchen floor," Minde said. "They taped his hands. I cut him free and he stood up and said what he was going to do when he caught them, not I should've done something when they were here."

That was Ricky, tough guy till he had to prove it. O'Clair was watching the dancers, fixing his attention on a dark-haired girl with a pair of melons that were trying to bust out of her workout shirt. He turned back to Minde as she slid onto the floor and did the splits.

"You don't mind, I have to stretch while we talk," Minde said.

O'Clair said, "What's it like dancing for the basketball fans?"

"It's okay. Most of us model and appear in commercials. We do this to stay in shape. Not for the money, we get like twenty bucks a game."

O'Clair wondered what would happen if he tried to do the splits. He didn't know if he'd be able to get up.

Minde looked up from the floor, her eyes on him. "Oak, do you know who hurt Smoothie?"

"That's what I was hoping you were going to tell me." He took the photograph of Bobby out of his shirt pocket, handed it to Minde and watched her eyes light up.

"He's the one that came out of the closet," Minde said. "I knew he wasn't a cop."

"What about Johnny?" O'Clair said. "You see him that night?"

"He was over earlier, playing cards with Ricky," Minde said. "Left about eight-thirty. He came in the living room and said good night to Smoothie. Yalda locked up after him."

Johnny could've set the whole thing up without being there, without taking part in the actual robbery. Johnny knew Bobby, had loaned him money, and Johnny knew Karen. But again, he doubted Johnny would rob his uncle. It was totally out of character.

O'Clair used his contacts and found out the Bloomfield Hills police department had impounded a black BMW the day before. It was registered to a John Karmo of Troy. Jim Simoff, a former Detroit cop O'Clair had worked with, also told him the car had been left in the Kingsley Inn parking lot with the key in the ignition.

The concierge at the hotel said he'd called a cab for a good-looking woman with red hair and a big suitcase. Metro Cab had taken the woman into Birmingham and dropped her off at Pierce and Merrill the dispatch record said.

O'Clair followed the trail. Across the street was a hotel called the Townsend where all the visiting rock bands stayed. He remembered reading that the Rolling Stones and their entourage spent more than fifty grand there in a week. A woman fitting Karen's description had checked in the day before, a bellhop told O'Clair after O'Clair handed him a $100 bill and said he was a process server. He had to give her divorce papers, put them in her hand.

"I'll take them up for you, sir," the bellhop said.

"It's a legal thing," O'Clair said. "I've been empowered by the 48th District Court," O'Clair said. "Is she still in the hotel?"

"As far as I know, she's upstairs in 326," the bellhop said. "I carried her bag."

"Three twenty-six, eh? How do I get up there?"

Twenty

Karen heard a knock on the door and thought it was room service. She turned down the TV and crossed the room. Another knock. She looked through the peephole and saw a big meaty face, features distorted in the wide-angle opening, but she knew who it was. She saw the handle turn, and swung the safety bar in place just before the door opened a couple inches and locked. She could see him clearly now as he tried to slide his hand through the opening and grab her, but his hand was too big and she turned and leaned her weight against the door and felt it jam him and heard him groan.

She ran into the living room and picked up the backpack. She opened the sliding door and moved out on the balcony, and felt the hot heavy summer air. Behind her she could hear O'Clair driving his weight against the door, trying to break the safety bar. She didn't have much time. There was a lot of traffic below her on the street in front of the hotel, cars double-parked and cars slowing, trying to pull up to the entrance. Two big custom rock band buses were parked down the street. A horn honked. She picked up the backpack with both hands, swung it and let go, and watched it fly toward the next balcony and land on the concrete floor.

Inside the room Karen heard the molding shatter and the door give. She stepped on the seat of a black wrought iron chair and put her foot on top of the metal railing, unsteady, trying to balance— the ground three stories below, and then just went for it, airborne as O'Clair appeared behind her and tried to grab her, reaching over the railing for her leg, but he was too late.

She jumped to the next balcony, landed on her feet, picked up the backpack and glanced over at him as he pulled a gun and aimed it at her. She didn't hesitate, opened the sliding door and went in and locked it. The room was freezing, but it felt refreshing, com- ing in from the heat. There was a suitcase open on the bed that was unmade. She lifted the backpack on the mattress and squat- ted down and slipped her arms through the straps. There was a newspaper on a little captain's table like the one she had in her room. A section of the *Detroit News* was spread open under a plate with breakfast scraps: leftover scrambled eggs, a slice of bacon with too much fat on it, a half-eaten piece of toast, a coffeepot, but no cup. She heard the shower and moved past the bathroom.

She opened the door a crack, expecting O'Clair to be standing there. She looked down the hall toward her room, heart pound- ing. Where was he? She looked left and saw the exit sign, and knew she had to go for it, and do it now. She swung the door open and took off, glanced back and saw O'Clair coming out of her room, running after her, limping on his bad knee.

She made it to the stairs, opened the door and started down, taking them two at a time, getting some rhythm going. She was halfway to the second floor when she heard the door above her open and snap closed. She glanced up and saw O'Clair and felt his weight send tremors through the staircase.

O'Clair took the stairs as fast as he could with his knee that was still mushy and numb ten years after a bank robber shot him with a Taurus 9. The round shattered the patella, and put him in the hospital for two weeks, and then had three months of physical therapy. He remembered the scene like it was yesterday, Terry Booth, an FBI agent squatting in a catcher's position next to him, telling O'Clair he'd been shot and not to move. O'Clair said he knew he'd been shot, he was in fucking agony and there was blood everywhere, and not to worry, he couldn't move if he had to.

O'Clair made it to the bottom and opened the door that said "One" in white block type on the brown wall, and walked into the lobby. He crossed the marble floor, went out the front door and looked down Townsend Street toward the parking structure, and saw her or thought he did at the end of the block, crossing the street, red hair, wearing a backpack. He ran now, limping but moving pretty well, made it to the end of the street, saw her enter the parking structure half a block away, sweat rolling down his face, the air hot and thick.

Bobby was crossing Merrill Street, carrying two Cokes and two Quizno's Italian subs, starving and sore after sleeping in the car all night, listening to Lloyd snore and fart, waiting for Karen to come out of the hotel, and there she was running into the parking structure. Where in the hell was Lloyd at? He dropped the food and drinks on the street and went after her. He knew her car was parked on the fourth level. They'd driven through the parking garage till they found it. Lloyd had this strip of metal he slipped in the driver's side front window and popped the lock in two seconds. Bobby was impressed. Lloyd was a real pro. They searched the car but didn't find anything, no money anyway.

As he got closer he could see Karen through the glass wall just inside the entrance, just part of her going up the stairs. Bobby ran in after her, dodged an SUV pulling out and ran up the stairs to the third level. He'd take the ramp up to four and surprise her as she was coming down. He had the .32 in his pocket. He took his cell phone out and dialed Lloyd while he was moving.

"Where the fuck're you at?" Lloyd said. "I'm starving."

Bobby heard loud rock music in the background. "I'm in the parking garage, chasing Karen," Bobby said.

"Who?"

"Karen," Bobby said. "The girl who stole the money, the girl we've been looking for, remember her?" Fuck Lloyd. He flipped his phone closed. He was on the ramp almost at the fourth level when he heard tires screeching and saw a Mercedes sedan coming at him, and stepped out of the way. And right behind it was a silver Audi. He drew the .32 and aimed it at Karen as she blew by him, Jesus Christ, and ran down the ramp after her.

O'Clair was walking in the entrance to the parking structure as a silver Audi came toward him, Karen behind the wheel. She slowed down and then accelerated and swerved around him, and drove past the exit booth, the windshield frame hitting the wooden parking gate, snapping it off. She accelerated, braked, swerved around the Mercedes, horns honking, took a hard right, moving down Pierce Street.

O'Clair ran out the entrance lane. There was a line of cars waiting to drive in. He walked up to a white Land Rover, glanced in the driver's window. There was a gray-haired guy with a pony-tail, talking on a cell phone. O'Clair opened the driver's door, stuck the barrel end of the Browning 9 against his chest and told him to move over. He needed the car. The guy closed the cell phone, flipped the armrests up and scrambled over the console into the passenger seat.

O'Clair got in behind the wheel, accelerated and drove through the stop sign at Merrill. It felt good in the air-conditioned car, although it was heavy with the smell of cologne. Pony's cell phone rang, a loud annoying instrumental. O'Clair reached over, grabbed it out of his hand, opened the window and threw it.

"Thanks," Ponytail said. "That had my whole life programmed on it."

He had an annoying voice with a lispy whine.

O'Clair saw the silver Audi up ahead, stopped in traffic. He watched it swerve around a Jag that was double-parked, and take a hard left down an alley behind an apartment building.

Ponytail said, "Will you at least tell me where you're taking me?"

O'Clair went left on the next street that ran parallel to the alley and gunned it, the Land Rover surprising him with its power. He slowed for a stop sign, rolled through it, took a right on a street called Henrietta and watched the Audi come out of the alley, turn right and stop at the traffic light at Maple Road.

It couldn't have worked out better. He was behind Karen in a luxury SUV, and she didn't have a clue. O'Clair looked straight ahead at a storefront with the word "Anthropologie" on it, and wondered what kind of stuff they sold in there until he focused on women's clothing on mannequins in the windows.

The light turned green and Karen took a left. O'Clair followed, giving her room.

Pony started in again: "If you let me go, I won't say anything."

O'Clair couldn't take any more of his whiny voice. He reached in his sport coat pocket and brought out the Browning 9, reached across the console, aiming it at his face, and said, "One more fucking word . . ." O'Clair didn't finish, but Pony looked at him and seemed to finally get it. He didn't say anything else. Jesus, he was annoying.

Bobby came out of the parking garage and watched the silver Audi head down Pierce and take a left in the alley just south of Maple, right behind the exclusive Pierce Street condos. Lloyd pulled up in the Mustang and he got in and Bobby said, "How'd she get past you?"

"I don't know," Lloyd said.

"What the hell were you doing?"

"Nothing."

They went after Karen but Bobby didn't hold out much hope of finding her. Lloyd took a left on Merrill, heading west and Bobby couldn't believe it, a silver Audi appeared, coming out of the alley, moving parallel to them on the other side of Shain Park. He watched it turn right on Henrietta, disappearing in traffic.

Lloyd took Merrill to Chester and went right, Bobby thought they'd circle around and catch her driving by on Maple. This was trendy Birmingham, rated as one of the best walking towns in the country Bobby had once read, a square mile of boutiques, coffee shops, restaurants and bars. They waited at a traffic light, a store called Linda Dresner on his right, a few mannequins posing behind the glass in high-style gowns. Smith & Hawken was across the street with its window displays of plants and gardening equipment. He saw the silver Audi turn left on Maple, heading toward them. "Turn," Bobby said to Lloyd, but he couldn't. He saw the Audi go right on Bates. The light turned green but they couldn't move, cars were still blocking the intersection. Lloyd honked and said fuck and started giving people the finger. When the intersection cleared, he floored it, crossed Maple, taking Bates that turned into Willits, curving around a four-story apartment building with restaurants on the first floor and a valet stand on the sidewalk. They drove all the way to Old Woodward and crossed it.

Bobby said, "She must've gone the other way. Turn around."

Lloyd gave him a sour look and said, "Yes, sir."

Karen waited for the light to change. What was taking so long? She checked the rearview mirror, watched a Land Rover pull up behind her. She scanned the cars creeping by in front of her searching for O'Clair, searching for Bobby and Lloyd. A skateboarder appeared out of nowhere, glided by the side of her car and took a right down the sidewalk next to a store called It's the Ritz. Karen was jumpy, nervous. She took the Mag out of her purse, not sure of anything, and put it on the seat next to her. She watched a group of teenagers crossing with the light in front of her, the girls looking full-grown mature, breasts showing under skimpy tank tops, and the guys looking like little kids, short and scrawny, waiting to hit their growth spurt.

The light turned green and Karen eased the clutch up and accelerated. She took a left on Maple, cruised to Bates and went right. The Land Rover appeared in her rearview mirror again. She went left on Willits, gunning it now, the Land Rover disappeared and then reappeared, trying to stay with her.

At the top of Willits Hill she floored it and hit fifty at the bottom and seventy going up the incline on the other side. She looked back and saw the Land Rover come over the crest of the hill, airborne, landing hard, off balance, the shocks taking the punishment.

Karen took a hard right through a residential neighborhood, the Audi bouncing hard on the uneven blacktop. She held the wheel in both hands, looked in the rearview. The street was empty and she let out a breath.

She pulled in the driveway of a house that had a "For Sale" sign in front and drove behind it and parked, hoping the people weren't home. She got out of the Audi and went to the side of the house where she had a view of the street and saw the white Land Rover speed by. She ran out and watched it go to the end of the block, slowing down at a stop sign and then accelerating.

She got back in the Audi and did a 180 and rumbled down the driveway. She looked right and saw the Land Rover coming back down the street, and gunned it. The back end slid out as the tires made contact with the asphalt, and she shifted into second.

Karen saw the Land Rover closing in fast, its grille filling the rearview mirror. She thought it was going to ram her until the turbocharger kicked in and the Audi picked up speed. She took a hard left at Willits. The Land Rover didn't make the turn and went off the road into the woods behind a small apartment complex and crashed into a tree. She could hear a horn blaring like it was stuck, and drove back up the hill and passed Bobby and Lloyd going by her in the red Mustang.

Bobby saw the Audi pass them and said, "Jesus, that's her."

Lloyd hit the brakes and spun the wheel. They went off the road, down an embankment and shot back up to the top of the hill. Lloyd braked hard, the engine rumbling. Willits, the street they were on, met Haynes, which turned at a forty-five-degree angle around a building.

Lloyd looked at him and said, "Okay, now what?"

Bobby looked one way and then the other. He didn't see a silver Audi A4 in either direction. But he knew she wouldn't have gone left and risk getting caught in slow-moving traffic in town. He said, "Go right."

Lloyd looked at him and said, "How do you know?"

Bobby said, "You're just going to have to trust me."

Lloyd popped the clutch and the rear tires squealed and locked on the pavement and they were moving. They went right again and Bobby saw the Audi about three hundred yards ahead on Maple Road, making the turn up the hill. Lloyd went through a red light at Southfield. Bobby was looking for police cars. He looked left and looked behind them on Maple, and then looked down the side streets they passed, going up the hill toward the waterfall at Quarton Lake. They went all the way to Telegraph Road, had to be six miles, without seeing a silver Audi with a good-looking redhead driving it.

Lloyd pulled into a gas station, glanced over at Bobby and said, "Got any more ideas, smart guy?"

He didn't. Not at that particular moment. Karen had gotten away from them again and he wondered if they'd get another shot at her.

The force of the collision set off the airbags. O'Clair's face made contact with the one that came out of the steering wheel and it felt like somebody hit him with a bag of sand. The hood was buckled and steam was pouring out of the radiator, and the horn was stuck on, making a racket. He was dazed, trying to focus. Ponytail was slumped over, unconscious, leaning against the passenger side airbag. O'Clair pulled the door handle but the door wouldn't open. He put his shoulder into it, but couldn't budge it. He pressed the window button and the glass went down and now he brought his legs up and squeezed through the opening head first, hands making contact with grass and dirt. His legs came out the window and he landed on the ground.

A voice said, "Sir, are you all right? Do you need help."

O'Clair looked behind him and saw a good-looking woman about forty, coming across the street, wearing a gardening belt, carrying pruning shears in her hand. He got on his feet and took off moving into the woods. He was unsteady, trying to find his legs. The air was dense and humid, sweat rolling down his face, as he followed the terrain downslope to a creek that wound its way through the woods, mosquitoes feasting on him. He crossed the creek, doing a balancing act on a tree trunk that had fallen across it, and went east up a steep slope and came out at Southfield and Maple, his shirt drenched, breathing hard.

It occurred to O'Clair at that moment he was getting old, tired from walking up a hill. He heard sirens and saw cars pulling over, a police car zipped by, followed by a mobile rescue unit and a yellow fire truck speeding through the intersection. It looked like this rich suburban town had been waiting for a little excitement and now they had it.

O'Clair waited for the parade of emergency vehicles to pass and the light to change, then he crossed Maple and walked three blocks back to the hotel. In the lobby, he ran into the bellhop who'd helped him earlier. His name was Colin, a thin little guy with white-blond hair and skin that was so fair it almost looked blue.

Colin said, "What happened to you?"

"Get me a copy of her bill." O'Clair could feel sweat running down his face that stung from the impact of the airbag and the mosquito bites.

"I don't know," Colin said. "I'd have to find a computer."

O'Clair handed him a damp, crumpled $20 bill.

Colin took it in his hand, made a face like he didn't want it, opened his fingers and saw the amount. He looked at O'Clair and said, "I don't know if I can—"

"I'll be in the coffee shop."

"Okay," Colin said, "but it's going to take some time."

"You've got ten minutes," O'Clair said. "Don't make me come looking for you."

Colin put the bill in his pocket now, figuring he was going to earn it, and headed toward the reception area.

O'Clair was drinking the hottest fucking coffee he'd ever had in his life, scalding his tongue, sitting at a tiny white circular wrought iron table in the coffee shop of the Townsend Hotel. The coffee and blueberry muffin he ordered came to $4.51 including tax. O'Clair asked the girl behind the counter if she'd made a mistake.

"No sir, it's a $1.75 for the coffee and $2.50 for the muffin.

See, it says so right here," she said pointing to a menu open on the counter between them.

O'Clair saw Colin, the bellhop, come in the room, looking around and he waved him over.

Colin handed him an envelope. "Sir, here's your bill."

O'Clair took it from him and pulled out a piece of neatly folded off-white stationery, the paper heavy, the hotel name in shiny gold type. Colin said he had to get back and moved away from the table. O'Clair opened the bill, studying it. Karen had made four phone calls, two to the same number. The cost for two nights, including room service and a couple movies, came to $963—more than O'Clair's mortgage payment.

Twenty-one

Bobby had dropped Lloyd off at the trailer park about 7:30, listening to him complain the whole way there, and then drove home to rethink things. He'd definitely underestimated Karen. She'd made fools of all of them. He parked and went to his apartment, searching his brain on his way up the stairs, trying to remember anything Karen had said that would help him find her. Where would she go? With over a million dollars, anywhere she wanted.

Bobby opened the door, went in and stopped. He couldn't believe it, the place was trashed. His fish tank was shattered on the living room floor. He saw the piranha on its side against a wall, beached on a strip of shoe molding. He saw his golf clubs in a pile on the soggy carpeting. Saw a cocktail glass on the coffee table, like whoever broke in was sitting there having a drink, Jesus, drinking his booze. Bobby had the .32 in the waistband of his pants, his olive button-down J. Crew hiding it. He drew it and went into the kitchen, tiptoeing through an inch of water. He saw the Green Giant pack ripped open on the counter. He went to the bathroom and checked the Band-Aid box. They'd found that money too. Just about everything he had. He left the apartment, walked down the stairs to his car and got in. He was nervous looking around the parking lot, thinking for sure someone was watching him. He drove out of the lot, checking the rearview mirror, no one was following him. He pulled out, cruised past cars parked on the street. Didn't see anything suspicious, nobody sitting in a car watching him.

Karen had it all planned that was obvious. They'd rob the safe; she'd take off, direct Samir's men to Bobby's apartment. "You want the mastermind, the one who organized it?" Bobby could hear her saying. "He lives over in Troy. Take I-96 to 75 and get off at the Big Beaver/Crooks exit. Somerset Apartments, 2335 Sprucewood, you can't miss it."

He drove back to the Chateau Estates Mobile Home Community in Southfield, and parked down the street from Lloyd's trailer as a precaution. He'd looked in the rearview mirror, checking to see if anyone was following him on the way over. No one seemed to be. Bobby walked to Lloyd's trailer and knocked on the door. Lloyd opened it and Bobby said, "I need a place to hang out for a while."

"I thought you didn't like mobile homes," Lloyd said, a can of beer in his hand. "And now you want to stay here, huh? Sure this is good enough for a royal Canadian such as yourself?"

The shit Bobby had to put up with anymore. But it was only for a night he told himself. Then he told Lloyd about the apartment. Someone was on to him.

Lloyd said, "You think they're going to come here?"

"I don't know." And he didn't. He'd been wrong about everything, lately.

"Well if they do," Lloyd said, "we're going to be ready for them."

Lloyd's bravado made him feel better. "You still have the .45?" Bobby said.

"Yeah," Lloyd said, "and I've got something better."

What could be better than a .45? Did he have a machine gun

in there somewhere? Lloyd left the room and came back carrying a strange-looking bow and a quiver full of arrows.

"It's a Hoyt Pro-Star," Lloyd said, handing the bow to Bobby.

It looked like a weapon designed by aliens, the strange shape with its lacquered curves. "It's a real beauty," Bobby said. What were you supposed to say about a bow?

Lloyd took the bow back and gave Bobby one of the razor-tipped arrows. "These are Zwickey 2310 broadheads. You can bring a grizzly down with this rig."

"Keep it handy," Bobby said, picturing a gang of Chaldeans attacking the trailer park on camels, carrying those swords with the curved blades. Scimitars, he thought they were called.

Lloyd said, "Since you're staying, I'll give you the grand tour?"

The grand tour? Bobby was in the main room, could see the whole trailer without taking a step. Was this Lloyd's dormant sense of humor kicking in?

Lloyd said, "My bedroom's in the back next to the bathroom. Check it out. It's got a sliding door that opens onto the deck. This model is called the Ver-sales. It's a French word."

Bobby liked the fact that they didn't abandon the chateau theme. This was good, a trailer named after a famous French chateau and Lloyd didn't have a clue. "What are the names of the other models?"

"There's one called the Vouv-ray and another called the Char-trez," Lloyd said.

Somebody had a sense of humor: the contractor or the marketing people who named the place.

"Well make yourself at home." Lloyd headed toward his bedroom with the bow and arrows.

There was a brown armchair, a beat-up old plaid couch, a coffee table piled with carry-out containers and empty beer cans.

Lloyd was quite a little homemaker. The TV in the corner was turned on to the WWF. Lloyd came back in carrying two cans of Molson Ice, handed one to Bobby, and Bobby said, "Who's your favorite wrestler?" Lloyd just stared at him for a couple seconds.

"Psychosis." He said it as if there was no other choice. "Who's yours? Don't tell me Little Guido." Lloyd grinned. "Not Booker T."

Bobby didn't know who he was talking about, but assumed they were wrestlers. "I'm between favorites right now," Bobby said.

"What kind of smartass answer is that? You making fun of me? Because if you are, you can go find another place to stay." Lloyd grinned then and said, "I got you. You should've seen your face."

Bobby figured Lloyd had slipped into one of his multiple personalities. But, which one? He'd identified at least three. Lloyd, the laid-back country boy; Lloyd the boastful con; Lloyd the bow hunting survivalist—and Bobby was sure this was another one. Oh yeah, he was also Floyd, the boozehound, who got dead drunk and turned into Avoid.

Bobby slept on the couch, a spring popping through, digging into his back, the .32 within easy reach. He couldn't believe the way his luck had soured—everything going wrong at the moment like a black cloud hanging over his head. That's what his mother, Zsuzsa, would've said, delivering the line in Magyar, the official language of Hungary and the Gal family.

Bobby felt the presence of his mother in the trailer and could've sworn he smelled onions cooking, the smell he associated with his mom and goulash, his favorite dish.

Bobby's mother believed bad things happened in threes. He could hear her saying:

"A baj hàromig meg sem àl."

And you had to get out of bed on the same side you got in on or you had bad luck. Bobby's bed was against the wall so that wasn't an issue. His mother also said if your left hand itched, you were going to be rich.

"Ha a ball kezed viszket, pénzt kapsz."

And if your right hand itched, you were going to be poor.

"Ha a jobb kezed viszket, pénzt kötesz."

He didn't believe in these crazy notions but at that moment he wanted his left hand to itch. He lifted his arm and stared at his hand. He'd take anything. But he didn't feel any unusual sensation and it bothered him.

He thought he heard a car, got up and looked out the window. It was a pickup truck parking in front of a trailer down the street. He went back to the couch. He heard a dog bark. In the odd silence the bark sounded like a guy calling someone named Ralph. "Raaaalph," a long bark followed by two short ones, "Ralph, Ralph." Maybe the dog was calling his buddy.

"Barney, shut the hell up, that's enough," a voice said.

The dog stopped barking. All Bobby could hear now were crickets and he wondered why they made that noise. When he was a kid someone said it was because the crickets were doing it, having sex and that's the sound they made. He started drifting off . . .

Next thing Bobby heard was the floor creaking. He opened his eyes and saw Lloyd moving toward him with the bow in his hand, an arrow ready to go. It was dark out. Lloyd put his index finger over his mouth and pointed toward the window. Bobby thought he heard the sound of a car door closing.

They went to the window, crouching, looking out. There was a guy standing next to a dark-colored Cadillac, an old Seville, the car was between the guy and Lloyd's trailer. Bobby thought he was the shylock who had grabbed him at the casino, and he was probably the one who trashed his apartment and followed him here. Bobby watched him coming around the car, holding a semi-automatic with a suppressor on the end of it that was almost as long as the barrel.

Lloyd slid the window open, pulled the bowstring back and let fly. The arrow sliced through the front passenger window like it was made out of paper, and now the guy was on his knees, scrambling to get on the other side of the car. Lloyd moved into the kitchen ready with another arrow. Bobby saw the shylock's head appear, looking over the hood of the Seville, and an arrow went through the windshield inches from him.

The shylock ducked behind the car again and then rose up and started firing. With the silencer, the big semi-automatic sounded like a BB gun. Rounds were punching holes in the thin aluminum walls across the front of the trailer. Bobby hit the deck, got on his belly and stayed as low as he could, and called to Lloyd, "You all right?" No response. "Lloyd . . ." Nothing. Bobby crawled the length of the trailer on his stomach. When he got to Lloyd's room he looked out the sliding door. There was a deck and beyond it, a grassy area and a pond. The shooting had stopped. He didn't see anyone. He slid the door open went out on the deck, moved down the stairs and started to run.

O'Clair'd gone back to Bobby's apartment and waited till Bobby showed up, knowing he'd open the door, take one look and make a run for it. And that's what he did. O'Clair followed Bobby to the trailer park—Chateau Estates—hanging back giving him plenty of room. He figured Bobby was going to the Diehl residence. Dumbshit put his real address on the warehouse rental contract, a bonehead move that reminded O'Clair of dimwits he'd arrested over the years. The moron who robbed a Comerica Bank during a snowstorm came to mind. O'Clair followed his footsteps from the bank to his house three doors away. The man was at his kitchen table, counting the money, when O'Clair came through the door and drew down on him. Another good one was the guy who held up a liquor store and wanted all the money and a fifth of Jack Daniel's. The store owner said he couldn't give him the booze unless he was twenty-one. The guy took out his license and held it up and it was recorded by a security camera. O'Clair was first on the scene, got the guy's address, went there and arrested him. Unbelievable.

O'Clair pulled up in front of the trailer with his lights off and killed the engine. He picked up the Browning, racked it and opened the door. There was a glow on the eastern horizon, the sun starting to rise. He got out and pushed the door to close it, trying not to make noise, and started around the car. He heard it before he saw it, an arrow that blew through the front passenger window and took out the driver's side window too. He got down and crawled around to the other side of the car. He waited and peeked over the hood and another arrow just missed him, went through the windshield and through the front and rear seats and landed in the trunk.

O'Clair rose up and fired eight rounds across the front of the trailer, reloaded and grouped four more shots in a tight circle where the last arrow had come from. Now he made his move, running to the trailer and went in. It was the kitchen. There were bloodstains on the cabinet doors and more on the greasy linoleum floor, spots of blood and smears. He got one of them, he hoped the Indian, but it appeared as though he was still alive, the blood trail going across the floor of the kitchen into the main room. He followed it through the main room into the bedroom. Checked under the bed and in the closet, and went in the bathroom and slid the shower curtain open.

O'Clair went back in the bedroom and glanced out the sliding door, opened it and saw the blood trail continue across the deck. He went outside and looked around. There was a pond. He saw people staring at him from the windows of their trailers, and then he heard the wail of a siren in the distance.

Lloyd sat hunched under the deck holding the bow as best he could. He'd been hit in the thigh, the round had punched through the aluminum wall of the mobile home and slammed into the meaty center of his upper leg. The velocity had knocked him off his feet and probably saved his life as rounds continued to punch holes in the beige laminate cabinets above him. The pain was intense. There was no other word he could think of to describe it. The wound was through and through, a little hole in front, and the back of his thigh was blown out, blood and tissue on the cabinet door below the sink.

He'd heard Bobby call him, but he was in too much pain to open his mouth. The son of a bitch didn't even check to see if he was okay. Lloyd dragged himself the entire length of the trailer, thinking at the time, he should've rented a Vouv-ray model, which was a little shorter—five feet—but might make a difference if the guy came in and caught him.

Lloyd heard movement and felt the floor above him sway and held the bow, watching the backyard through a section of lattice-work. He could see a couple canoes beached at the edge of the pond. People fished its murky depths, kids mostly, catching gold-fish and carp.

Lloyd rubbed his leg trying to get some relief from the pain, and had to breathe a certain way or it hurt more. The pond reminded him of a lake he swam in when he was a boy in northern Minnesota. He'd float in the warm clear water and then dive into the cold depths, the water temperature changing as he went down, getting colder and darker until he touched the bottom and scooped up a handful of sand, and then shot up toward the light, lungs ready to explode, coming out of the water, taking gulps of air. He'd show his friends the sand, proof that he made it all the way down.

He was directly above Lloyd now, the metal creaking. Then he was on the deck, his footsteps sending dust through cracks in the plank floor. Lloyd sat up with the bow ready to fire as a khaki leg appeared and then another one. He took a breath and knocked a broadhead, aiming at the guy's leg and he heard the wail of a siren.

Twenty-two

Karen parked on the street four houses north of Lou's in front of
the Robertses, Jeff and Shelley. She knew them and liked them. It
was Friday night and they were having a party. There were cars
lining the street and her Audi blended right in. It was 9:30 and
dark, and still hot, a sliver of moon hanging over the lake. She
could hear music and voices from the party as she walked between
the Robertses' house and their neighbor's down to the water, and
moved along the beach back to Lou's house. He didn't care about
swimming and let the reeds grow tall along his 150 feet of water-
front.

The house was dark. Karen knew he was back from Vegas and
had been trying to reach him. She had called his cell phone and
left a message. She tried his office at the restaurant and got his
answering machine. Well as long as he wasn't home. In her current state of mind Karen was in no mood for a confrontation with
Lou. She'd had enough excitement for one day. She was exhausted,
drained.

She crossed the backyard and took the steps up to the deck,
and used her key to open the sliding door. She went into the family

room with its comfortable couches and chairs and great view of the lake, locking the door behind her. The house was hot and stuffy. The air wasn't on and hadn't been on for some time. She stood and listened, but didn't hear anything. It was dark and she waited till her eyes adjusted. She had come back to get letters her dad had written, and a one-karat diamond wedding ring that had been her Grandmother Nonie's.

She moved through the house to the living room and looked out. There were cars parked along the street all the way to the Robertses'. None she recognized—just dark shapes in the dim light. She went in the front hall and saw a pile of mail (days worth), on the floor, confirming that Lou hadn't been home for some time. She went through the living room into the bedroom, and thought about the night Bobby and Lloyd broke in, the night it all started.

Karen opened a drawer in the antique desk and found the letters and her grandmother's wedding ring. She decided to take some of the clothes she'd forgotten when she walked out. She went in the dressing room and got her small suitcase and put it on the bed and unzipped it and folded the top open. She went back in the dressing room, opened dresser drawers and grabbed a pair of jeans, her white shorts and a couple blouses. She couldn't see very well so she turned on a small lamp that was on top of the dresser, and picked up a pair of boots and a pair of shoes and took everything in the bedroom and laid it on the bed. She went back in and grabbed the pearls she'd bought herself at Tiffany's, and a couple necklaces and bracelets and turned off the light.

Ricky was in the back seat of the Escalade, watching Lou Starr's house on Walnut Lake for the second night in a row, talking to the Iraqis, Tariq and Omar. They were lucky tonight, someone was having a party, and it must've been a big one. There were cars parked down four or five houses.

Once Ricky realized Samir might not make it, and he was in charge, running the show, it was easy. He was the boss now and didn't have to take shit from anyone. All Samir's collectors: Romey, Saad, Joey, Nasir and now Moozie reported to him. They brought the money they collected and gave it to him, and he couldn't believe it. He was rolling in dough. He'd paid off Wadi Nasser, and still had plenty left over, and more was coming in every day.

Ricky was thinking about the night of the robbery. He'd heard a girl's voice, and that girl he believed was Karen Delaney. She had lived in the house, slept with the man for six months. She probably had an idea how much money was in the safe, and he wouldn't doubt it if she also knew the combination. He didn't know why Samir had hit her and knocked her down and thrown her out of the house, and then burned her clothes in the backyard, first dousing them with gasoline. His uncle wouldn't let anyone mention her name after that. Ricky was thinking, do that to a woman and she would be angry, and he believed an angry woman was capable of anything.

He had contacted the Iraqis a couple days after the robbery. He'd gotten Tariq's cell number from a friend at the Chaldean Social Club, realizing there was no one on his payroll qualified for this kind of work except O'Clair, and there was no way he was going to involve him. So who? And the Iraqis popped into his head. They'd be perfect.

He invited them to Samir's house, and received them in Samir's office, sitting behind Samir's massive oak desk, commanding authority and feeling good about himself. He was the boss now and the Iraqis gave him their full attention and respect as he laid out his plan to find Karen. He gave them photographs of her, shots

Samir had taken on their many trips together, close-ups of her face, smiling, happy, white teeth, red hair cut short in one and longer in another, the photographs capturing her with unmistakable clarity.

The Iraqis, as it turned out, were interesting. Tariq told Ricky how they had left Baghdad on the second night of the American air strikes that shook the city, and believed, as did many of their countrymen, that the American weapons were far superior to anything Saddam had. They snuck out of the garrison, stole a car and drove into Syria.

Ricky said, "How'd you get from Syria to Dearborn?"

"We drive to Damascus," Tariq said, "and then Beirut."

"How far is that?"

Tariq looked at Omar and Omar said, "I think is eighteen hundred kilometers, maybe two thousand."

"And then what?"

"We take flight to Naples, Italy," Tariq said, "another to Amsterdam. From there, we fly to Toronto, Canada. My cousin drive from Dearborn to pick us up."

Ricky was impressed. They'd traveled halfway around the world and made it look easy and he'd get lost driving through downtown Detroit. He liked these wacky Iraqis. That's how he thought of them: strange and weirdly formal, but they got the job done.

Ricky was watching the dark house and thought he saw a light go on in one of the side windows. "Hey, you see that?" he said, looking through the space between the front seats where the console was. Tariq, behind the wheel, looked over his shoulder at Ricky.

"What is it?"

When Ricky looked back at the house the light was off. "Someone's in there," he said.

They got out of the Escalade, Omar had a crowbar in his hand,

Tariq had a shotgun. Ricky walked behind them up the driveway to the two-car attached garage that had a glass-paneled entrance door. It was still hot at 10:30. Ricky had soaked through his nylon warm-up pants and tank top. He said, "Be quiet. Try not to make any noise. We'll sneak in and see who's there." He looked both of them in the eye when he said it, and they glanced back at him blank-faced like they didn't understand.

Omar turned with the crowbar and punched one of the glass panes out of the door, glass shattering on the concrete floor inside the garage. "Hey, what did I just fuckin' tell you? Why don't you ring the doorbell, tell her we're here."

Omar gave him another blank look and reached his hand through the busted pane and unlocked the door.

Tariq said, "We go in now?"

"No," Ricky said. "I thought we'd stand here with our thumbs up our ass."

The garage was empty except for the usual stuff: garbage cans by the door, rakes, brooms and shovels mounted on a wall, a wheelbarrow, snow blower. Omar stuck the crowbar between the jamb and the lock and popped the inside door open and they went in the kitchen.

Karen was putting clothes in the suitcase when she heard glass shatter and a loud bang that sounded like it came from the kitchen or family room. She walked into the living room and listened. Now it was quiet, not a sound. Maybe she was hearing things. Or maybe Lou was home. Then she heard hushed voices, and footsteps on the hardwood floor, moving through the house.

She ran back into the bedroom, glanced at the suitcase on the bed—there was no way—and went in the bathroom and locked the door, her pulse throbbing, heart banging in her chest. She had to get out of the house. The room had a white marble floor and white walls with a cathedral ceiling. There was a big tub in the corner of the room with windows on two sides.

She heard voices in the bedroom and then something with weight behind it slammed against the bathroom door. She was conscious of her own breathing, taking short quick breaths, trying to get air into her lungs. There was a loud bang as the sharp end of a crowbar punched a hole through one of the wood panels of the door. Karen stood in the tub, her body frozen, like an electric current was going through her, unable to move, unable to think.

The crowbar came through the door again, and she forced herself to pull the window up, and kick out the screen. She went feet first through the opening, dropped four feet to the ground, landed in a boxwood, lost her balance and fell over. She got up and crouched in the shadows. She could see the deck behind the house. There was no one on it, and she made a run for the lake, heading downslope thirty yards, thinking she could hide in the reeds till they were gone.

Halfway there she heard them come out of the house and looked over her shoulder and saw three men on the deck, coming down the stairs now as she ran toward the water and disappeared in the reeds that were taller than her, feet sliding in the muck. Karen stepped out of her sandals, squatting at the water's edge, trying to hold her breath, trying not to make a sound as they came toward her, crashing into the reeds. She got down on her stomach and felt the cool water soaking her blouse and shorts and lay there, trying not to move. She couldn't see them but could hear them thrashing around. And then a foot appeared and she looked up and saw a muscular guy in a tank top and dark track pants with white stripes, and recognized Ricky. He moved past her, and she caught a glimpse of a guy with a dark beard she'd never seen before. He looked in her direction, but didn't see her and kept moving. She slid into the water, knee-deep, waist-deep, and then dove down, gliding into cool depths.

Karen came up for air about twenty yards from shore and saw them on Lou's neighbor's beach. She was treading water, nose and eyes barely above the surface. She moved a few yards closer to shore and felt her toe touch the mucky bottom. She studied Ricky and the other two, who she didn't recognize, looking out at the lake. Karen knew they couldn't see her or they'd be in the water.

She did the sidestroke; gliding slowly, trying not to ripple the water or make noise. Ricky and his men moved along the beach and then disappeared in the shadows of the neighbor's property.

Karen could hear music, the Marvelettes doing "Beechwood 4-5789" and saw her neighbors dancing on the Robertses' patio a couple houses over as she came toward shore, body flat in the water, looking around. She came crouching out of the lake and ran barefoot up the lawn to the Robertses' neighbor's, a colonial with the lights on—but didn't see anyone as she went along the side of the house, looking in the windows.

She made it to the front of the house and could see her Audi parked on the street in a long line of cars that extended in both directions. Ricky wouldn't know the car. She had leased it after she left Samir. She'd earned enough for a down payment after doing a couple of Red Tag Sale commercials for the Metro Chevy Dealers.

Karen took the car key out of the back pocket of her shorts and ran to her car. She was unlocking it when she saw headlights coming at her. She moved around the back of the Audi and ducked down as a black Escalade roared by. It went down to the end of the street and turned around and came back. Karen could see Ricky in the rear driver's side window and wondered how many of Samir's men were looking for her?

   She got in the Audi and waited till people started leaving the party and drove out behind three other cars, passing the black Escalade, which was sitting in Lou's driveway, and let out a breath. Jesus.

Twenty-three

Karen rang the doorbell, waited and rang it again. No answer. She went around to the back of the house to a small patio and saw Schreiner in the window watching TV. Karen pounded on the back door and now Schreiner looked over at her. He picked a joint up out of the ashtray, took a hit and got up. She watched him come across the room toward her and open the door.

He grinned and blew out a cloud of smoke. "How about a toke?"

"Maybe later," Karen said.

Now he looked at her and seemed to focus on her wet hair and clothes.

"Jesus, what the hell happened to you?"

"I need a place to stay for a night," Karen said, stepping past him into the family room. He swung the door closed and grinned at her, lids swollen, eyes little slits.

Karen said, "I'm not interrupting anything, am I?"

"God no," Schreiner said. "Peace in the valley."

"Can you put me up?"

"This have something to do with Samir?"

"Aren't you perceptive," Karen said. "Do you have an extra tee shirt and a pair of shorts I could borrow? I wouldn't mind taking a shower too."

"Anything I can do to make your stay at the Schreiner Hotel and Spa more comfortable," he said, grinning, powerless to stop it in his stoned-out condition. He held the roach between his thumb and index finger, the skin around his fingertips yellow from excessive toking.

They went upstairs and he got her a maize and blue University of Michigan tee shirt, and a pair of khaki shorts. The same outfit he was wearing, although his shirt had food stains all over it. "We'll be twins," Karen said.

"Whoopee," Schreiner said.

He showed her where the bathroom was and gave her a folded maize and blue University of Michigan towel. Karen took a hot shower behind a maize and blue University of Michigan shower curtain and felt better. Seeing Schreiner helped too, his laid-back hippie attitude and dry-as-kindling sense of humor made her feel more relaxed, less tense.

After what happened at the Townsend and the Red Roof Inn, there was no way Karen was going to risk staying at a hotel or motel in suburban Detroit. She assumed O'Clair and Ricky would have their people out, checking every place in town. She couldn't go to her mom's or her sister's or her friend Mika's, they were too obvious. So where? And just like that, Schreiner's face popped into her head.

Karen changed and went downstairs. She put her wet clothes in the dryer and joined him in the family room. They sat on the couch, watching a fifty-inch Sony flat screen, a program about praying mantises on the Discovery Channel. He looked gamey, like he hadn't shaved or taken a shower in a few days. His white-veined legs, the color of travertine marble, were stretched out on the coffee table, his bare feet with yellow toenails. The air was on and it was cold, like being in a meat locker.

"Know how they get their name?" Schreiner said.

"Something to do with how they fold their legs," Karen said. "Like they're praying."

Schreiner said, "You know the female runs the show, right?"

Karen met his gaze, but wasn't listening.

"What happens," Schreiner said, "she has sex with the male and then bites his head off."

Karen was mad at herself for going back to Lou's. She'd have to be a lot smarter if she was going to get out of town.

Schreiner looked at her and put the roach in an ashtray on the coffee table. "You haven't heard a word I've said, have you?"

She met his gaze but didn't say anything. On TV a female mantis began to devour the head of her mate, whose body continued to move, gyrating as if he still had all his parts.

"You want to tell me what's going on?"

"Do you have anything to drink?" Karen said.

Schreiner got up and Karen followed him into the kitchen. He opened the refrigerator and said, "Corona or Bass?"

"Bass." She glanced in at the leftovers and takeout containers. Schreiner took a bottle of Bass Ale out and popped the top and handed it to her.

Schreiner looked at her and said, "Do you need legal representation?"

"We tried that," Karen said. "Remember? All I need is a place to stay." She drank the Bass. It had a bitter taste that she liked and it was ice cold.

"I can have a restraining order slapped on him," Schreiner said.

He seemed lucid now, the prospect of a job bringing him out of his marijuana fog.

"You want to tell me what's going on?"

She did, most of it, hiring him first and handing him a hundred dollars as a retainer. Then she got his assurance that anything she said was protected by attorney-client confidentiality; a signed document Schreiner drafted on his MacBook Pro attesting to their new relationship.

It felt good to let it out, get it off her chest. Karen told him how she did it, holding back a few details here and there, but giving him most of it in straightforward sequence. When she finished she felt relieved, like a weight had been lifted off her. She took a swig of ale. Schreiner leaned against the counter and fixed his stoned gaze on her.

"So you committed armed robbery and you're an accessory to murder and you've got Samir's army looking for you. Did I leave anything out?"

"No, that sounds about right," Karen said.

"You seem pretty cool," Schreiner said, "under the circumstances."

"You ought to see me from the inside," Karen said. "I'm scared out of my mind."

"I can get you a bodyguard. I know a former Secret Service agent. His name's Ray Pope, formerly on Presidential Protection Detail."

"I don't need a bodyguard," Karen said.

Schreiner said, "You're right, you need a platoon, a battalion."

"If you're trying to make me feel worse," Karen said, "you're doing a good job."

"Should I just shut up?" Schreiner said.

Karen said, "That's not a bad idea."

"I want to help you," Schreiner said.

"You are," Karen said, "more than you know."

Schreiner said, "Where's the money?"

"In a safe place," Karen said.

"I can hang on to it for you, if you want. Put it in the safe in my office, ease your mind while you're getting ready to leave town."

"That's okay," Karen said.

"You sure you don't want me to help you," Schreiner said, trying again.

"I'm all set," Karen said, trying to convince herself, but knew she wasn't even close.

Twenty-four

Megan knew she shouldn't have taken him back so fast. He'd lied to her and cheated her out of her share of the money from the Greek, contrary to his bullshit story. He might even be lying now. But there was something about him. She couldn't help herself; she liked him.

Megan thought about Bobby showing up at her door, quarter to six in the morning, looking like he'd been put through the wringer.

"I'm in trouble," Bobby had said.

Megan had said, "You sure are." She opened the door and he walked past her into the living room.

He told her about stealing the safe, and about the guy coming to Lloyd's trailer. Then he said he was going to give Megan half his share.

"Sweetie, I figured we'd each clear better than a hundred grand, I was going to take you to Hawaii, start our new life together."

Megan had known some bullshitters in her life, but Bobby took it to a whole new level. Christ, he was Ninja. She said, "I don't want to ruin your day but the police are looking for you too. A Detective Conlin was here asking questions about you."

Bobby looked like he was going to cry and Megan felt bad for him. She wanted to take him in her arms and comfort him. But first she had to make him pay a little more. She had some of the bitch gene in her. What her dad used to say to her mom. "There's even a reward—now up to $7,500 for information leading to your arrest and conviction," Megan said, making it up.

"I've been such an asshole," Bobby said. "I wouldn't blame you if you turned me in."

Megan put her arms around him. "Honey, I'm not going to do that."

She hugged him and put her face against his chest. She could hear his heart beat. "I might worry about your friends at the apartment complex, though, if I were you." Megan took Bobby's face in her hands. She could feel the bristly stubble of his whiskers. He let out a breath that smelled sour and kind of stinky, and seemed to lose what remaining energy he had at the same time, leaning against her now, so tired he'd have fallen to the floor if she wasn't there to support him. "Everything's going to work out, you'll see." She guided Bobby into the bedroom and undressed him and put him in bed. He was so out of it she just took charge. "Lay back and relax, let me do the heavy lifting." She winked at him and now he smiled.

Megan thought about the money while she was searing lamb shanks and peeling potatoes. Bobby was snoring so loud she could hear him all the way in the kitchen. Megan believed in intuition and believed she was one hundred percent intuitive. Her feelings about people and the inevitability of situations had been proven true over the course of many years. And her intuition told her—make no mistake about it—Karen Delaney was still in Detroit. Where exactly, Megan didn't know, but Bobby had said something that got her thinking, gave her a place to start.

She browned the shanks and took them out of the pan and put them on a sheet of tinfoil, and covered them. She sliced potatoes with a mandolin and left them soaking in water to get the starch out. She grabbed her purse and walked out of the apartment. Bobby'd be asleep for hours.

"Guess what I did while somebody was teepee house?" Megan said.

"I give up," Bobby said, glancing at her with puffy eyes. He was still groggy from sleeping all day. He had his elbows on the table and it was a major fucking effort to sit up. Megan was across from him, pulling a piece of lamb off the shank with her knife and fork. Bobby hadn't touched his yet.

"I went to the library and looked at yearbooks—Garden City High School—the Cougars. Their colors are blue and orange. I started with 1980 and went all the way to 2000."

Megan cut a piece of potato and put it in her mouth. It was hot and she drank beer to put out the fire. "Be careful." She fanned her mouth.

Bobby was staring down at his plate. God, he was tired, really out of it.

"What's the matter," Megan said, "aren't you hungry?"

Bobby didn't answer. He wished she'd stop talking. He wished she'd sit there and not say anything for a while. She was driving him crazy.

Megan said, "How many twirlers named Karen do you think I found?"

He looked up at her.

"How about one? Karen Delaney—class of '88."

She handed Bobby a folded piece of Xerox paper. He opened it and saw a shot of Karen in her majorette outfit, short-shorts, gauntlets and white go-go boots from the yearbook, page seventy-four, and a quote from the majorette herself. "Toughest thing was catching the baton at night games in November—you have no idea—it would be like freezing out, and my fingers were numb."

"She was also voted biggest flirt."

Bobby wished she'd just get to the fucking point.

"Her mom still lives on Schaller Drive—thirty-eight years." Megan took a bite of lamb. "Mr. D. passed eighteen years ago, killed by a drunk driver." She said, "When Dad died, Frisky did too. Frisky, bless his heart, was Dad's buddy, a miniature schnauzer who couldn't live without his master. Isn't that so sad?"

No what was sad was he had to listen to this schmaltz-o-rama. He tried the potatoes first. "What's this stuff on top?"

"Nutmeg."

"It's good."

"How do I know all this," Megan said. "Is that what you're thinking? I went over and met Mrs. Delaney. Spent some quality time with her. She's a nice silver-haired old lady hopes Karen and her other daughter, Virginia, give her a lot of grandkids."

"That's really interesting," Bobby said with a mouthful of lamb. Her words were like puffs of ether, zoning him out.

"I told her I went to high school with Karen. A group of us was getting together for a reunion and I wanted to get in touch with Karen to invite her. She thought I was a friend of Virginia's. No, Mrs. D., I said, I'm Missy O'Hara, my hair used to be dark." Megan took a sip of beer. "You know what she said to me? 'Oh, dear, how have you been?' She thinks she remembers me. Isn't that something?"

Bobby looked up from his plate. "Are you trying to make a fucking career out of telling this?"

Megan gave him a dirty look. "If you're so bored and disinterested, I'll stop right there."

They ate, not talking for a few minutes.

Judy came in and jumped up in Megan's lap.

Bobby said, "Can I eat one meal without a fucking cat staring at me?"

"Please don't talk like that in front of Judy. Vans are very perceptive. She'll think you don't like her."

Were all people who loved animals fucking loony?

Megan said, "Do you want to know what I did today?"

The cat purred.

"See, Judy doesn't think I'm boring. Do you girl?"

"I don't care what happened to their fucking dog, or how many grandchildren the old bag wants, has she seen Karen? That's all I want to know."

"She's going to see her, okay? If you'd let me finish. They're planning to get together before Karen leaves town. Did you know she was a model? Oh yeah, and she's moving to Europe—has a big contract."

Bobby was giving Megan his full attention now. "She say when?"

"You sure you want me to tell you? You might get bored again, and I'd hate to see that."

They made up after dinner, Bobby apologized and they had dessert, homemade key lime pie, on Megan's bed, watching a movie. Bobby couldn't think of a more uncomfortable way to eat, lying down with a plate on his chest, but she wanted to see *Eternal Sunshine of the Spotless Mind.* She'd seen it eight times and Bobby said, "Why do you want to watch it again?"

"It's my favorite movie of all time."

Bobby had watched part of it and thought it was about a girl who dated a guy and they had a big fight so she went to a special doctor, and had the memory of their relationship erased from her mind. That's what Bobby wanted to do, have his memory erased so he'd stop thinking about his apartment getting trashed, and losing the money, and Karen making a fool of him. He felt one of the cats rubbing against him.

Megan sat up and said, "Snickers likes you, I can tell."

She picked up the plates and said, "Pause it, will you? I'll be right back," and walked out of the room.

Bobby punched the remote, turned off the DVD and put on the TV—*Wheel of Fortune*, watching Vanna reveal a letter. Snickers moved along the bottom of the bed, glancing at him with an expression that said, What do you think you're doing? This is my bed, asshole. Bobby sat up, reached out and grabbed the cat. He held the little guy up at arm's length, staring into his whiskered cat face. "Hey, Snickers, fuck you." Bobby threw the cat across the room, and watched him bend and twist in midair, somehow landing on his feet on top of an end table, sending picture frames and a terra-cotta planter crashing to the floor.

Megan yelled from the kitchen. "What was that?" He could hear her coming back to the bedroom, shoes clicking on the hardwood floor. He was still watching Snickers, amazed by his moves. Bobby would've given him an 8.5 if he were judging a cat-throwing contest.

Megan came in the room looking pissed off. "What happened?"

"Your cat jumped on the table and knocked all that shit off," Bobby said.

Megan went to Snickers, picked him up and stroked his back. "He's shaking. What did you do to him?"

Bobby got up and went into the bathroom and turned on the shower. He wondered if maybe he'd done something in a previous life—thinking about his luck again—how everything had gone from bad to worse.

Twenty-five

Karen woke up in Schreiner's maize and blue University of Michigan themed extra bedroom, staring at a Lloyd Carr bobble head figure on the bedside table. The room had a dark blue Michigan Wolverine curtain valance, a maize and blue bedspread and pillows and a Michigan wallpaper border.

Karen got dressed, put on her own clothes and brushed her teeth and went downstairs. Schreiner was sitting at the kitchen table, a cup of coffee in front of him, reading the *Free Press*. He looked up when she came in the room. He was wearing the same outfit he had on the night before.

"There's coffee," Schreiner said. "Cups in cupboard in front of you, second shelf."

Karen opened the cupboard door, reached up and took out a cup and filled it from the glass Krups pitcher that was in the coffeemaker on the counter. She took her cup and went over and sat across from him at the table.

Schreiner said, "How'd you sleep?"

"Not bad, considering," Karen said. "I woke up thinking I'd turned into a University of Michigan booster. The excessive use of maize and blue distracted me and took my mind off my problems. If you ever sell this place, it better be to a U of M fan."

Schreiner laid the newspaper on the breakfast room table. He stretched and yawned. Karen picked up the pint container of half & half and poured some in her coffee, stirred it with her finger and licked it.

Schreiner looked up from the newspaper and said, "In case you're wondering, I do have spoons."

"That's good to know," Karen said, and grinned. "What are you doing today?"

"Working," Schreiner said.

"It's the weekend," Karen said.

"Look outside," Schreiner said. "Can you tell what day it is?"

That surprised her. She thought of him as more of a slacker than a worker, and wondered if he smoked weed at the office.

"How about you?" Schreiner said.

Karen said, "I've got to run some errands."

"Are you crazy? I wouldn't go anywhere till it gets dark," Schreiner said.

"There are some things I have to do," Karen said.

"I'll go with you."

This was her deal. She wasn't going to involve Schreiner or anyone else. "I'll be fine, but I need a place to hang out till this evening, if you don't mind. I'm meeting my sister to say goodbye."

"Be careful," Schreiner said. "You see anyone following you, I want you to call me."

"Peace in the valley," Karen said and Schreiner grinned.

Karen decided to pick the money up first. She borrowed one of Schreiner's dark blue University of Michigan caps with a maize-colored M on the front and a blue windbreaker that was too big. She had to roll the sleeves up. She put the cap on and pulled it down so the brim was just over her eyes. She went in the kitchen where Schreiner was still sitting and said, "How do I look?"

"Unbelievable. You're one of us, a member of the U of M nation. I wouldn't have recognized you in a million years."

She drove to Target on Coolidge and bought an Eddie Bauer Northlake duffel bag in a dark color called volcanic gray that looked almost black. The description on the tag said it was made out of lightweight, water-resistant, tear-resistant polyester, and it had a shoulder strap, which was perfect for carrying heavy loads.

Karen paid for the bag and drove back to Birmingham. She parked in a small lot on Hamilton Street. She looked around before she got out of the car, and went in the rear entrance door of Comerica Bank with the Eddie Bauer duffel bag over her shoulder. A young stylish Comerica customer service representative named Pam Glefke escorted Karen downstairs to a private room with a desk and chair and a Picasso print, *Three Musicians*, framed on the wall. Pam disappeared for a couple of minutes and came back with two long narrow safe deposit boxes.

"Take all the time you want," Pam said. "When you're finished, or if you need anything just call me."

There was a phone on the desk. Pam Glefke left the room and Karen got up and locked the door. She unlocked the first box and lifted the top off and stared at the rows of bills in banded packs. She couldn't believe what she was doing or what she'd done. Yeah, Karen had gotten her money back, but at what cost? It seemed unimportant now weighed against all that had happened. She kept picturing Johnny dead on the bed, and Yalda in the kitchen, blood all over the walls and floor. She couldn't get those images out of her head, but it was too late for that now.

She started filling the Eddie Bauer duffel, emptied the first safe deposit box and locked the top back on it. She opened the second box and did the same. The duffel held all the money. She zipped it closed and called Pam Glefke and said she was finished.

Ricky went to the hospital for a meeting with Samir's sisters, Noor and Huda, who Ricky thought looked like men in drag because of their big hands and receding hair. The sisters decided, after an emotional tug-of-war, to take Samir off life support. The doctor had told them that Samir might have brain damage as a result of the beating he received. He could be a vegetable. Ricky wondered what kind? He pictured a head of wet cauliflower from the produce aisle at one of the stores.

The sisters stood over Samir, crying and dabbing their eyes with tissues. They loved their younger brother. They said he was a great man. Ricky was thinking, you ought to work for him, see how great he is. He embraced his aunts and pretended to be sad, but the truth was he'd never been happier in his life. With Samir out of the way, he was in charge, the one giving orders and collecting the money.

They pulled the plug, but Samir didn't die, and Ricky believed, he chose that moment to come out of his coma.

Samir's older sister, Noor, said, "Look his eyes are open."

"It's a miracle," Samir's younger sister, Huda, said.

To Huda everything was a miracle. If the sun shined on a day it was supposed to rain, it was a miracle.

Samir looked at Ricky and said, "Did you find the bastards who stole my money?" Raising his voice, challenging him the second he regained consciousness. The man was a freak. Ricky was so stunned he couldn't talk. He stood there in shock while the sisters embraced Samir, crying again until Samir said something loud and guttural in Arabic and silenced them. They got up and moved away from him, afraid now. They moved toward the door and walked out of the room.

Ricky looked down at Samir and said, "Don't worry, I know who did it."

Samir said, "You know who did it, what are you doing standing here? Why aren't you out finding them?"

Dr. Kirshenbaum came in the room and said, "My God, you're awake."

"Yes, I'm awake," Samir said, "and I'm getting the hell out of here."

"You're not going anywhere," he said. "You've been in a coma for two days. Your condition is profoundly unstable."

Samir said, "I take full responsibility. Get me a release form and I'll sign it."

Dr. Kirshenbaum walked out of the room, shaking his head. Samir tried to sit up, got about a foot off the pillow and crashed back down. He didn't look good.

"Yo," Ricky said. "You okay?"

Samir glared at him. "Who did this? Who stole my money?"

"It was Karen," Ricky said. "And I think Johnny." Ricky didn't know for sure, but he was dead and couldn't defend himself.

Samir took a breath. "Where is O'Clair?"

"I don't know," Ricky said. "He's disappeared, vanished. He could be—"

"Not O'Clair," Samir said. "I do not believe it."

"Well where is he then?"

Samir closed his eyes like he was in pain. "Tell me why this happened?"

"How should I know?" Ricky couldn't read minds, predict what people were going to do.

Samir said, "Johnny's weak . . ."

It sounded like it was an effort for him to talk. Ricky said, "Not anymore, he's not. He's dead."

"What happened?"

Ricky told him.

Samir shook his head. "I want you to find her and bring her to me."

He still wouldn't say Karen's name, like he'd be cursed or something if he did. He closed his eyes, and Ricky wondered if he was dozing off.

"I've lost respect," Samir said, eyes open, back on Ricky. "Robbed in my own house. My enemies are laughing, and also my friends."

Ricky found his clothes, black pants and black shirt, in the closet. He helped dress Samir, thinking this was going to be his new job, dressing the man and taking him to the bathroom, and waiting while he did his business. He went down the hall and got a wheelchair at the nurses' station. He went back to Samir's room and helped him into the chair, and rolled him along the clean shiny hallway. He took the elevator down to the first floor and wheeled him to the front entrance.

When the valet brought Ricky's car up, Ricky lifted Samir out of the chair like he was a child and put him in the front seat of his Lexus. Ricky was sweating, Jesus, exhausted from the effort, and he was in shape.

On the way to his house, Samir told him that anger, the buildup of rage in his subconscious, was what brought him out of the coma, and anger was again his ally, pumping adrenaline into his weakened condition, giving him the strength to leave the hospital against his doctor's advice. Ricky wasn't buying it, the man looked like an extra in *Alien Dead*, a zombie movie he just seen on late night TV.

He pulled up in the circular drive and carried Samir through the front door that had been repaired, up the stairs to his bedroom. He helped undress him and helped him in bed, propping pillows behind him, working his ass off to make the man comfortable and never once did Samir thank him. All he did was give him orders:

"Get me some water," Samir said. "Hand me the switcher for the TV."

It was right there on the table. What, he couldn't reach over and pick it up? Samir was treating him like a servant. Ricky went in the bathroom and filled a glass with water and took it to his uncle.

"Just leave it there," Samir said. "And bring up the money you owe, and everything that you collected while I was in the hospital."

Ricky felt like he was going to be sick. He wasn't expecting that. He'd spent $82,000 of Samir's money, $57,500 to pay off his gambling debts and interest, and $15,000 to get his watch back. What could he say? I gambled and lost my ass and used your money to bail myself out. He wondered what Samir would say if he told him that. He could put his uncle off for a little while, but there was only one way out of this. He had to find Karen and the money.

Twenty-six

"Is she a dom or a sub?"

O'Clair had no idea what she was talking about. He didn't say anything, just glanced at all the strange things on the wall behind her: whips and chains and handcuffs and leather masks. What kind of wacko bought this stuff?

The girl said, "I'll bet she's both, huh?"

Lou Starr said Virginia worked at this place in Royal Oak called Noir Leather, and that's where he was, standing across a glass counter from this girl with purple hair and a stud under her lip. She wasn't that good-looking but there was something weirdly sexy about her.

"I'm fifty percent dominant," she said, "thirty percent submissive, and the other twenty percent, I like to get kind of crazy and experiment."

Now he was looking in her mouth at the tongue stud while she talked. His forehead itched and he rubbed the swollen area around the stitches. She stared at him and he looked down into the glass case at the fireman pumps—whatever they were—on display. He felt like he was in grade school, tongue-tied in the presence of a girl.

"How old is she, your lady? Or is it your mistress? Or your slaveboy?"

"She's forty," he said, making it up.

"What's she into? Bondage? We're having a sale on restraints. A bondage table, maybe? Body suspension? A spanking bench?"

A skinny guy with long hair and tattoos covering his arms like shirt sleeves came through the beaded curtains behind the girl and said, "Ariana, I need you."

"I'm with a customer," she said.

She turned and grabbed a small whip off the wall and cracked it across her hand.

"Or, how 'bout a penis whip for that naughty penis in her life," she said, giving him a sly smile.

O'Clair could feel his face turning red.

"I know a beautiful Domina who's accepting applications for slaves and pantyboys. Kinky sissies preferred, but she will train the right applicants."

O'Clair had had enough of this freak show bullshit. He said, "You know a girl named Virginia works here?"

"Never heard of her," she said. "What's she look like?"

"If she worked here," O'Clair said, "I think you'd know."

"I don't but I'd like to know you."

She wrote her address on a store business card and handed it to him.

"I'm off at five," she said.

O'Clair didn't get it. Why was this girl with a tongue stud coming on to him? He watched her pull out in a red Tempo, trying to decide what year it was, '87 or '88. O'Clair knew the car, his sister Mary Beth drove one just like it that leaked oil.

Two of the calls Karen had made from the hotel were to the weird store he was just in. Karen's sister supposedly worked there, but this girl Ariana he was talking to had never heard of her. Something wasn't right.

O'Clair followed the Tempo, taking Main to the Freeway and cutting over to Woodward, hanging back giving her plenty of room. He didn't know what she was up to, but this weirdo girl with purple hair sure turned him on. He couldn't explain it, what she did to him, how he felt when she was standing across the counter from him. He wanted to reach over and touch one of her perfect pure white cheeks. God she was sexy. O'Clair had stood there, staring at her, hoping she couldn't read his mind.

He saw the Tempo slow down and turn right on Albany. The houses were old and close together, California ranch style, with big front porches. He watched her pull into a driveway, park and get out. O'Clair cruised by and saw the address over the front door as the purple-haired girl walked up the driveway to the side of the house. He noticed there was a two-car garage in back.

He drove around the block, searching for 310 and found it and parked behind a Ford F-150 with a camper top over the bed. He sat back against the cracked leather seat checking things out. There was no hurry. He saw a teenager pushing a stroller along the sidewalk. She glanced at O'Clair and looked away, minding her own business. In this neighborhood he could've been serving a warrant or repossessing a car or arresting someone who'd skipped bond.

O'Clair was thinking about the bowhunter from the trailer park. He'd found out the guy was a hick with a police record from Eagle Bend, Minnesota, named Lloyd Henry Diehl. He was in police custody, Beaumont Hospital in Royal Oak, a second floor private room. The Southfield cops that showed up in response to a 911 emergency—gunshots fired at the Chateau Estates Mobile Home

Community—found a .45 semiautomatic handgun, and a ring stolen from the Lou Starr residence in Bloomfield Hills, O'Clair connecting Bobby and Karen now.

Lloyd was going to be moved to the Oakland County Jail hospital in twenty-four hours, O'Clair had learned. So if he was going to pay him a visit, he better do it quick.

He drove to Beaumont and picked up a bouquet in the gift shop, cheapest one was $15, and hung around the second floor waiting room, watching the nurses' station, and when it seemed like something crazy was happening—all the nurses freaking out and running down the hall—O'Clair made his move, got up with the bouquet and walked down the hall.

Lloyd was watching TV and glanced up when O'Clair entered and said: "Dude, you're in the wrong room."

"My sister dated a guy from Minnesota, Jim Dudley," O'Clair said. "You don't by any chance know him, do you?"

"The hell're you talking about?" Lloyd said.

"These are for you," O'Clair said. He picked up a water pitcher on the table next to Lloyd, pulled the top off and stuffed the freshly cut ends of the flowers in it. Lloyd was flat on his back in bed staring at the TV. It looked like a Seagal action film, the one where Seagal was in a coma for seven years and woke up the day someone was coming to kill him. Lloyd's leg was in a cast elevated by a contraption of silver chains. "You eat a lot of hot dish up there, I understand." O'Clair could see one of the silver hoops of the handcuff locked around the steel bed frame, the other one attached to Lloyd's left wrist. The bed had metal sides that flipped up and locked in position to keep patients from falling out. The only way Lloyd could get out of the room was to drag the bed on one leg. "What exactly is hot dish?"

Lloyd looked at him now. "You start with a can of Campbell's mushroom soup." He split the name Camp-bell's making it two names. "After that it's anything you can think of. There's hamburger and wild rice hot dish. Chicken and potato hot dish. And my personal favorite, ham and lima bean hot dish."

Hot dish sounded like the food O'Clair grew up on, casseroles his mother used to overcook. He glanced down at Lloyd, "Where's Bobby? You going to take all the heat while he's out having fun?"

"You with the A-rabs?"

"What difference does it make?"

"I don't have the money," Lloyd said.

"I know," O'Clair said. "How'd you get hooked up with Karen?"

"We broke into her house one night," Lloyd said.

"Got seduced by her charm, huh?" O'Clair said.

Lloyd said, "I never bought it myself."

"But you went along with it," O'Clair said. "Where is she?"

"Somewhere with a whole shitload of money is my guess."

Lloyd turned away, fixing his attention on the TV now. Seagal was in a karate outfit practicing his moves. O'Clair wondered where he got the outfit and what it was called. "You seen this one?" he said. "Hit men coming to kill him."

"No," Lloyd said, "and I don't want to know, okay?"

O'Clair studied his leg hanging in traction. "That nine hits with some force, doesn't it?"

"What do you know about it?"

"I know if you don't tell me where Bobby's at there's going to be some serious complications."

Lloyd picked his cup up off the table and took a sip of water. "Doctor said I shouldn't get excited."

"We're talking," O'Clair said. "Just lay back and relax."

Lloyd put the cup back on the table and said, "What is it you want to know?"

"Where's your sidekick?"

"If I had to guess, I'd say his girlfriend's."

"See," O'Clair said, "that wasn't so tough was it?"

As soon as he finished with the girl with the purple hair he'd drive downtown and visit Megan, and if he was lucky Bobby would be there this time. He got out of the car and walked up the driveway, hoping someone didn't come out of the house and ask him what he wanted. In the tan sport coat and Hawaiian shirt, he didn't look like he was from DTE or Edison. He saw the back of Ariana's house and her garage. Smoke was pouring out of the grill next door and a guy in a tank top rushed out and threw the top open, releasing a white cloud that drifted up over the backyard and disappeared. The guy was dousing it with water now, and the grill hissed and more smoke rose.

O'Clair crossed a short expanse of burned-out grass and swung his leg over a short rotting picket fence that separated Ariana's property from her neighbor's. He moved along the side of a garage that needed paint, to a door. He turned the knob. It was locked. He leaned his shoulder against the wood and put his weight behind it pushing with his legs. The wood groaned. He tried it again, putting everything he had into it, and the door gave and now he was in the semidark garage that was filled wall to wall with stuff.

There were stacks of old newspapers, tools and boxes piled up to the ceiling, motorcycle frames and parts. He glanced at the front page of a *Detroit News* dating back to 1969. The headline said, "Man Walks on Moon." Another paper had Kirk Gibson on the front page raising his arms in victory after the Tigers won the

World Series in '84. O'Clair had gone to the game, remembered Gibson's game-winning home run.

There were boxes of records. He pulled out several albums scanning the covers: *Live at Leeds,* The Who; Big Brother and the Holding Company with Janis Joplin; and a group called Electric Flag, he'd never heard of. Behind the wall of boxes he saw a vintage Harley with a custom paint job. Sweat dripped down his forehead into his eye. He had to catch his breath and sucked in air that was stale and musty and he coughed. He was way out of shape and had to do something about it after he got the money. Start exercising again.

It was a two-car garage and there were two small windows in the garage door. He wiped a line of dust away and could see the house.

"What's he doing here?" Fly said.

"Looking for Karen," Virginia said. "I want to find out what he wants." The truth was, she was also attracted to him.

"Maybe he's an old friend," Fly said, "that ever occur to you?"

"I doubt it," Virginia said. "My sister doesn't have friends like that."

"What's he doing in the garage?" Fly said. "Better not be messing up my shit."

Virginia said, "How could you tell?"

Fly gave her the evil eye. His real name was Gary Garringer. He'd gotten the name Fly before Virginia ever met him. Fly said he used to take acid at parties and think he'd turned into a fly. He'd put on his leather aviator helmet and goggles and move around buzzing at people. That all stopped one night when a guy who called himself the Lizard blew a flaming mouthful of Jack Daniel's into Fly's face. He lost his eyebrows but the name stuck.

Most of the people who knew Fly had no idea what his real name even was.

She watched the big guy come across the burned-out lawn to the back of the house. Virginia swung the door open and said, "Won't you come in. I've been expecting you."

His face had the same confused expression it had at the store. She didn't have a plan—just invite him in and see why he was looking for Karen. But, as usual, Fly screwed everything up. He came in behind the guy and hit him in the back of the head with this thing he called his *schlepper*, a leather sack filled with ball bearings.

The big guy didn't go down, it was amazing. He turned and threw an elbow that caught Fly and knocked him off his feet. Virginia lifted the heavy iron skillet off the stove and swung it and hit him on top of the head. His knees buckled and he dropped to the floor. She didn't mean to hit him that hard and hoped he was okay.

Fly was slow getting up.

"I wanted to talk to him," Virginia said. "How am I going to do that now?"

"Don't blame me," Fly said. "You're the one who clocked him with the fry pan."

"You didn't give me any choice," Virginia said. "He was going to kick your ass."

"He got lucky," Fly said going through the guy's pockets now.

Virginia said, "You're lucky I was here to save you."

Fly had the guy's wallet. He opened it and took out his driver's license. "His name's O'Clair. That mean anything to you?"

Virginia shook her head, but the name did sound familiar now that she thought about it. He worked for the Arab guy Karen used to go out with.

Fly dragged the guy by his feet to the basement door, bent over trying to pick him up. He was a load. She could hear his body bang on the steps as Fly took him down to the dungeon.

Virginia was rolling a joint when Fly appeared a few minutes later, breathing hard.

"Why's this dude looking for your sister?" Fly grabbed her arm, wrapping his hand around her biceps. "This have something to do with the car I picked up? You know something you're not telling me?"

"Stop it," Virginia said, "that hurts."

Fly said, "You holding out on me?"

"No," Virginia said.

Fly let her go. "You better not be. Where's Karen at?"

"I don't know. I've been calling her cell phone all day. She doesn't answer."

Fly gave her his mean biker look, trying to be a badass.

"You think she calls me up," Virginia said, "tells me what she's doing every minute? Hey, Gina," she said in a voice trying to sound like Karen, "I'm going to take out the garbage, I just wanted to let you know."

"Don't get smart with me," Fly said.

He had the same look on his face the night he hit her. Hauled off and decked her because she didn't bring him a beer fast enough. I'm not your slave, Virginia had said at the time, and he'd lost it. Her cheek was black-and-blue for weeks. She split after that, went to live with her mom.

Fly showed up a week later and said he was sorry and asked her to come back, and against her better judgment, she did. Karen told her she was nuts. If he hits you once, he'll do it to you again. Virginia realized she was afraid of Fly and always would be. "I'm going to see her tonight, you forget? Me, Mom and Karen—it's girls' night out."

"You have all the fun, don't you? If you're lucky, Mom will tell you a few of her entertaining choir stories. Or what she did yesterday."

Fly could be a real dick.

Twenty-seven

Karen wanted to drive to the Bingham Center and say goodbye to her friend Mika, a former model from the Czech Republic who ran the Elite Model Agency, the company that had represented her for fifteen years, but realized it was too dangerous. Karen phoned her from Schreiner's house.

"I can't believe you're leaving," Mika said, a hint of an accent still there after twenty years in the U.S. "I'll miss you."

"Me too," Karen said.

"Listen," Mika said. "There were two men here looking for you earlier. One asked for you by name. He said he wanted to hire you."

"Hire me for what?" Karen said.

"A new clothing line, but it didn't sound right, like he was making it up on the spot. I said, give me your card. But he did not have one," Mika said.

Karen said, "What was the name of his company?"

"I asked him," Mika said, "but he did not answer."

"How many clients walk in off the street," Karen said, "and ask for a specific model?"

"They are the first in twenty years," Mika said. "They give me the creeps. Do you know them?"

"No," Karen said. But she knew who they worked for. She was nervous now. "What did they look like?"

"The one that did the talking had dark hair and a fancy beard, you know like it was sculpted, perfect. The other one was tall and thin and never spoke, not a word. He just stare at me."

Mika had just described the two guys who were with Ricky at Lou's house the night before.

"I told them you are not available," Mika said, "you quit the business and left town."

Karen said, "What'd they say?"

"Nothing," Mika said. "They walked out. Ever see the movie *Men in Black*? That's who they remind me of—those two guys who wear sunglasses, there was something strange about them. They are not from around here, I can tell you that."

This was one of four locations on the list from Ricky, 3945 Schaller Drive in Garden City. The name confused Tariq. There was no city and there was no garden, just small houses lined up one after another. They had been sitting in the splendid Cadillac Escalade, a gift from Tariq's uncle, since two o'clock in the afternoon and it was now five o'clock. He saw no one enter or exit from the house. Tariq had read *Sada Alwatan*, the *Arab American News*, every word, from the front to the back. The large headline on the cover page said: "Uncertainty Hangs over Mideast." He was thinking, of course, what else? He was thinking about his four years in the elite Republican Guards, the Hammurabi Mechanized Infantry Division, wondering what so was elite about marching behind Soviet T-72 tanks on maneuvers in the desert for weeks at a time. Or loading shells into Austrian GHN-45 howitzers, firing at targets they could not see, even with the aid of binoculars. He wondered too about the namesake of his military unit and its connection with the ruler who established the greatness of Babylon in 1792 B.C., uniting Mesopotamia with his code of laws.

He was also thinking of his good fortune to be living in America, away from the suicide bombers and the craziness of Baghdad. To Tariq it made no sense—Arabs killing Arabs. Why? But that part of his life was over. Now he was looking to the future and saw himself as a man of great wealth. When they found Karen Delaney and brought her to Ricky, he would give each of them $25,000, a considerable sum of money. If they found her within forty-eight hours, he would give each of them $50,000. Ricky was desperate to find this woman, but he did not tell them why.

They sat in silence, Omar was not one for conversation. Words seemed precious to him. He did not want to give them away. Talking to Omar was the same as talking to a wall made out of bricks and mud. Instead, Omar sat next to him, singing the lyrics to "Kol El Aarab" by Marwan Khoury, and at the same time ejecting the magazine from his Beretta semiautomatic and snapping it back into place—*click click*, *click click*, *click click*—until Tariq could not listen any longer and said, "Enough." Omar turned his head staring at Tariq but not saying anything. "Put the gun away. If someone sees the gun they call the police, and then we have problem."

Omar had no expression, his face was blank as always.

Tariq studied the piece of paper Ricky had given to him. He turned the ignition, watching the navigation screen rise up in front of him, displaying a map. The second address was in Birmingham. He entered 564 Wallace Street, Birmingham, Michigan, on the screen, and a voice said, "Turn right in fifty yards . . ."

Karen saw someone come across the patio and moved to the glass-paneled French doors. She thought it was Schreiner until he got closer and pressed his face close to one of the glass panes, looking in the house. He had a dark beard and dark hair. He was one of Ricky's men she'd seen at Lou's the night before, and one of the guys Mika had described. She heard him turn the door handle, moving it up and down. Thank God Schreiner had locked the door.

She was in the breakfast room. She heard the doorbell ring. She moved through the kitchen and looked down the front hall past the dining room to the front door. She could see someone standing on the porch. He knocked on the door. She heard glass break and looked behind her and saw Beard's hand come through the busted-out pane, trying to unlock the door.

Karen got down on her hands and knees and crawled back into the breakfast room. She crawled through the room and down three steps and opened the garage door. It was dark. Her car was parked, pointing out, Schreiner's suggestion. She got in and turned the key and heard the engine trying to start. It sounded weak like the battery was going. She turned off the radio and air-conditioning and tried again. It cranked a couple times and then started. The garage door opener was on the console between the seats. She pressed it and the door started to go up and light came across the floor. That's when Beard came at her out of the darkness and startled her. The window was down. He reached in, grabbed her arm and tried to pull her out of the car. She panicked, trying to fight him off, and then buried the accelerator, taking him with her, Beard hanging on to the doorsill, fear in his eyes now, then letting go as she blew out of the garage, just missing the door that was still rising.

She saw him go down hard on the concrete, and looked through the windshield and saw the other one standing in front of her on the driveway. She turned the wheel, aimed the front end at him, tried to run him over, and he jumped out of the way. She went right on Wallace and saw them running to the Escalade that was parked on the street two houses away.

Karen took a right on Stanley and crossed Lincoln and went left on Bates, a boulevard, pulse accelerating, speeding past parked cars through a residential neighborhood, going seventy in a twenty-five. She checked the rearview mirror but didn't see them, tension easing, letting up as she went left on Fourteen Mile Road.

Karen went to Lim's Palace, a Chinese restaurant in Clawson. This was the last place anyone would come looking for her. She parked in back and went in the rear door and sat in a red Naugahyde booth in back. The inside was so dark nobody would recognize her even if they knew her. The bar was to her right and most of the seats were taken by serious drinkers with boozy lowball cocktails in front of them. She ordered a Coke and sat there waiting for Virginia.

She saw a flash of light as the front door opened and Virginia came in and stood next to the cashier, her eyes trying to adjust to the darkness. Virginia moved through the tables in front, and came toward Karen down the narrow aisle that separated the bar and the booths. Karen waved. Virginia saw her and slid in the booth across from her.

"Could it be any darker in here? I'm going to need a seeing-eye dog when I go back outside," Virginia said. "What's with the hat? I barely recognized you."

"I'm trying to keep a low profile," Karen said.

"You're doing a good job," Virginia said. "What's this, your incognito outfit?"

Karen didn't say anything.

"Are you going to tell me what's going on?"

"I got my money back from Samir," Karen said.

"He must've been in a good mood that day," Virginia said.

A petite Asian girl in a red dress trimmed in gold brought menus and asked Virginia if she wanted something to drink. She ordered egg rolls and a Bud Light. Karen said she was fine.

"He didn't give it to me, I took it," Karen said and told her how she did it.

Virginia said, "No wonder they're looking for you."

"Who're you talking about?" Karen said.

"This big dude named O'Clair came in the store."

Karen said, "How do you know it's O'Clair?"

"Fly's got him in the dungeon," Virginia said.

"What? Why didn't you tell me?"

"That's what I'm doing," Virginia said. "I'm telling you. It just happened. I invited him over."

Karen shook her head. "You invited him over? Tell me you're kidding."

The waitress brought Virginia's beer and walked away.

Virginia picked up the bottle and took a drink. "And Mother told me some girl came to the house looking for you. Said her name's Missy O'Hara and she went to Garden City with you."

"Missy O'Hara's got MS," Karen said. "She's in a wheelchair." Well it wasn't Missy O'Hara, so who was it?

"Things are a little crazy, aren't they?" Virginia said.

"You could say that," Karen said. "What did you tell Fly?"

"It's girls' night out. He thinks I'm having dinner with you and Mother."

"What's he going to do with O'Clair?"

"What do you want him to do?"

"Keep him till I leave town. Did you bring the passport?"

"I couldn't find it," Virginia said, and drank her beer.

"Mother said she was going to leave it on the kitchen counter."

"I'm sorry, it wasn't there and she wasn't either."

Now what was she going to do? "When I get somewhere you can mail it to me."

"Let's just go get it."

"It's too dangerous. Somebody could be watching the house."

Karen didn't want to involve her mother and sister in this mess. She had stayed away from her mom's on purpose, thinking that whoever was looking for her would go there first.

Virginia said, "I've got an idea."

Her idea was to have Karen drive them to Garden City and park on Burnley, the street behind their mom's house. Virginia would run through the backyard, get the passport and come right back. It'll take like two minutes.

"Somebody might see you," Karen said.

"It's dark out," Virginia said. "And I'm going to be so fast nobody will have a chance to see me."

Karen didn't like it.

Virginia told her she was overreacting, and Karen finally gave in, thinking maybe she was right. Now she was sitting in the Krippendorfs' driveway, looking at the back of her mother's house. There were lights on in the kitchen and her mom's bedroom. Virginia had been gone five minutes and Karen was getting anxious. She tried her sister's cell phone, and it went to voice mail. She tried her mother's phone and it was busy. Her mom didn't have call waiting, didn't think it was necessary. Karen pictured Virginia waiting for their mother, a talker, to get off the phone. She sat there for five more minutes, regretting coming here. It was dumb, but it was too late to change it. She got out of the car and snuck through the Krippendorfs' yard to the back of her mother's house and looked in the kitchen window. She didn't see anyone. There was a freshly lit cigarette—a Virginia Slim—her mother's brand, in an ashtray on the counter, smoke drifting up to the recessed lights in the ceiling. She moved across the back of the house and looked in the dining room. It was dark. Karen didn't see anyone or hear anything. She went around the side of the house, ducked behind an evergreen and scanned the street. She didn't see a red Mustang or a black

Escalade or Ricky's Lexus, and moved back around the house and opened the door and went in the kitchen. The cigarette had burned down to ash and filter. She closed the door and heard someone behind her. Bobby came out of the pantry, a grin on his face, aiming the .32 at her.

"I wondered if I'd get another chance," Bobby said, "and here you are."

"Where are my mom and sister?" Karen said.

"Where's my money?"

"It's in a safe place," Karen said.

"It better be."

They went in the living room. Her mother and Virginia were on the floor, looking up at her. Their wrists and ankles were ducttaped together, and there were strips of tape over their mouths. A little blonde was sitting in one of the blue wingback chairs, holding a gun, a revolver that looked big in her tiny hand.

Bobby said, "Look who's here." And to the little blonde he said, "I told you she'd come in."

The blonde looked at him and yawned. "Yeah, you really know what you're doing." She said it sarcastic.

"Mom, I'm sorry about this," Karen said.

"Isn't that precious," Bobby said.

Karen could see tears in her mother's eyes, and she felt awful. She hadn't wanted to involve her family and now they were in the middle of it. Bobby slipped the .32 in the front pocket of his khakis and picked up a roll of silver duct tape that was on the coffee table.

"Give me your hands," Bobby said.

Karen put her hands together and moved her arms toward him. He ripped a twelve-inch strip off the roll and looped it twice around her wrists, taping them together.

"Where's the money?" Bobby said to her.

"At a friend's house," Karen said.

"A friend's, huh? Must be somebody you trust a whole lot," Bobby said. "We're going to go get it, and we're going to leave Mom and Sis here with my associate."

The blonde got up and stuck the revolver in the waist of her black capris and said, "I've got an idea, why don't you stay here with Mom and the freak and I'll go with her and get the money."

"What's the matter," Bobby said, "don't you trust me?"

The blonde said, "Are you going to screw up like you did last time?"

"I guess you'll just have to wait and see, won't you?"

Twenty-eight

O'Clair opened his eyes. He was groggy, trying to focus, trying to figure out where he was. A voice said, "It's about fucking time." And now the biker appeared, standing in front of him. "Hell, I was starting to wonder about you."

O'Clair was sitting in a chair in a basement room, wrists held tight by leather restraints attached to chains that were bolted to the wall. His mind flashed back to the biker coming up behind him and hitting him, and then something heavy crashed into the back of his head. He couldn't believe these two amateurs had taken him. Jesus Christ, it was embarrassing. "What'd she hit me with?"

"Cast iron skillet," Fly said.

"You going to tell me what you want?" O'Clair pulled on the chains with his arms but couldn't budge them, the leather restraints strained but held his wrists tight.

"Give it a rest, " Fly said. "That's high tensile steel. You're not going to get out till I let you out. Now tell me what you're doing here?"

"Looking for Karen," O'Clair said, and noticed he had a blue-green fly tattooed on his neck and barbed wire that wrapped around his biceps, the tat for idiots with no imagination.

Fly said, "What the hell you want her for?"

"She stole some money," O'Clair said.

"It must've been a lot," Fly said. "You're a real high roller, aren't you? Got that '99 Caddy and twenty-eight bucks in your wallet. Man, I'm impressed."

Fly wore a black leather vest with nothing under it, his fat gut hanging over his belt. "Belongs to a guy I work for," O'Clair said. "She ripped him off for over a million."

Fly rubbed his chest. He had a heavy beard but not much body hair, and he smelled.

"Help me," O'Clair said. "I'll cut you in."

"You will, huh? Oh, boy." Fly flashed a crazy grin. "We gonna be partners?"

"You know where she is?" O'Clair pulled on the chain with his right hand.

"I might," Fly said. "Tell me, what the hell I need you for?"

"How're you going to open the safe?" That stopped him, got his brain in gear.

Fly said, "How do I know there is a safe?"

"I work for a bookmaker," O'Clair said. "He had a million dollars in a safe stolen from his house. Karen lived with him. Karen was seen the night of the robbery in front of the house, positively identified by a neighbor. You think I'm making this up? Where is she?" If that didn't get through to him, he might have an easier time breaking the chains that were holding him.

Fly said, "You got the combination?"

"That's what I'm saying," O'Clair said.

"Let me see it," Fly said.

O'Clair said, "It's in my head."

"Maybe I should just beat it out of you." He held up the black-jack like he was going to use it and grinned. "All right, I believe you."

He unlocked the restraints, first one then the other, dropping them on the floor. O'Clair rubbed his wrists, stood and stretched, glancing around the room now. "What do you do in here?"

"All kinds of crazy shit," Fly said. "It's our dungeon."

O'Clair shook his head. He didn't get it. "So where is she?"

"Karen? Right now, at her mom's with Virginia, the girl you came to visit."

So it was her after all. "They were calling her Ariana at the store."

Fly said, "That's her pretend name, you know, when we go to the dress-up parties and such."

"How'd you get involved in all that?" O'Clair said.

"Just lucky, I guess," Fly said. "Want a beer?"

O'Clair wanted a beer more than anything. They went upstairs to the kitchen and Fly pulled two bottles of Miller High Life out of the refrigerator, popped the tops and handed one to O'Clair. He stared at the cold bottle before he brought it to his mouth and guzzled half of it. He didn't know if a beer had ever tasted so good.

"Jesus," Fly said, watching him, "you're a beer drinker, aren't you?"

O'Clair was staring at a photograph of Fly with hair down to his shoulders on a motorcycle, Virginia standing next him with a joint in her mouth. "What happened to your hair?"

"I was out at a farm one day buying weed and this dude was shearing a horse," Fly said. "It was ninety-seven degrees out and I had long hair as you see. When the dude finished the horse, I asked him if he'd clip me."

O'Clair said, "Shave it yourself?"

"Or Virginia does me in the shower," Fly said.

O'Clair tried to picture Virginia naked and wet with her purple hair, shaving Fly, the image stirring his loins. He drank his beer.

"She said she was lookin' out for Karen, that's why she invited you over here," Fly said. "I just wanted to make sure."

O'Clair slugged down the rest of his beer and said, "Who're you looking out for?"

Fly said, "Who do you think?"

O'Clair raised his empty. "Got another one?"

He held the Caddy—with the new windshield that cost twelve hundred bucks, and the two side windows that were three bills each—steady going sixty. There were still holes in the front and back seats where the arrow had gone through, but he didn't care about that.

O'Clair had gotten his keys and wallet back, including the twenty-eight dollars that Fly had folded and stuffed in the front right pocket of his jeans. Fly wore a silver skull and crossbones ring on one hand. O'Clair had noticed it when he handed him the money.

"You've got to admit you don't appear to have much going for you," Fly said. "Dude, you seen a mirror recently. Look at you, your clothes. That sport coat's a fuckin' relic."

O'Clair said, "What convinced you?"

"You mentioned he was a bookmaker with a safe. I remember Karen going out with him—an A-rab, isn't he? And then it all made sense. Maybe you knew what you were talking about. There was something else that was strange. She paid me two hundred to pick up her car at this motel. I think she was shacking up with some dude."

Right, O'Clair was thinking. He had to pick up her car 'cause she took Johnny's. Why exactly, he couldn't quite figure out. They were on 696 heading for Garden City, a town O'Clair had never been to in his life, Garden City the gateway to Romulus. Fly hadn't stopped talking since he got in the car. Now he was bragging about his days riding with the Renegades, a Detroit biker gang.

"Sixty of us badasses would rumble into a small town, scare the shit out of people. I mean like a western movie. Grown men ducking into stores, mothers pulling their children to safety. Cops would just watch us, too afraid to do anything. We'd go into a bar challenge the whole place." He glanced over at O'Clair. "What's the matter? Am I boring you?"

O'Clair looked out the window, saw a street sign that said "Windsor." They were in a residential neighborhood, passing parked cars and small brick ranch houses.

Fly said, "Take a left up there. It's the third house on the left."

O'Clair made the turn, pulled into the driveway and turned off the engine.

"Okay, let's go get her," he said to Fly.

Twenty-nine

The first day back from the hospital Samir had slept all afternoon and all night, and was still sleeping when Ricky went to check on him the next morning. He hoped and prayed Samir would die in his sleep, but no such luck. Ricky listened to his labored breathing and watched his chest rise and fall.

He went back to check on him an hour later and Samir was awake, but groggy. His eyes would open and look at Ricky and then close and open again.

"How you feeling?"

Samir said, "Where's the money?"

"What money?" Ricky said, playing dumb. "Oh you mean the money Karen stole from you? No word yet, but I'm on it."

"The collections," Samir said.

Ricky said, "You've been asleep since you got home."

"Now I'm awake."

Ricky thought he had a few days before Samir would bring this up, and by then the Iraqis would have Karen and he'd be able to pay Samir back the $82,000 he'd lost, and be rich. "The doctor said you shouldn't work or even think about business for two weeks at least."

"Bring me my money," Samir said, raising his voice. He started coughing and couldn't stop.

Ricky went over and picked up the water glass on the bedside table and handed it to him. He drank some water and it helped. He drank more and stopped coughing. "I'm not going to jeopardize your health." Ricky remembered the doctor saying something like that at the hospital. Ricky thought it sounded good. What could Samir say to that?

"I'm not going to ask you what you did with the money," Samir said. "You have till tomorrow to give it to me—all of it."

"Take it easy," Ricky said. "I've got it."

Ricky went downstairs and called Tariq. His phone rang three times.

Tariq said, "Yes?"

"What's going on?" Ricky said. "Talk to me, tell me something good."

Tariq told him they went to the lawyer's house and almost had her.

Ricky said, "Almost had her? What're you doing? Two of you can't handle a girl? You've got to find her today. I'm going to give you each $50,000. You know how much money that is?"

"If you pay $150,000," Tariq said, "I guarantee we will find Karen Delaney."

Now the Iraqis were trying to take advantage of him. "I'll go one twenty but you better deliver." He hung up and thought, but what if they didn't find her? What if he didn't recover the money? Ricky needed a backup plan. He called Wadi Nasser. He hated to do it but didn't have a much of a choice. He asked Wadi if he could borrow a hundred grand for a few days, a week at the most.

Wadi said, "I don't know Ricky, that's a lot of money. I'd have to charge you 20 percent."

Ricky said, "That's fucking robbery."

"Listen," Wadi said. "I'm doing you a favor. You want it or not?"

Thirty

"Your mom's very disappointed you're mixed up with someone of my ilk," Bobby said. "That's a direct quote."

"I am too," Karen said.

Bobby said, "You propositioned me, remember?"

Yeah, she remembered, and regretted it every time she thought about what happened. They were in the kitchen ready to leave. The little blonde was standing a few feet away. She looked bored.

"Do it quick," she said, "okay? I want to get out of here."

Bobby looked at her and said, "What do think I'm going to do, take my time, make a night of it?"

"I never know with you," the blonde said.

"Yeah, well don't worry about it."

The blonde said, "I'm not worrying, I'm just telling you."

"We're going to take your car," Bobby said to Karen, "so it looks like you're coming back from wherever you've been."

He had gone through her purse and found her keys. She'd left her gun in the trunk.

Bobby said, "Who's at the house watching the money?"

"A friend of mine," Karen said. "A guy named Bingo." She thought using a real name would sound more believable.

The blonde said, "What kind of name is that? Is he a clown?"

"No," Karen said. "He's a security guard, big teddy bear of a guy. You don't have to worry about him." She did know a security guard named Norm Darwish who had worked auto shows with her and his nickname was Bingo, but he didn't have anything to do with this.

"Okay," Bobby said, "but I'm warning you. You try anything . . ." His words trailed off.

He opened the back door and they went out. Bobby had his hand on Karen's biceps, guiding her across the lawn and through an open gate in the fence to the neighbor's yard. It was dark out and still hot. The Audi was sitting in the Krippendorfs' driveway where she'd left it. Virginia had mentioned they were out of town and suggested that Karen park there.

Bobby opened the front passenger door for Karen and helped her get in. He went around to the driver's side and got in behind the wheel. He reached across her and grabbed the seatbelt and pulled it around her and buckled it. He started the car and backed down the driveway.

"Imagine my surprise when the safe was empty," Bobby said. "But then again, it isn't over till it's over, is it?"

She could see a little grin on his face.

"My mother used to say, '*Ha a ball kezed viszket pénzt kapsz,*'" Bobby said. "Know what that means?"

"My Hungarian's a little rusty," Karen said.

"If your left hand itched, you're going to be rich," Bobby said. "And my hand is definitely feeling itchy."

He was already counting the money. Karen took him out to an area in West Bloomfield where the lots were big and the houses were far apart, and picked a place that didn't have lights on. "Think you could loosen this tape a little so I could get some feeling back in my hands?"

"We're going to be there in a couple minutes," Bobby said, "aren't we?"

"My fingers are turning blue," Karen said.

Bobby said, "I can't help you. Let me tell you something else. If the money isn't there—"

"Slow down," Karen said, cutting him off. "It's right up here."

Bobby downshifted. They were out in the middle of nowhere. There were no streetlights and it was dark now and hard to see. The houses were single-story on enormous lots. Karen said, "There it is."

Bobby turned left into the driveway. It was forty, fifty yards to the house, a brick ranch with no lights on.

"Where's your friend?" Bobby said.

"He must be at work," Karen said.

Bobby stopped about halfway to the house. He glanced over at her. "If he's in there with a gun, you're the one I'm going to shoot first."

"If he was home his truck would be parked there," Karen said. "Do you see a red Chevy Silverado jacked up like Big Foot? If you don't, he's not here."

"Maybe it's in the garage," Bobby said.

"It doesn't fit in the garage," Karen said. "You need a step-ladder to get in it."

Bobby slowed down and stopped the car about halfway to the house, and turned off the engine. He pulled the key out of the ignition and put it in his pocket.

Karen said, "What're you doing?"

"Going to the house," Bobby said, "surprise any security guards named Bingo who might be waiting for me." He reached behind him and pulled the .32 from the waistband of his Levi's. He got out and walked up the driveway toward the house.

Karen's wrists were taped, but she could use her hands. She unhooked the seatbelt, but waited till Bobby was almost to the house before she opened the door and got out. She kept a spare key in a little magnetic box under the rear fender, her dad's advice. God bless Dick Delaney. She got it and got in behind the wheel. She opened the box and took out the key. She started the Audi and put it in gear, and gunned it, doing a 180 on the grass and then headed back down the driveway. She saw Bobby in the rearview mirror, running after the car. She buried the accelerator and he disappeared.

Bobby wanted to know where she got the key. Why didn't he check the car? His spirits were at an all-time low. He was walking in the pitch fucking dark in the middle of bum fuck and had no idea what he was going to do when he saw headlights approaching.

Now he stood in the middle of the road, waving his arms. The car flashed its brights and swerved around him and came to a stop about twenty yards down the road. Bobby ran to it, a white Dodge Neon, coming up on the passenger side. The window was down. There were two clean-cut black dudes in the front. They were wearing white shirts and ties.

The one in the passenger seat said, "Sir, do you need help?"

The driver said, "Can we give you a ride?"

What was this? Were they putting him on? Bobby pulled the .32 out from under his shirt and said, "I think I'll just take your car." They were Jehovah's Witnesses and Bobby hoped they learned a lesson here today. "Never stop and offer to help someone, understand? You might get car-jacked."

Bobby went back to Karen's mother's to get Megan and it looked like the set of a cop show, police cars everywhere, lights flashing.

He wondered what could've happened. He saw Megan come out of the house in handcuffs escorted by two Garden City cops. He saw his Mustang parked down the street but he didn't dare go near it with all the police around.

Bobby drove downtown to Megan's apartment in the white Neon that had about forty horsepower, and a Bible on the seat. He sat in the parking lot, staring up at the dark windows of her apartment, overcome by paranoia. The cops could be up there waiting for him. He picked up the Bible and felt a vibe. Maybe this was the way it was meant to be. He didn't have the money, but considered himself lucky. Wade was dead. Lloyd was in jail. And Megan, it appeared, was on her way. Bobby had a couple grand and a fresh start. He'd learned a shitload about trusting people where money was concerned too. You didn't.

He decided to go back to Canada, lay low for a while. He could see the shoreline of Windsor across the river. He took Jefferson to the tunnel, paid his toll and drove the mile and a half under the Detroit River into Windsor, Ontario. Traffic moved fast. He was back in Canada in a couple of minutes, then stopped in a line of cars waiting to enter the country.

When it was his turn, Bobby pulled up to the customs booth and grinned. The guard, a petite brunette in a blue uniform, didn't look at him for at least a minute, staring down at a piece of paper, pretending to read. Bobby liked the situation, the fact that this girl, who'd probably gone only as far as high school, was trying to intimidate him with her sophisticated customs guard tactics. Bobby was going to say something he'd just read in the Watch Tower Bible. "No discipline seems for the present to be joyous, but grievous; yet afterward to those who have been trained by it yields peaceable fruit, namely righteousness." Hebrews 12:11.

The guard beat him to it, she looked up and said, "City, where you were born?"

"Montreal," Bobby said, not thinking. It just came out.

"What were you doing in the United States?"

"Working," Bobby said. "I have a green card." He almost said at Tad Collins Buick-Lexus, forgetting for a second he was in a stolen car.

"Can I see some identification?"

Bobby handed her his driver's license and green card.

"Sir, are you the owner of this vehicle?"

"It belongs to the ministry where I work," Bobby said.

She came out of her booth and stuck a white card on the windshield and told Bobby to drive over and park the car, they wanted to ask him a few more questions. Bobby said, "Sure, no problem, officer, happy day." Happy day. Where'd that come from? Just popped into his head, but sounded like something a God Squader'd say.

Bobby put the car in gear and considered his options. He could floor it right now and probably not make the street in this dog of a car before they shot his tires out and maybe shot him. Or he could pull over and answer their questions while they searched the car. What would they find? He had thrown the .32 out the window in the tunnel on the way over. He was a Jehovah and had the Watch Tower Bible to prove it.

What he didn't expect was a customs inspector pulling a bag of weed out from under the front seat. And now Bobby was in a detention cell, thinking you couldn't trust anyone.

Thirty-one

When Karen got back to her mother's the street was blocked off. She had to park on Windsor. She could see Garden City High in the distance. It was dark now and there were four blue and gold Garden City police cars and an EMS van in front of her mom's, lights flashing. Karen wandered over to where crime scene tape had been strung across the front lawn. Neighbors were coming out of their houses, starting to gather as if it were a block party.

She had stopped on the way and pulled the tape off her wrists. She found the seam and dug it open with her front teeth.

Karen asked a Garden City cop, what was going on? His nametag said, "Officer Swinney." He was standing next to a patrol car. The driver's door was open and she could hear the static chatter on the police radio. The lights on the roof flashed across his face. He looked young, too young to have a Glock 9 on his hip. He wore his hat low over his eyes, maybe trying to look older, or look tougher. He had his hands on his hips, flexing muscular arms under a short-sleeve shirt.

Karen said, "Can you tell me what happened?"

"There was a shooting," Officer Swinney said, "a homicide."

"Was Mrs. Delaney hurt," Karen said. "She's the woman who lives here?"

"Are you a relative?"

"No, a neighbor," Karen said. "Mrs. Delaney's a friend of mine."

"She's okay," the cop said. "A little scared, but fine. A forty-three-year-old white male was shot and killed." He tilted the brim of his hat up.

"Do you know his name?" Karen said.

"I'm not at liberty to disclose that information."

He sounded like a cop now. Karen thanked him and walked down the street lined with pickup trucks and SUVs to her car. She hoped her mother was okay and wondered how she was going to explain all this to her. Karen went past the Cardells' house and pictured Mr. Cardell, a retired lathe operator, sitting on the front porch after work in his undershirt, drinking beer. Now she was passing the Griffis, Paula and Larry, who lived on the corner, their lawn perfect, like a golf course fairway. Karen was approaching the Audi; she could see her old high school in the distance and thought about how she used to twirl a baton all the way from her house to the parking lot, three blocks away without stopping. She took out her key, pushed the remote and heard the beep, and saw the taillights flash. Then she saw someone appear coming around the side of a Ford Explorer parked behind her. She stopped and looked, she was almost to her car now, but it was too dark to see his face. Karen pulled the door handle up and someone grabbed her from behind. She tried to get her right hand in the bag that was hanging from her shoulder, but her arms were pinned to her sides.

There were two of them, and now she was lifted off the ground and carried to a dark SUV. The bearded one opened the back end and pulled up the lift gate, and laid her flat on the cargo floor. He tied her feet together and her hands behind her with pieces of thin plastic rope. She caught glimpses of their faces and recognized them as the Arabs from Lou's house the night before and Schreiner's a few hours earlier.

Beard said, "You are Karen Delaney?" He had a thick Middle East accent, sounding like relatives of Samir's who had come over from Beirut.

Karen said, "Who're you?" The tall one with the bad complexion picked up her bag, unzipped it and reached in, and took out the Mag and put it in his pants pocket. He took out her wallet too, opened it and studied her driver's license.

"Is Karen Delaney," he said.

She said, "Did he tell you about the money?" Beard glanced at her, but moved away and closed the lift gate. They were speaking Arabic when they got in the front seat. She heard the engine turn over and the Cadillac Escalade rolled away from the curb and picked up speed, cruising down Windsor. She couldn't believe it, kidnapped in her old neighborhood with half the Garden City police department fifty yards away.

Karen was on her side and her shoulder was digging into the plastic cargo liner. She turned on her back and that was worse, the weight of her body pressing on her hands. She tried to undo the knot with her thumb and index finger but couldn't budge it. The Escalade made a couple of turns and they were on Middlebelt now. She saw lights from storefronts and heard the sounds of traffic. She worked at the knot, which was small and tight, trying to loosen it.

She had a pretty good idea where they were going and figured she had about twenty-five minutes to do something before they handed her over to Ricky and Samir. She turned on her left shoulder, still working at the knot trying to loosen it. It was hot in the Escalade, her skin wet where it stuck to the plastic liner. She heard a window go down, the whir of the electric motor, and felt the rush of hot air swirl around her. They were talking, speaking Arabic again. Karen said, "I have the money. Isn't that what this is about? I stole a million six hundred thousand from him and he wants it back. Unless you guys want to make some kind of a deal." She didn't even know if they understood what she was saying.

The SUV slowed down and made a turn into what looked like a strip mall; she could see a big asphalt lot and cars parked and stores in the distance. The Escalade came to a stop. She heard the front doors open and close. She saw the lift gate swing up, and they were standing there looking at her. Beard grabbed a fistful of hair and yanked her head over to the edge of the cargo bay.

"This money," Beard said, "where is it?"

He pinched her shoulder, found a nerve and sent a bolt of pain through her neck and chest. She tried to move away, but the other one held her, hands on her breasts, groping her, and when she thought she was going to pass out from the pain, Beard let go and bent down, getting in her face. His breath reeked of garlic, the smell choking her, making her gag.

"Where is the money?" he said.

Karen said, "At a friend's house."

She saw his fist come up and felt it drive into her chest, blowing the wind out of her, a new pain taking over. She was conscious of them smiling, seeing her in pain and getting pleasure from it. Karen wheezed as her lungs lost air and now tried to get it back.

Beard said, "The money?"

He was in her face again.

"I'll show you," Karen said. "I'll take you there."

With his trim beard and dark eyes, he looked like one of the 911 terrorists she'd seen in the *Free Press* when the Trade Center was destroyed.

After that it seemed surreal, like a movie scene in slow motion. A car cruised into the frame, a blue and gold Garden City patrol car. The Arabs were moving. She saw the tall one go past the window on his way to the front seat. She heard the door open and saw him come back along the side of the Escalade, carrying a rifle. She saw Beard pull a semi-automatic from under his shirt and hold it against his leg, before he pulled the lift gate down and swung it closed. Karen dug at the rope with her index finger. She got a nail in the knot and felt it move.

Officer Jason Swinney watched the good-looking redhead walk down the street. He wanted to see where she lived, maybe stop by later with some news about her neighbor. She didn't appear to have a wedding ring. After he looked at her face that was the first thing he checked. He was going to ask her name, but didn't want to seem too obvious. She was older than him, ten years, at least, but that was okay. She sure was good-looking.

He tracked her to the end of the street. She was standing next to a car—some kind of foreign sedan, when two guys appeared. They grabbed her and picked her up. What the hell was going on? Were they kidding around? Jason wasn't sure what to do. He'd been a patrolman with the Garden City police department for a week shy of three months. He didn't want to make a mistake and screw up, do something embarrassing and call attention to himself. But his instinct told him to get in his car and follow the black SUV.

He didn't tell dispatch what he was doing. He got in his cruiser and left the crime scene. He would follow them and see what happened. If he needed backup, he'd radio in. He tailed the Escalade down Windsor onto Middlebelt and then into the Midway Shopping Center. He wondered if he had misread the situation, if he had overreacted. He watched them park in a remote corner of the lot. What were they doing?

Swinney pulled into a parking space between a conversion van and a Silverado 4×4. He had a good angle on the SUV about a hundred feet away. He sat and watched. Nothing happened for a couple minutes, then the front doors opened and the two guys got out and opened the back end. He saw the redhead stretched out in the cargo area, and it looked like they were roughing her up. Jason had his hand on the radio about to call for backup, but changed his mind. He thought he could handle these two pussies beating up a girl.

He put the Crown Vic in gear and came up behind them in stealth mode, headlights off, speedometer needle climbing to fifteen, twenty. He pictured himself on TV, a news flash: rookie Garden City Police Officer Jason Swinney receiving a commendation from Governor Granholm after saving the life of a citizen.

He saw one of them close the lift gate, and then he saw the second one appear, coming around the side of the SUV, firing an automatic weapon, and Jason ducked for cover. He got down on the floor as low as he could go as bullets ripped up the interior, blowing out the windshield and side windows. He also heard the report of a semiautomatic handgun as rounds thudded into the side of the car. He unsnapped the clasp on top of the holster and drew his own department-issue Glock .40, but didn't dare risk looking up. When the shooting stopped, he reached for the radio handset, brought it to his mouth and said, " Officer down . . ."

Once the knot was loose, Karen untied her hands and went over the backrest into the rear seat, dragging her legs, which were still bound. The shooting had stopped. She could hear a siren somewhere in the distance. She slid over the console between the front seats. Her .357 Smith & Wesson Airweight was on the floor in front of the passenger seat. She leaned over and picked it up. The keys were in the ignition. She glanced in the rearview mirror and saw the Arabs moving toward the police car. She turned the key and shifted into drive and pushed down on the accelerator. Her bound feet felt big and clumsy on the pedal, but the Escalade took off and she could see the Arabs turn and start firing, trying to blow out the tires.

Karen swerved around a Ford F-150 backing out of a parking space. She sped across the lot, slammed on the brakes and just missed a Honda minivan. Now a police car entered the strip mall lot, flying past her, lights flashing. She heard speed bursts of machine gun fire behind her.

Karen drove out of the lot and took a left on Middlebelt Road and took a right into a neighborhood subdivision. She wound her way back to her mother's house, taking an intersecting series of dark side streets. She parked the Escalade on Windsor, the scene at her mom's was still playing out: police cars were still parked, lights were still flashing, and the neighbors were still gawking, standing behind the yellow crime scene tape.

Tariq watched Omar fire a long burst at the oncoming police car, first shooting off the flashing lights on top and then shooting out the windshield. The police car swerved off course, and slammed broadside into a parked car with impact, moving it out of its fixed position.

Omar ejected the spent magazine and reloaded, removing a new one from a satchel he wore over his shoulder. The asphalt around him was littered with shell casings. Omar turned as another police car approached from a different direction, speeding toward him. Omar raised the AK-47 to his shoulder and fired five-shot bursts. The second police car made contact with a row of shopping carts, sending carts airborne, carts in motion.

Tariq could see people emerging from stores in the shopping center, looking over at them and running back inside. He could see people in the parking lot disappearing behind their cars. He could hear more sirens in the distance, the sound of the sirens here much different from the sirens in Iraq.

He saw Omar fire at the storefronts, shooting out windows. People were running, scattering, afraid. Tariq shot a man with silver hair as he was opening the door of a Jaguar. He shot him at close range in the back of the head and the man dropped on the asphalt next to the car.

Tariq sat behind the wheel of the Jag. He turned the ignition switch and heard the engine start. He backed out of the parking space and picked up Omar, and drove slowly out of the parking lot, not wanting to attract further attention. He pushed the turn signal indicator in the upright position, turning right onto Middlebelt Road. In the side mirror, he could see more flashing lights approaching.

Karen drove to Schreiner's and parked in the driveway. She could hear laughter hang in the air, and music as she moved along the side of the house to the patio. There was a party in full swing two houses away. She could hear snippets of conversation, and then the music got louder and she could identify the singer, Shania Twain, and the song "Man! I Feel Like a Woman," sung by a chorus of buzzed partiers, mostly girls, by the sounds of their voices.

Although the weather had cooled down, Karen could feel herself sweating under her tee shirt. The back of Schreiner's house was lit up. She went through the family room into the kitchen and turned off the bright ceiling lights. There were empty beer bottles and bottle caps, and an ashtray with a roach in it on the counter. She could hear the TV on in the family room, the announcer said: "It took five years to build the five-mile-long Mackinac Bridge, making it a modern marvel."

With the kitchen lights off, Karen could see outside and saw three people appear on the patio. They were laughing as they came in the house. She heard Schreiner say who wants to catch a buzz?

She went into the pantry and closed the door.

A girl's voice said, "Nice place. What do you do, anyway?"

"I'm a lawyer," Schreiner said.

"And you smoke weed?" the girl said.

Karen wanted to open the door and say by the truckload.

Another voice, a guy's, said, "Got any beer?"

Schreiner said, "I'll fix you right up."

Then they were in the kitchen. Karen could see them, dark shapes through the slats in the door.

"How about some music?" The girl said, "I feel like dancing." She started to mambo, showing some moves, grooving to some tune in her head.

The ceiling lights went back on. Karen could see Schreiner. He was wearing his *Make Love Not Law Review* tee shirt again, the shirt saying, hey, I'm an attorney, but I'm fun. The refrigerator opened and closed, she heard the clinking of bottles, Schreiner put three Coronas on the counter and popped the tops and let the caps fly, pinging off the counter onto the floor. Schreiner picked the roach up out of the ashtray and lit it with a plastic lighter. He took a long hit, held it in for ten seconds and blew out a cloud of smoke. He handed the roach to the girl. She was wearing a short black skirt and a pink top, and looked about twenty-five.

The girl said, "Is this stuff any good?"

Schreiner said, "Remember Helen Keller? Two tokes, you can't walk, talk or hear."

The guy laughed.

The girl said, "I don't want to get blown away."

Schreiner said, "It's really polio pot, one hit you need a walker."

The guy laughed again, pinched the roach between his thumb and index finger and took a long dramatic pull, sucking in air.

The girl said, "I'm going back to the party."

She walked past the door, heading toward the family room. Schreiner and the guy picked up their beers and went after her. Schreiner said wait, we're coming with you. She heard them walk out of the house and close the door.

Karen stood in the center of Schreiner's two-car garage. There were no cars so it looked big and almost empty. There was a built-in worktable with shelves over it against the south wall. Underneath, a cord of dry aged wood was stacked in rows. On the other side, lawn and gardening tools hung from hooks on a Peg-Board. There were three green trash cans lined in a row next to the door leading to the house. Schreiner had a big green and yellow John Deere riding mower and a red Honda track-drive snowblower and a black Schwinn mountain bike.

Karen, on her knees, cleared a row of stacked aged oak logs, tossing them on the garage floor behind her. She cleared another row and could see the molding around the crawl space. She'd had one just like it at her place down the street. That's where she got the idea. Karen reached in and felt the strap of the Eddie Bauer duffel. She dragged it out and zipped it open on the garage floor, staring at over a million six in banded packs of bills.

Thirty-two

O'Clair said, "Know where your sister is?"

"If anybody did I would," Virginia said. "We're close. She'd tell me, but she didn't."

"Ricky hired a couple Iraqi hit men to find her and they will," O'Clair said.

"If you took money from someone like Samir, what would you do?"

"Run like hell," O'Clair said. They were cruising south on Woodward in light traffic, passing storefronts in Ferndale, neon lights ablaze.

"Exactly. That's what Karen's probably doing. I can't help you though."

"You wouldn't be helping me," O'Clair said. "You'd be helping her."

"I can't tell you what I don't know," Virginia said.

"Where would you go?" O'Clair said. "Didn't you say you're a lot alike?"

"I said we're close. You want to know where I'd go? I'd go to Argentina and you'd never find me."

"Why Argentina?"

"I've got a friend who lives in Buenos Aires."

"Is that where your sister's at?"

"I've already told you two times, I don't know."

O'Clair was driving Virginia home from her mother's after hanging around the house, waiting for the police and then talking to two Garden City detectives, telling them what happened, and telling them he had been a Detroit cop for fifteen years, and then telling them about some of his exploits.

When the police had gone, Virginia asked him if he'd give her a ride home. She sat with her body angled on the seat, facing him. He'd been thinking about her since he saw her at the store. She had a nice smile and nice teeth and perfect skin. Get rid of the lip stud and the purple in her hair, she'd be pretty.

"I wish she hadn't shot him," Virginia said. "Fly did a lot of bad things but he didn't deserve that."

O'Clair didn't think it was any great loss to mankind. In a flashback, he recalled the scene: he and Fly had walked in on the little blonde, who was holding down on Virginia and her mother. Fly had approached the girl, who looked like a teenager. She gripped the Colt Python in her hand like she'd never fired a gun in her life.

Fly said, "You better hand that over puss before somebody gets hurt." He figured he could take it from her 'cause she didn't look threatening. He took another step and she shot him point-blank in the chest and he fell backwards and that was it. Fly was gone. O'Clair grabbed the gun from Megan and made her free Virginia and her mom and then sat her on the couch till the police got there. Virginia got on her knees next to Fly and cried for a while.

"Are you okay?" O'Clair said.

Virginia said, "I think so but I don't want to be alone tonight."

O'Clair didn't know if she was coming on to him or not. "You got a friend you can call?"

"Karen used to say 'Gina, you're a magnet for freaks and weirdos. What do you see in Fly?'"

O'Clair wondered if he qualified as one or the other.

"Sorry for hitting you with the skillet," Virginia said. "Is your head okay?"

He had a lump the size of a golf ball on top of his head. "I've got brain damage," O'Clair said. "But with therapy they say I'll be able to live a useful life." He smiled to show her he was kidding.

Now she broke into a grin. "You're not mad?"

O'Clair shook his head. "No."

Virginia said, "Are you sure? Fly would've been pissed."

He turned right on Albany Street and cruised down and took a left in her driveway. He put it in park and looked over at her.

She said, "Want to come in for a beer?"

Tariq was driving the Jaguar well within the speed limit, exercising caution in a stolen automobile. They were on a street called Woodward Avenue, en route to the final address on Ricky's list, and if luck was with them, this is where they would find Karen Delaney and the money.

Omar had his back to him. He was turned in his seat, looking for a street called Albany, which, as Tariq remembered from an American geography course, was also the capital of New York state.

Tariq was more surprised than embarrassed by the strange turn of events. They had Samir's woman. All they had to do was deliver her and collect their money, but now they had nothing. Even the magnificent Cadillac Escalade was gone. Yes, certainly it was a concern. How would he explain this to his uncle?

A more pressing issue, however, was recovering the money. He tried to imagine one million dollars and more than half of that amount again. With this money Tariq could live like a king. He could purchase twenty Escalades. Tariq saw himself wearing expensive clothes from Paris and New York. He saw himself in the company of many beautiful women.

Omar said, "Is Albany. Turn here."

Tariq did, driving slowly, looking for the address Ricky had given to them. According to the numbers the house would be on the left side of the street. There was a car with its lights on parked in a driveway twenty meters ahead. Passing it, Tariq identified the automobile as a Cadillac Seville, 1998 or '99. There was a woman standing at the open front passenger door of the vehicle, talking to someone inside. This was the correct address. The house was dark, no lights.

He drove to the end of the street, and turned around driving back toward the house. When they were within fifty meters he turned off the lights, moving closer, parking behind a Toyota Tundra pickup truck, two houses away. Tariq saw a man emerge from the Cadillac and walk with the woman, who he believed was Karen Delaney's sister, to the front door and enter the house.

Virginia said, "Do you like what you do, chasing people around, collecting money?"

She opened a bottle of Miller High Life and handed it to him.

"I'm going to retire and buy a motel on the beach. The kind with efficiencies." He sat at the kitchen table. She cracked a beer and sat across from him.

"What're efficiencies?"

"Rooms with kitchens. So people can go down and stay for a couple of weeks or a whole season, and they don't have to eat all their meals out."

Virginia said, "Where is this motel going to be?"

"Florida," O'Clair said. "Somewhere on the Atlantic side, Delray, or further south, Pompano, maybe." He'd rent out rooms and take it easy. No more muscling people for money. No more Detroit winters. O'Clair knew for a fact that he never wanted to see snow again as long as he lived. "Now's a good time to buy because most motel owners haven't seen a tourist since Easter."

Every couple of weeks he'd buy the *Sun-Sentinel* at Borders and check out the real estate prices. He'd mix himself a cocktail and think of names for the place. He kind of liked Pirate's Cove. Get a sign with a pirate in a bandanna winking at you—a friendly pirate. Somebody you'd like to drink rum with and tell stories. He also liked Treasure Island for a name—another one where you could use a pirate on the sign, or a big treasure chest full of loot.

"We went to Fort Myers once," Virginia said, "for a family vacation." She sipped her beer.

O'Clair said, "That's on the Gulf side."

"We'd drive straight through," Virginia said. "Twenty-four hours. My dad would only stop for gas."

"I do it in two days," O'Clair said. "Spend the night in Valdosta."

"Where's that at?"

O'Clair said, "Southern Georgia. It's down near the Florida border. You think 'cause you're close to Florida you're almost there and you've got another eight hours of driving ahead of you."

Virginia said. "Can I come down and visit you?"

"I've got to get a place first," O'Clair said. He took a sip of beer.

Virginia got up and came around and stood next to him. He wondered what she was doing. His chair was out about a foot from the table.

She said, "Will you kiss me?"

He was hot and sweaty and wondered about his breath. "I better not."

"Come on," Virginia said.

She sat in his lap and brushed her mouth against his. It was clumsy at first until she zeroed in on him and locked her lips on his, and stuck her tongue in his mouth. He noticed her eyes were closed. The kiss lasted about ten seconds. Then she pulled away and looked at his face.

"You're a good kisser," Virginia said.

O'Clair was thinking, I am?

"Want to hang out sometime?"

"What do you mean?" O'Clair said.

"You know," Virginia said, "go to a bar or a club, hang out."

"That'd be nice," O'Clair said.

"What's your number?"

"What do you want my number for?" O'Clair said.

Virginia said, "Why do you think? So I can call you."

He checked his shirt pocket for something to write on and pulled out a business card that said, Bobby Gal, Sales Consultant, Tad Collins Buick-Lexus. "Do you have a pen?"

She got off him and went to the counter and got a pen and gave it to him. He wrote his number on the back of the card and handed it to Virginia. He got up and held her hands and looked her in the eye and said, "I'm going to ask you one more time. Know where your sister's at?"

She smiled at him and said, "And I'm going to answer you one more time. No, I honestly do not."

"Would you tell me if you did?"

"Yes," Virginia said, "because I believe you'd help her."

It sounded like she was telling the truth the way she said it. "I better go."

She walked him to the front door and kissed him again.

"Take it easy," O'Clair said.

"Yeah, you too."

He thought about her as he walked to the car, imagined her in a bikini, bringing him a beer while he cleaned the pool. O'Clair barefoot in a pair of Bermuda shorts, working the long handle of the skimmer. Or better yet, Virginia would do the cleaning. He'd watch her from a lounge chair, drinking a beer. He liked looking at her. He could sit there all day and look at her.

Tariq watched the man exit from the house twenty minutes later. He watched the Cadillac drive down the street and disappear. Five minutes after that a light appeared in a second floor window. Omar saw it and pointed.

He said, "You see?"

"Yes," Tariq said. "I see." He was thinking about the money, Ricky instructing him: call me, update me, keep me posted. But what did Tariq have to update? Did he know the whereabouts of Karen Delaney? No. He glanced at the clock on the dashboard again. The time was 1:48 A.M. He glanced at the house and saw the light turn off. Omar looked at him and Tariq nodded.

They exited from the vehicle, closing the doors as quietly as possible. They walked to the house. The air was still hot, the street dark and quiet. They moved along the side of the house to the rear. There was a door with four glass panels. He peered in and saw a stove and refrigerator. Tariq tried turning the door handle, it was locked.

Omar had another idea. Occasionally, Omar would surprise him. He was ten feet away, removing a window screen with his knife. He stood on a patio chair and hoisted himself up and through the window and less than one minute later he unlocked the door for Tariq. They crept through the house to the front door. He was looking up the stairs ready to move when he heard a phone ring and stood there quietly. The phone was ringing. It rang five times before stopping. He could hear a woman's voice talking in the upper level of the house.

They waited until it was quiet again and started up.

Thirty-three

Virginia said, "Do you have any idea what time it is? I was sound asleep."

"I just wanted to make sure you were all right," Karen said, looking out at the skyline of Chicago.

"Where are you?" Virginia said.

"In a safe place." She picked up her drink, sipped Stoli on the rocks, her second, trying to relax. "How's Mother?"

"That little blonde killed Fly."

"What're you talking about?"

"Fly and O'Clair showed up while you were gone. Fly's dead."

"My God," Karen said. She was confused. What were Fly and O'Clair doing there?

"I loved him," Virginia said.

"You were afraid of him," Karen said. "And now you're better off without him." She decided to tell it straight, not sugarcoat it.

"You should talk," Virginia said, anger in her voice. "The winners you've been involved with."

It was true. Karen's taste in men was as bad as her sister's. Maybe worse. "Tell me how Mother is."

"You brought some excitement to her life," Virginia said. "To say the least."

"Is she all right?" Karen walked across the room and sat on the bed.

"It depends what you mean by all right," Virginia said.

Karen said, "What do you think I mean?"

"Well she's not hyperventilating anymore," Virginia said.

"What . . . ?"

"She was breathing into a paper bag," Virginia said. "That's what can happen when someone gets shot right before your eyes."

"I tried calling her," Karen said. "Where is she?"

"Aunt Jean came and picked her up," Virginia said. "She didn't want to be in the house alone after what happened. Can you blame her?"

"I'm sorry, I tried to keep you out of it," Karen said. She could see cars ten stories below, cruising along Lake Shore Drive.

"Mom's worried about you."

"I'm worried about me too," Karen said. She'd have to talk to her mother and try to explain things.

Virginia said, "You going to tell me where you're at?"

"Chicago," Karen said. "If two Arabs in barber shirts show up looking for me, tell them I left the country."

Virginia said, "Are you really going to?"

"Yeah, but I need my passport," Karen said. "Will you try to find it and send it to me?"

"It's the middle of the night," Virginia said.

"Not now," Karen said, "in the morning. FedEx it overnight Priority. Send it to—"

"Wait a minute," Virginia said. "You think I sleep with a pen in my hand?"

Karen heard her put the phone down, and heard her open a drawer and rattle what was inside.

"Okay," Virginia said back on the phone.

"Drake Hotel, 140 East Walton, Chicago, 60611. I'll send you some money. I'm sorry I woke you," Karen said and hung up.

It was strange Karen was waiting for the passport again, like the passport was bad luck, a bad omen—holding her here, preventing her from leaving. She looked at the clock on the bedside table. It was 1:20 A.M., Chicago time. She'd stopped at a twenty-four-hour Walgreens on the way to the hotel and bought a Clairol Nice 'n Easy hair coloring kit, chestnut medium brown. Karen knew she had to do something. Her hair was like a neon sign. She went in the bathroom and opened the box and read the directions, which were in English and Spanish. She had never colored her hair. Why would she?

Karen wrapped a towel around her shoulders and got her hair wet and dried it till it was damp. She put on the rubber gloves and poured the colorant into the activating creme. She put her finger over the tip and shook the bottle. The directions told her to part her hair in even sections using the colorant nozzle. She started at her hairline and squirted the stuff through the length of her hair and then rubbed it in with her hands until the red was gone and she was a brunette.

Her eyebrows didn't look right so she rubbed a little brown through each one. There were splotches of color on her forehead and temple. She wet a washcloth and wiped them off. She let the dye set for ten minutes and got in the shower. The kit came with a conditioner. She rubbed it through her hair, waited a couple minutes and rinsed.

Karen dried her hair and looked in the mirror. She barely recognized herself. How would anyone else?

Thirty-four

"Are they gone?" Virginia whispered.

"Yeah," O'Clair said. He stood looking down at her on the bed. There was blood on her face and neck and more on her pillowcase. She was naked, on her side, knees curled up to her chest. He covered her with the sheet.

"You're sure?"

"Don't worry," O'Clair said.

"There were two of them," Virginia said in a low voice he could hardly hear. "Arabs looking for Karen."

O'Clair said, "Where is she?"

"Chicago."

He touched her cheek with a warm washcloth and she winced. "Did you tell them?"

"I would've told them anything they wanted to know," Virginia said. "I was begging to tell them."

By the look of her, he was surprised she could talk, surprised she was conscious, surprised she was alive. They'd broken her nose and beat her body with pieces of broom handle. O'Clair saw the straw broom head on the floor and two broken lengths of wood.

They'd pulled the stud out of her lip with a pliers. That's where most of the blood had come from, the wound in her face. They beat her for the hell of it, for the sport. He tried to clean her up before he called 911.

Virginia told him what happened in her quiet voice. How she opened her eyes and saw the barrel of a pistol pressed against her lips and then pushed into her mouth, the second man holding her arms behind her back. This was how she woke up, scared out of her mind.

"The man with the gun had a heavy accent. 'Where is Karen Delaney?' It sounded strange the way he said it, using her first and last name in a formal way. I couldn't answer, the gun was in my mouth. I gagged and I saw his face in the dim light, grinning. When I didn't answer, the second man hit me with something that stung the back of my legs. He let go of my arms and hit me on the bottom of my right foot. Ever been hit there? It hurts more than you can imagine. I said 'You want Karen she's at the Drake Hotel in Chicago.' He hit me again with the stick and kept hitting me till I passed out.

"I woke up and heard the door close downstairs. I saw the card you gave me on the table next to the bed. It was all I could do to pick up the receiver and dial your number. I put the phone on the bed and got my face next to it and listened to it ring ten rings before I heard your voice."

O'Clair said, "Just lay there and don't talk, okay?"

"Do you remember what you said when you answered the phone?"

Yeah, he remembered, but it didn't seem particularly memorable.

"You said, 'This better be important.' Your voice deep and angry."

He saw her try to smile and then make a face, knowing she hurt bad.

"It was the best sound I've ever heard," Virginia said, her eyes holding on him, trying to smile again.

"Don't talk anymore," O'Clair said. He touched her chin with the warm washcloth trying to wipe away some of the blood and she turned her face away from him in pain.

"I'm sorry," he said. He could see right through her lip to her teeth and it made him angry, and he knew if he had any chance of catching them he had to get going. He sat on the edge of the bed, leaned over, and kissed her forehead. "I have to go, but I'll be back soon."

"You've got to find Karen," Virginia said, her sad eyes locked on him. "Promise me you'll help her."

"Don't worry," O'Clair said.

He was in his car now parked across from Virginia's house, watching an EMS van pull up in front, lights flashing. Two med techs got out and went to the front door that was open, and went in. O'Clair considered his next move. It was 4:56 A.M. The Arabs had a forty-five-minute head start. He assumed they were driving. How else could they could get to Chicago with their guns? It was 284 miles. But maybe he could close the gap, make up some time on the road. At seventy miles an hour, it was a four-hour drive. If he drove ninety he could shave an hour off and get there before them.

According to Virginia, Karen was at the Drake on East Walton in downtown Chicago. He'd been to Chicago a number of times and had a pretty good idea where it was—a block from Lake Michigan. O'Clair wanted to find Karen and the money, but his priorities had changed in the past hour and now he wanted the Arabs more. He felt anger he hadn't felt for a long time. Things didn't set him off like they used to. He actually thought he was mellowing till he saw what they did to Virginia and the adrenaline started pumping and hadn't stopped.

What was it about this oddball girl with purple hair and a tongue stud that made him feel so good? He felt something inside, in his gut, and it made him happy, the feeling so new and unexpected he didn't know what to make of it at first, and now he couldn't get her out of his head.

He was on I-94 passing the exit for Saline when he began to doubt himself. Maybe he was seeing something that wasn't there. What did Virginia, this wacko kid fifteen years younger, see in a fat old guy like him? But in O'Clair's mind it didn't matter, it was right. She trusted him. Who'd she call to ask for help, and to help her sister? She called him.

He was approaching a road sign that said "State Correctional Facility Exit 139"—Jackson Prison, Michigan's largest, housing more than five thousand inmates, and O'Clair thought back to his twenty-seven months in protective custody. He wouldn't have lasted a day in general population after the gangs found out he'd been a Detroit cop.

A deputy director of MDOC—Michigan Department of Corrections—told O'Clair he should apply for a job. He said, "Inmate labor goes hand in hand with our mission to help you successfully reenter society and become a productive, contributing citizen."

O'Clair wanted to deck the ignorant bureaucrat, thinking he'd been a productive, contributing member of society when he was convicted and sent to this godforsaken shithole.

Just past Jackson he was tired and started to nod off. He stopped at a McDonald's and got two cups of coffee, a sausage McMuffin and hash browns, and ate while he drove. It was 6:05 A.M.

From there it was just O'Clair and a parade of semis. He got to the outskirts of Chicago two hours later, pushing it, cruise control set at ninety, passing through Battle Creek and Kalamazoo, passing woods and farm fields and orange and white construction cones lining the highway on both sides, passing Dowagiac and Holland and Benton Harbor, passing through the top edge of Indiana into Illinois.

He followed the Dan Ryan into town and looked for a parking space on East Walton across from the hotel, but there weren't any. The street was lined with trucks and delivery vehicles at 8:30 in the morning. O'Clair didn't see two guys who looked like the guys Virginia had described. He wasn't sure how to play it from here. Should he go in the Drake and call Karen? And tell her what, her life was in danger?

He took East Walton to Michigan Avenue and went right again. He cruised by the west side of the Drake. There were cars parked to his left in the metered spaces on Oak Street that extended from Michigan Avenue all the way to Lake Shore Drive. He noticed a man sitting behind the wheel of a Jaguar sedan, parked across from the faded canopied Oak Street entrance to the hotel. Just sitting in the car like he was waiting for someone. O'Clair drove around to the front of the hotel. He sat in a "No Parking Zone" for fifteen minutes, watching taxis pull up to the hotel to drop people off and pick people up. He was thinking about the guy in the Jag and went around the hotel again to see if he was still there. He was.

This time he got a better look, studied him and thought he might be one of the Arabs who attacked Virginia. O'Clair drove to the end of the street, saw the bright blue expanse of Lake Michigan in the distance, and made a U-turn and found a parking space halfway up the block. The Jag was about twenty cars down the street. He took the Browning out of his sport coat pocket and screwed the suppressor on the end of the barrel.

Four-thirty in the morning Ricky heard his cell phone ringing. He picked it up and said, "Tell me you've got her."

"We are driving to Chicago, Illinois, in search of Karen Delaney," Tariq said.

He always said her last name too. Ricky thinking, you don't have to say Delaney. She's the only Karen we're looking for. They were a couple of oddball dudes, but he had to admit they were persistent—still on the job at 4:30 in the morning, while everyone else on the payroll was sacked out, snoring. Ricky said, "Where the fuck you at?"

"We are on Interstate 94, approaching Marshall, Michigan," Tariq said in his straightforward, no bullshit way. He sounded like a Middle East robot.

Ricky said, "You don't have to say Michigan. I know where Marshall's at, okay?"

When Tariq told him Karen Delaney was staying at the Drake Hotel on Walton Street in Chicago, Illinois, pronouncing the "s," Ricky said, oh Chicago's in Illinois, huh? I didn't know that, thanks for telling me. He'd decided he'd better get up and go there himself, protect his interest. He wouldn't need the hundred grand from Wadi Nasser now. He'd be able to pay off Samir and be set for life.

Ricky called Northwest and booked a seat on the 7:00 A.M. nonstop to O'Hare, flight 1235, arriving at 7:23. He'd fly in, get there before Karen got out of bed. But it didn't go that way. Ricky was in first class, drinking a screwdriver and the plane was taxiing on the runway when the pilot said I've got good news and bad news. The good news is we're the next plane to take off. The bad news is we have a mechanical problem and have to go back to the terminal. Ricky couldn't believe a pilot would talk like that: good news, bad news. Like it was a fucking joke.

The flight was delayed for an hour while they fixed the plane and Ricky didn't arrive in Chicago till 8:22. He rented a car and called the Iraqis.

Thirty-five

Karen woke up at 8:45 and ordered room service: an English muffin and coffee. She drank the coffee and took a couple bites of the muffin, but wasn't hungry. Her nerves were still frazzled. She went in the bathroom to brush her teeth and was surprised to see the face looking at her in the mirror, still not used to her new hair. She got dressed and went down to the lobby. She bought a Chicago Cubs baseball cap in one of the gift shops. She went in the ladies' room and ripped off the tags and adjusted the cap low over her eyes, hiding as much of her face as she could.

Instead of going out the main entrance on Walton, she went out the Oak Street side of the hotel. There was something going on. Two police cars, lights flashing, were parked right there on the street. Karen could see four cops standing next to a Jaguar. She went south and crossed Michigan Avenue and walked a couple blocks to Emporium Luggage and bought a black twenty-six-inch roll-along suitcase that looked like it would hold a million six in banded currency. She stopped at a newsstand and bought a *New York Times*, *Chicago Tribune* and *Sun-Times*, *Wall Street Journal*, *Investor's Business Daily* and *USA Today*. She took a cab back to the hotel and asked the driver to drop her off at the Oak Street entrance, but the street was blocked off, so she got out on Michigan Avenue. The cops were still there and two med techs were putting someone on a gurney in the back of an EMS van.

Karen went in the hotel. She rolled her suitcase along the corridor of shops and got behind a group of conventioneers coming out of a meeting room. She followed the group to the lobby, and took an elevator up to her room. She'd transfer the money in her new bag and leave the Eddie Bauer duffel and a couple of blouses in the closet to make it look like she was still using the room.

The suite had been cleaned while she was out. She went in the bedroom and pulled the covers back on the bed and messed up the pillows. Karen went in the bathroom and wet a couple of bath towels and dropped them on the floor. She left her toothbrush and toiletries on the counter next to the sink. She was tired and stressed from worrying, and wondered if she was going to be looking over her shoulder for the rest of her life.

O'Clair got out of the car. He slid the Browning in his belt and buttoned his sport coat that was too small for him. It bulged against his belly and the buttons strained, trying to hold it together. He walked along the row of parked cars toward the Jag. There was a park on his right, bordering Oak Street. The Drake was on his left. Except for an occasional car he didn't see anyone around.

He flashed back to Virginia, the way he found her, all busted up. He could feel himself getting angry, getting pumped again. As he got closer to the Jag, O'Clair could see the guy's face watching him in the side mirror. He walked up to the car, the window was down and he stood behind him—an old cop trick—so the guy had to turn to see him. O'Clair was holding the Browning at arm's length down his right leg. The guy's face was pockmarked and expressionless the way Virginia had described him. The guy's right hand was in his lap, his left was hidden by the door. O'Clair said, "I noticed your license plate. I'm from Michigan too." He grinned. "Where you from?"

The guy looked at him but didn't say anything.

"You don't by any chance know Virginia Delaney, do you?" O'Clair saw him turn in his seat and saw his left hand come up over the doorsill, holding a gun, and shot him three times in the chest and watched him twist and grunt and slump forward, head touching the steering wheel. "I thought that might get your attention," O'Clair said.

Ricky sat in his rental car parked in a loading zone on Walton Street across from the Drake Hotel. It said "Louis Vuitton" on three first floor windows of the building next to him. It looked like a luggage store. Trucks lined the street behind him. There was a stake truck in front of him and workers were unloading construction equipment. It was so fucking hot he had to keep the engine running to keep the air on.

Ricky had gotten a call from Wadi Nasser, who told him he'd gone to a hell of a lot of trouble to get the hundred grand for him, and was he going to pick it up or what? He'd also gotten a call from Samir, who'd left an angry message: Where the hell are you? If you're not back here by noon, don't come back. You're through. You hear me? Yeah, Ricky heard him. He wasn't going to make it.

Hearing Samir's voice got him thinking. He could sit here and wait for Tariq to find Karen, or he could go in and try to find her himself. He got out of the car, crossed the street and went through the revolving door. He walked upstairs through the lobby to the front desk. A cute young girl in a blue suit was standing across the dark wood counter from him, smiling.

"Sir, may I help you?"

"I'm looking for a friend of mine, Karen Delaney," Ricky said. "What room's she in?"

The girl typed something on the keyboard in front of her. She studied the computer screen and looked up at him. "Sir, there is no guest named Karen Delaney registered at this hotel."

"She's five six, a hundred and fifteen pounds, red hair, nice-looking girl. Maybe you've seen her around."

"No sir."

"Try Karen Starr with two r's."

She looked down at the computer again and said, "I'm sorry, we do not have a guest named Karen Starr registered here either."

Ricky didn't know if this chick was jerking him around or not, but what could he do about it? He looked behind him and saw Tariq sitting at a table in the restaurant that was half a dozen steps above the lobby.

He went back outside and heard sirens and saw cop cars speeding by on Michigan Avenue. Something was happening on the other side of the hotel. He walked around the block to Oak Street. Two police cars were parked, lights flashing, blocking the street. As he got closer he could see Omar slumped forward in the driver's seat of the Jag. Ricky asked one of the cops what happened. Guy told him to please step back on the sidewalk. Police were investigating a possible homicide.

Ricky had no idea who popped Omar. Maybe Karen had someone working with her. He decided not to say anything to Tariq. He didn't want him distracted. He wanted him to keep his eye on the ball.

Tariq was thinking about Omar before he saw the woman. He had tried to contact him three times without success, and now believed Omar was outside the hotel asleep in the car. He saw her enter the lobby, coming behind a business group from Millennium Software, the people wearing the plastic-coated cards around their necks. Tariq was sitting at a table in the Palm Court restaurant above the lobby, watching her from his elevated perch. This woman did not appear to be with the group. She was rolling a suitcase across the red carpeting. It was the way she was walking, angled forward that caught his attention. That and she seemed to be hiding behind the cap and sunglasses like someone who did not want to be recognized. He studied her as she passed by him and waited for the elevator. There was something familiar about her. Yes, the color of her hair was different, but he was convinced this was Karen Delaney.

He stood up and moved down the stairs. He was halfway across the lobby, moving through the group of conventioneers when the doors to the middle elevator opened and Karen stepped inside and the doors closed behind her. Tariq watched the elevator rise up to the tenth floor and stop. He pressed the button on the wall and watched as the elevator to his left returned to the main floor. The doors opened, Tariq entered and pushed the button quickly before anyone could walk in. The doors closed and the elevator started up.

He walked along the deserted hallway, which was covered with blue carpeting. There were many rooms. How would he find her? He walked to the end of the hall and around the corner to his right. There was a maid's cart. The door to room 1026 was open. He could hear the electric hum of a vacuum cleaner. He peered in the room. The maid had her back to him. She was vacuuming the floor next to the bed.

Tariq entered and closed the door. He approached her from behind, bringing his right arm around her neck. She released the handle of the vacuum cleaner, and tried to free herself. He was squeezing with all of his strength and she was flailing, trying to kick him and gouge his eyes. The maid was thin, fine-boned and slender but very strong. The motor of the vacuum was still humming. He clamped his arm tighter around her neck and lifted her off the ground. When she stopped moving he laid her on the floor and turned off the vacuum cleaner. She was Asian and young. He found the master key, a white plastic card, in the pocket of her apron. He dragged her into the bathroom, bent with his knees and lifted her into the tub and closed the shower curtain.

Tariq opened the hotel room door. He glanced in one direction and then the other. The hall was deserted. He rolled the maid's cart around the next corner and pushed it against the wall, and retraced his steps, going back to the first room next to the elevators to begin his search. He tapped on the door with the knuckles of his right hand. He listened but he could not hear a sound. He slid the plastic card in the lock and opened the door.

Karen heard a knock on the door and heard a card slide in the lock. She had forgotten to use the safety bar. The door opened and a maid came in carrying a pile of towels. She was Asian and slightly built and said excuse me.

Karen took the towels and thanked her.

When she walked out of the room fifteen minutes later the maid's cart was in the hall to her right, a couple rooms away. Karen wheeled her new suitcase down the hall to the elevator. She pressed the button and waited. She turned and saw someone, a man, come out of the room next to hers. He glanced her way and started toward her. Karen got in the elevator and took it down to the lobby. She carried her bag down the stairs to the street level and wheeled it through the revolving brass door to Walton Street.

The doorman hailed her a cab. He picked up her suitcase and put it in the deep trunk of the taxi.

Tariq walked out of the room and glanced to his left and saw Karen Delaney at the end of the hall. Seeing her surprised him. Again, she was so close. And again, she stepped into an elevator and was gone. He ran to the elevator bank and pushed the button, glancing at his watch, impatient as always, pressing the button again. He had to wait twelve seconds for the next elevator and rode down to the lobby.

He scanned the reception area and the concierge desk, but he did not see her. He ran down the stairs and pushed through the revolving door, and saw a glimpse of Karen Delaney in the right rear window of a yellow 2006 Mercury Marquis taxi driving away. He ran after the taxi all the way to Michigan Avenue and watched the vehicle turn left and accelerate, blending in with the traffic.

Out of the corner of his eye Tariq could see an automobile drive up next to him, coming to a stop. The passenger window was down, Ricky leaning across the front seat.

"I've got a better idea, why don't you get in. Unless you think you can catch her," Ricky said, smiling at him.

Thirty-six

Karen stood at the picture window that extended the length of the living room and looked out at the Chicago skyline. She could see the Hancock building and Water Tower Place and the Affinia Hotel, and below her she saw the Water Works and Saks and Neiman Marcus on Michigan Avenue. If anyone was following her this move to the Peninsula Hotel would keep them off balance, keep them guessing.

She called Stephanie, her buddy. They'd been close for sixteen years. Stephanie had met a guy named Jerry Hilliker, married him and moved to Chicago. Karen hadn't seen her for six months, although they still talked on the phone every couple of weeks.

"I can't believe you're here," Stephanie said. "What's the occasion?"

"I'm making my run," Karen said. "I'm on my own for the first time in eighteen years."

"How's it feel?"

"Are you kidding?" Karen grinned.

"Judging by the sound of your voice," Stephanie said, "it must be good. Where's Lou?"

Karen said, "I left him in the dust." She looked out the window. There was a cloud drifting through the top of the Hancock building.

"I had a feeling something was wrong, you show up here by yourself."

"There's nothing wrong," Karen said. "Everything's right. I'm free and I can't believe how good it feels."

They agreed to meet at the Tavern on Rush Street at 5:15, Stephanie's suggestion. Karen remembered it, red awnings and sidewalk tables.

Ricky sat in the restaurant off the lobby and watched Karen check in. The black chick from the registration desk took her up to her room on the sixteenth floor. He saw them get on the elevator together. Saw the floor they went to and went up after them. The black chick came out of room 1616 and passed him in the hall. She said, good afternoon. Ricky said, hey, how you doing? He stood outside Karen's room considering his next move. He could knock on the door and when she opened it, go for her. But he had a better idea. Walked to the end of the hall. He liked the look of this hotel, everything all gold and white. Man, it was classy. There was a maid's cart in the hallway to his left. The door to room 1648 was open. The maid, a Latina in a beige uniform, looked at him from inside the room.

Ricky said, "I left my key in the room. Stupid, huh?" He smiled. Be friendly, he told himself.

She smiled back and said, "Sir, it happens all the time. What room are you in?"

"Sixteen sixteen, right down the hall." He took a $20 bill out of his wallet and handed it to her.

"Sir, that's not necessary," the maid said, still smiling.

"Sure it is," Ricky said. He wanted to say, you're a fucking maid you're going to turn down twenty bucks?

She thanked him and followed him down the hall. She slipped her card in the slot and Ricky turned the handle and opened the door a crack.

"Have a nice day, sir," the maid said and walked away.

Oh, he was going to have a nice day, all right. He was going to have a great fucking day. He went in and closed the door. He heard voices, sounded like a TV, glanced down a short entrance-way to the living room. He moved past an open door, and looked into a bedroom. No one was there. He moved to the living room, peeked in. The TV was on, looked like a news channel. There was no sign of Karen. No sign that anyone had been in the place.

He glanced out the big window at the Chicago skyline. He went into the bedroom. Went through the dressing room to the bathroom. He was hoping Karen was in there taking a bath, open the door, "surprise," but she wasn't. He checked the shower and the toilet room. Everything was perfect like the room had never been used. He went back in the dressing room and opened the closet and there it was, the black suitcase. Identical to the one Karen had rolled out of the Drake, and rolled in the Peninsula. He picked it up and put it on the floor. Ricky was so excited he could barely breathe. Here it was, the way out of all his problems. He was thinking he could take the bag downstairs, get in a cab and take off, leave Tariq in his rental car, wondering what the fuck happened.

He unzipped the suitcase and folded back the top. But it wasn't filled with money. It was filled with newspapers. He flipped the suitcase upside down and the papers fell out. He could feel himself getting angry, starting to lose it. There was a built-in dresser behind him. He yanked the drawers out and threw them on the floor. They were empty. He went in the bedroom, looked under the bed. Nothing. Went in the living room, flipped the couch over, getting more pissed off. Where was the fucking money at?

Then he thought, wait, maybe he was in the wrong room. No, a card on the desk in the living room said, "Karen Delaney, welcome to the Peninsula Hotel," signed by the hotel manager. Next to it on a notepad was an address written in blue ink. Ricky took out his cell phone and called Tariq. "Get over to 1031 North Rush Street. That's where she's going. I'll meet you there."

Karen stood staring at herself in the bathroom mirror. She had second thoughts about going out, meeting Stephanie in a bar, a public place, but decided she was being paranoid. Nobody knew she was in Chicago except Virginia, and Karen had changed her appearance and changed hotels. She wanted to see her friend and this was the only opportunity to do it.

She left the room and went down to the lobby. It was simple and elegant, with gold-tinted accents and a lot of light coming in from the twenty-foot-high windows in the lobby restaurant.

She stopped at the concierge desk and got a map of the neighborhood. She studied it and located the Tavern four blocks away on Rush Street. She walked down the wide gold marble corridor to the elevators. The lobby was on the fifth floor. She went down to the street level and walked outside. The doorman was in the street, hailing a cab for a group of Asian men in suits. Karen decided to walk. She took Superior Street to Michigan Avenue and went left. She regretted her decision halfway to the next block. It was hot and humid and she was already starting to sweat. She saw a taxi coming toward her, raised her arm and it stopped. She got in and took it to the Tavern.

Stephanie was waiting inside the door. She looked at her as if she wasn't sure and said, "Karen . . . ?"

They hugged, both grinning, happy to see each other.

"What's with the new look?" Steph said. "I loved your red hair. I know women who'd kill to have hair like that."

"It's a change of pace." Karen took off her sunglasses and put them in her bag.

"Well, I think you're crazy."

They sat at a table in the bar, drinking wine, Stephanie looking as good as ever, still a knockout at age thirty-six, Gwyneth Paltrow with long dark hair.

"I can't believe you're here," Stephanie said. She picked her wineglass up by the stem and said, "I didn't tell you. I'm single again myself. To freedom."

They clinked glasses and took sips and put their glasses back on the table.

Karen said, "What happened to Mr. Perfect?"

"He wasn't," Stephanie said. "I looked at him one day, coming home half in the bag in his golf outfit, giving me a hard time because dinner wasn't ready, and decided I'd had enough." She paused.

"There has to be more to it than that," Karen said.

Stephanie said, "I didn't see that much of him. He'd travel every week and come home, and get mad if his laundry wasn't done, or if I didn't pick up his dry cleaning. I work too I told him, pick up your own dry cleaning. One time he got back from a business trip and said, 'We have no food. There's nothing to eat. And we're out of plastic bags. Don't you make a list of the things we need?'"

Karen said, "No plastic bags, huh? That sounds like a real emergency. What'd you say when you left?"

"Get used to making your own dinner. I'm out of here." Stephanie sipped her wine.

Karen said, "And you took off?"

"I packed a bag and walked out the door while he stared at me in disbelief, geezing down Grey Goose on the rocks. What'd you say to Lou?"

"It isn't working and isn't going to," Karen said. "I left him a note on the refrigerator."

"How'd he take it?"

"He still won't talk to me," Karen said.

"You're lucky. Jerry wants me back. Calls all the time, won't leave me alone. I've gone out with a couple of guys. Nothing serious."

Karen said, "What about your first date's the beginning of the end philosophy?"

"It's still true," Stephanie said. "More so than ever."

Karen said, "How's it go again?"

The waiter put two glasses of wine in front of them. "From your admirers," he said, indicating two dudes in golf shirts, sitting at the bar. They held up their drinks and grinned.

Karen said, "Tell them thanks, but we'll buy our own."

Stephanie said, "You don't want to hear their rap, huh?"

"I'm not in the mood," Karen said.

The waiter picked up the glasses and walked to the bar and put them down in front of the men.

Stephanie said, "You know the relationship's doomed before he picks you up—when you're opening the door for him on the first date. It's all downhill from there."

"If you were so sure what was going to happen," Karen said, "why'd you get married?"

"I had twenty-one orgasms with Jerry one weekend and I was temporarily blinded by passion," Stephanie said.

Karen said, "Twenty-one, really?" She tapped a Marlboro Light out of her pack and lit it with a red plastic lighter.

"It took place over two days," Stephanie said. "I never told you that?"

"I think I would've remembered," Karen said. "So you let your guard down, huh?"

"Did I ever," Stephanie said. "I was in stage one of the relationship and didn't know it—infatuation bordering on lust."

"How long does stage one last?" Karen said.

Stephanie said, "Anywhere from a couple days to months."

"Then what happens?" Karen said.

"Stage two is the slow but sure buildup of contempt, which can go on for a long time—years." Stephanie paused, caught her breath and took a sip of wine.

Karen could see one of their admirers look over at them and get up.

"Stage three is the loathing," Stephanie said. "It's also a euphemism for marriage. It's the end of hope—when your soul is sucked out of you by your joyless, loveless life partner—crushing your will to live."

Karen laughed. "With that positive attitude, how can you miss?" The guy was coming toward them, almost there.

"But you know I'm right," Stephanie said, "don't you?"

The guy was tall and good-looking, wearing a tight-fitting black shirt. He had a weightlifter's shoulders and arms and the confidence of a someone used to getting what he wanted. He walked up and stood between them.

"Hi, I'm Gil," he said.

Like they were expecting him. He had dark hair combed back and long sideburns. He checked Stephanie out first, then turned and fixed his attention on Karen.

"My friend and I were taking bets on what you girls do for a living," Gil said. "Want to join us for a drink, find out what we guessed?"

Karen turned so she was facing him now. "Gil, listen, we're having a conversation here, okay?" She met his gaze. She was about to say—we don't give a shit what you think we do for a living, but when she looked past him she saw the Arab with the beard, sitting at the bar. It couldn't be, she told herself, but it was. She felt her heart begin to race and her body tense up.

He sat there staring at her, making no attempt to get up, letting her see him, letting her imagine what was going to happen. Karen said, "I'd like to have a drink with you, Gil, but I've got a problem. There's a man stalking me. He's sitting right over there. Don't look." But she knew he would.

Gil turned and stared at the Arab and flexed his upper body. "The dark-haired guy?" he said.

"Yeah," Karen said. "The one over there with the beard who looks like he's going to hijack a jumbo jet."

"Let me talk to him," Gil said. "Order me a drink, will you. Bombay Sapphire martini up. I'll be right back." He moved toward the bar.

Stephanie gave her a puzzled look. "What was that all about?"

"I've got to go." There was no time to explain it.

Stephanie said, "I think you're overreacting. He's harmless."

Karen didn't think anything would happen. She figured Gil would give him a hard time, and that would give her a chance to get away. She was almost to the door when she heard the gunshot.

Thirty-seven

Tariq, sitting at the bar, asked for a glass of water.

"That's all you want?" the bartender said. The man's tone saying, this is a bar, you come here to drink, to spend money. Tariq was aware of the reason people came to a bar. He would be enjoying a single-malt Scotch if the situation were different, an eighteen-year-old Macallan. Tariq was there to frighten Samir's woman, to create tension. He believed his presence would cause her to make a move she was not ready to make. What surprised him, what he did not expect, was the man approaching him, the man saying, Hey, Sheik, I'm only going to tell you this once, so listen up. Tariq had not experienced any overt anti-Arab sentiment since arriving in the United States. What did he do to provoke this stranger? He was sitting at the bar minding his own business, not bothering anyone. Tariq now wondering if maybe the man thought he was someone else. The man was angry, coming toward him. Or maybe he was a friend of Samir's woman, trying to protect her. He had seen them engaged in conversation across the room.

As he came closer, Tariq decided that it did not matter why the man was angry or what he wanted. Tariq reached behind his back, under his shirt and touched the Beretta. He felt the cool metal against his skin.

"Sheik, you hear me? Get up right now and walk out of here, we won't have any trouble."

The man's voice was loud and threatening, purposely so, trying to intimidate him.

"That's your first option."

Tariq was aware of the people at the bar watching them.

"Your second option is to continue to sit there, and get your ass kicked."

Tariq glanced toward Karen Delaney. She was on her feet, moving toward the door. He drew the Beretta and shot the man in the chest from three feet away. The discharge was deafening, like a mortar round exploding. The man went down. He heard the shell casing *ping* as it landed on the floor, and then it was quiet. He was aware of the silence, and the people around him, frozen as if it was stop action. Tariq slid off the barstool. He wanted to run, but told himself to move slowly, not to hurry. He stepped around the man, who was on his back, blood pooling on the floor to his left. Tariq was still perplexed, wondering why the man had interfered in a situation that did not involve or concern him.

He walked away from the bar with the Beretta in his hand. People moved out of his way. He slid the gun behind his back in the waistband of his trousers, and went outside, feeling the heavy heat and humidity. He walked through tables in the café area and stood on Rush Street, glancing in one direction and then the other. He could see Karen running twenty meters away. Tariq turned and scanned the cars parked along the street, looking for Ricky.

He heard a police siren and horns blaring behind him as he ran south on Rush Street. Tariq now understood the significance of the name Rush—all of the cars and people, all the activity—everyone rushing. He thought it was an astute observation. He came to Oak

Street and stopped. He glanced to his left and saw Karen, a brief glimpse, before she entered a store on the other side of the street.

Karen went through the door at Barney's, moving down the wide main aisle with its floor stands and elegant decorations. On her right were glitzy chrome and glass display cases in the cosmetics department. The men's department was to her left. Headless mannequins displayed the latest shirt/tie combos from top designers. She didn't think the Arab would follow her into a crowded department store. She was partway up the staircase that wound through the center of the store, looked down and saw Beard come through the door, and she ran up to the second level.

Karen glanced across the floor and saw two shoppers browsing in different areas of the department. A salesgirl behind a counter was ringing something up for a customer. She moved past racks of blazers and blouses and dresses. She stopped, crouching behind three mannequins in designer outfits, arranged like they were having a conversation. Karen gripped the .357, looking out across the floor, and heard a voice say, "Are you finding everything okay?"

She glanced back and saw a salesgirl approaching her from behind. Karen said, "Have you taken your break yet?"

The girl, early twenties, with a short mod haircut and heavy red lipstick, didn't seem to think it was strange to see a customer in the shooting position, holding a .357 Magnum in her hand. "This would be a good time to disappear for a few minutes."

The girl gave her a puzzled look.

Karen saw Beard approaching. "Do you see that man with dark hair? He's coming to kill me."

"Oh-my-God," the girl said, stretching it out like it was one word, and took off, running across the floor toward the rear of the store. Karen was on one knee, holding the .357 Airweight with two hands the way Lou had taught her—right hand on the grip, left cradled under the barrel and trigger guard to help balance it.

She saw Beard move, coming toward her through the department, checking behind the high-end clothing racks as he approached. She was on her knees behind the mannequins. She started to get up and heard a gunshot, and next to her the head of a mannequin in a cocktail dress exploded. Karen took off, crouching as she ran toward the back of the store, up the steps where the dressing rooms were, and saw reflections of her in the wall-to-wall mirrors.

There were four rooms, two on each side of the fitting area, with gold curtains instead of doors. Karen went in the dressing room furthest from the entrance, and stood in the corner behind the almost floor-to-ceiling curtain that you could pull closed for privacy. She was holding her breath, trying not to make a sound. If she was lucky, he'd come in take a quick look and leave.

But he didn't. She heard him sliding the curtains in the dressing rooms across from her all the way open. She could feel her heart beating faster, but this time she wasn't afraid, she was angry. She reached into her bag and gripped the .357, but decided against it. He wouldn't shoot her till he got the money. He came toward her, grabbed the edge of the curtain, pulled it open and stepped in the room, aiming his gun at her.

"You cause many problem," he said. "Where is the money?"

"I don't remember," Karen said.

He pressed the gun barrel against her cheek, his face close, inches away, staring with those dark eyes that had no feeling, no emotion.

"The money?"

"I don't know," Karen said.

He hit her with an open hand across the face that stung her cheek, and pulled her out of the dressing room. He cocked the hammer back now and said, "The last time I ask."

She looked in the mirror behind her and saw O'Clair come up the steps into the dressing area, two hands on his gun, arms locked in front of him like the cop he'd once been, aiming at the Arab.

Beard sensed something and swung his pistol toward O'Clair and O'Clair shot him twice, *pfffft, pfffft,* with his silenced Browning and Beard went down and didn't move.

He looked at her and said, "You want to get out of here, come with me."

Karen said, "Why would I do that?"

"'Cause the police are downstairs and I've got the money."

Karen said, "What money?"

"Play dumb if you want. Your sister asked me to come here and protect you."

"What're you talking about?" Karen said.

"Virginia's in the hospital," O'Clair said.

"I just talked to her," Karen said. "And she was fine."

He told Karen what the Arabs did to her and what time it happened. He sounded convincing, and now Karen wasn't sure what to believe. She'd seen the Arabs in action. They liked to hurt people, seemed to enjoy it.

"I'll tell Virginia I saw you and you're okay. You want to stick around, suit yourself," O'Clair said. "I'm going to get out of here."

Karen imagined herself being interrogated by the Chicago police, trying to explain why this Middle East thug was after her and ended up dead, and that was enough to convince her. She followed O'Clair back across the floor, past the elevators to a hallway where the restrooms were. From there they took the backstairs down to the first floor and went through a door that said

AUTHORIZED PERSONNEL ONLY. They walked across the stockroom with its floor-to-ceiling shelves to the loading dock. A semi was parked in one of the bays and men on Hi-Los were unloading pallets of merchandise.

They came out on Rush Street and headed back toward Oak. There were four Chicago police cars, lights flashing, parked in front of Barney's. The area was cordoned off with yellow tape. Karen could see gawkers behind the tape, watching the action.

Thirty-eight

Ricky took his rental car and met Tariq at 1035 North Rush Street. It was a restaurant-bar called the Tavern. Tariq would go in and let Karen see him, scare the shit out of her. Ricky'd be outside, parked on the street, waiting. When she came out he'd follow her. But Ricky got distracted watching two twenty-year-old blondes in hot pink bikinis on Rollerblades. He watched them cruise past his car. He turned his head following them, staring at their perfect little asses until they disappeared down the street. When he looked back through the windshield he saw Tariq running down the block, chasing Karen.

Ricky got out of the car and ran as fast as he could to Barney's, the store they'd gone in. He was at the bottom of the giant staircase when he heard the first gunshot. It sounded like it came from somewhere upstairs. He wondered if Tariq had lost his mind, firing a gun in a crowded store. He didn't want any part of this. It was time to go. A woman carrying packages ran down the stairs yelling, "He's got a gun. He's going to kill somebody."

Ricky moved toward the door and got caught in a stampede of people rushing to get out. He heard another gunshot and now the crowd was pushing and shoving with more intensity. A woman fell and was trampled. Ricky moved through the door, fighting to keep his balance. He heard sirens. Then he was outside. Three blue and white Chicago police cars had pulled up and parked, blocking Oak Street. More people had pushed their way out of the store and Ricky was standing in the middle of the panicked crowd.

He didn't know what he was going to do, but hanging here wasn't an option. He was thinking life was like a game of craps. Sometimes things went your way and sometimes they didn't. He pushed through the people, and there, coming toward him on the other side of Rush Street, were Karen and O'Clair. And just like that Ricky's luck had changed. Unbelievable. He wished he was in a casino with a pair of dice in his hand, but this was better. He watched them walk down the street and get into O'Clair's Cadillac that was facing south. There were two more Chicago Police cars and an EMS van parked next to the Tavern bar. More yellow tape was strung around the perimeter of the sidewalk café.

Ricky ran to his car and got in. He saw the Caddy take Rush to Delaware and go left.

He turned and faced her, leaning back against the door. Karen couldn't believe the strange turn of events, sitting in a car, having a conversation with O'Clair. She felt cold air blowing in her face and turned the air-conditioning vent away from her. She looked at him and said, "Let me make sure I understand this. You came here to protect me as a favor to my sister, is that what you're saying?"

"Uh-huh."

He had taken off the tan sport coat and was sitting there in a Hawaiian shirt, his big white freckled arms at his sides. "They beat her up and she called you, a total stranger," Karen said. "Why am I having trouble believing this?"

A green Jeep Wrangler drove by, stopped, and backed into the parking space in front of them. A young couple got out with a baby and wheeled a stroller down the street.

"She trusts me," O'Clair said, and sounded convinced.

"She trusts you?" Karen said. "How does she even know you?"

"I met her at the store where she works and then again at your mother's. I gave her a ride home. We hit it off."

His big sweaty face flashed a grin.

"Is there something going on between you two?"

"Ask Virginia," O'Clair said.

"I'm confused," Karen said.

"You're not alone," O'Clair said.

It was tough to see them together, too much to comprehend. O'Clair, the heavy, the over-the-hill ex-cop who made his living scaring the shit out of people, had a thing for her sister. Was he conning her? Was he making this up? O'Clair took out his cell phone and dialed a number and handed it to Karen.

It rang four times before a woman's voice said, "Providence Hospital."

Karen said, "Do you have a Virginia Delaney there?"

The voice said, "Room 650, I'll connect you now."

It just rang, but proved that Virginia was there. She had been admitted. "All right, I believe you," Karen said. "Where's the money?"

Ricky should've listened to himself. He'd suspected O'Clair right from the start, but didn't do anything about it. And now here he was with Karen. This was too good to be true. His luck was hitting on all cylinders. He watched O'Clair get out of the car and walk back and pop open the trunk. O'Clair took out a black plastic garbage bag that was loaded with something, and Ricky's guess was money. He went around to the passenger side of the car, opened the rear door, threw the bag on the back seat and got in.

Ricky took out his gun, the Walther PPK Tariq had given to him. He liked the look of it and the feel of it in his hand. He racked it, and looked through the windshield, thinking, do it. Make your move.

Karen turned so she could look over the top of the seat back. O'Clair picked up the bag and flipped it over and dumped the money, a pile of banded packs on the faded, worn-out leather seat.

"It's all there," O'Clair said. "A million six and change."

Karen said, "How'd you know where I put it?"

"I saw you come out of the Drake and followed you to the luggage shop."

"I was watching the whole time," Karen said. "Why didn't I see you?"

"I didn't want you to," O'Clair said. "I was thinking, if it was my money I wouldn't walk out and leave it in a hotel room, knowing there were some bad dudes after me." He kept his eyes on her. "And I didn't think you would either. You're too smart. So what did you do with it? I knew you drove, so that seemed like your first best option. Hide it in the wheel well under the spare tire."

"Aren't you clever," Karen said.

"No, I'm from Detroit," O'Clair said.

"How'd you find my car?"

"I described you and it, and gave the valet a hundred bucks. He brought the car up, I drove it around the block and brought it back."

"Samir stole three hundred grand from me."

"You don't have to explain it," O'Clair said, "tell me your motivation. And you don't have to worry about him coming after you. I got a call from Saad, friend of mine, one of his collectors. Samir's back in the hospital in bad shape. His chain of gourmet markets are in Chapter 11, and a team of auditors from the IRS showed up at his house, and want to see his books. His empire's crumbling around him."

"I'm sorry to hear that," Karen said. She could see people on the sidewalk moving past the car, shoppers and joggers and dog walkers.

"No, you're not," O'Clair said. "Why'd you go out with him in the first place? I've always wanted to ask you that."

"He was a charmer," Karen said. "Why'd you work for him?"

O'Clair said, "I was an ex-con, ex-cop without a lot of job prospects. He made me an offer."

Karen glanced down at the money. "How much did you take?"

He looked at it now, and then at her.

"Nothing," O'Clair said. "It's all there."

Karen said, "How much do you want?"

"Four hundred grand—I'm going to buy a—"

"You don't have to explain it," she said cutting him off, "tell me your motivation."

O'Clair looked at her serious and smiled.

Karen said, "Why didn't you just take what you wanted?"

"I figured we'd work something out," O'Clair said. "That leaves you a million two. At 8 percent that's a hundred grand a year."

"I'm glad you're looking out for me," Karen said.

He said, "You never know . . ."

He didn't finish but she had a pretty good idea what he was going to say.

"Don't you think maybe you're getting a little ahead of yourself?" Karen said.

He had that same goofy look on his face again. She couldn't believe it, couldn't get used to the idea that O'Clair was gaga over Virginia.

"What're you going to do?" O'Clair said.

"What do you think? Go see my sister."

O'Clair said, "I'll meet you there."

He took forty banded packs of bills, each worth ten grand, and loaded them into two grocery bags. He put Karen's share back in the Hefty trash bag and dropped it over the seat next to her. He drove to the Drake and pulled up in front.

"Want me to wait for you?" he said. "Ricky's still out there somewhere. You never know."

"I'll be all right," Karen said. "I'll meet you at the hospital. Providence, right?"

She got out and swung the plastic bag over her shoulder and went in the hotel. She checked out and had her car brought up from the garage. She opened the trunk and put the plastic bag in it. Then she got in the Audi and took off, heading for Michigan.

Thirty-nine

Ricky passed Gary, Indiana, saw smokestacks belching smoke in the distance, thinking there was a city that was uglier than Detroit and he was looking at it. Karen was five cars ahead of him cruising on I-94. He'd had to make a decision. O'Clair was in on it too. But he could only follow one of them and Karen had the plastic bag, and his gut told him that's where money was at. Ricky didn't know where O'Clair had gone to. He'd dropped Karen off at the hotel and driven away. Ricky just had to be patient, wait till she pulled over, stopped somewhere and make his move.

Twenty minutes later he got his wish. She got off the highway just outside Kalamazoo. Ricky wondered where she was going. He didn't see any gas stations or fast food places at the exit. He followed her for half a mile on a two-lane county road, cornfields on both sides, to an old Mobil gas station. She pulled in and he stopped by the side of the road and watched her get out, and go in the place.

Karen was hungry for the first time in days. She'd seen a small weather-beaten sign on the highway that said "Gas-Food Next Exit" and decided to stop and pick up a little something to hold her over till later. She hadn't eaten anything all day except for the two bites of English muffin that morning and her stomach was growling. She got off I-94 and drove about half a mile to a little run-down gas station with a cornfield behind it. She went in and bought a Coke and a bag of cashews, and came out humming "Runnin' Down a Dream," the Tom Petty song she'd just been listening to. She noticed another car had pulled in the small lot and parked next to hers. She had the can of Coke under her arm and it was cold as she dug her hand in her purse, trying to find her keys. She felt the presence of someone, and looked up and saw Ricky. He was aiming a chrome plate semiautomatic at her sideways like a bad guy in a TV movie. He was wearing blue track pants with red stripes going down the legs, and a black tank top.

"You better have my money," Ricky said.

"It's in the car," Karen said. "I've been holding it for you."

"You've been holding it, huh?" Ricky said. "Let me see it."

Karen opened the trunk and pulled out the plastic bag and dropped it on the oil-stained asphalt. Ricky squatted and opened the bag and looked in. He lowered his gun and reached in the bag and took out three banded packs of bills. He grinned, staring at the money, not paying any attention to her.

Karen reached in her shoulder bag and gripped the .357 and stepped toward him. "I've been holding this for you too."

Ricky glanced up at her with a nervous look on his face.

"Jesus, be careful," Ricky said. He looked down at his gun.

Karen said, "Don't even think about it. I don't want to shoot you but I will if I have to."

Ricky dropped his gun on the asphalt, got up and stepped back. Karen picked up the gun and said, "Put the money back in my car."

"Give it to me," Ricky said. "I'll let you go."

"You'll let me go?" Karen said. "I'd worry about myself if I were you."

Ricky picked up the bag of money and put it in her trunk and closed the lid.

"You're making a big mistake," Ricky said. "I don't care where you go . . . no place is safe, you take this money." He stood there looking cocky and self-confident.

"Open your trunk," Karen said, pointing the .357 at him.

"What the hell for?"

"Because I told you to," Karen said. "And I've got the gun." She kept the Airweight trained on him.

"Don't do anything dumb," Ricky said, realizing it was all Karen now.

"I was going to say the same thing to you, but you can't help yourself," Karen said, "can you?"

He moved behind the white Ford Focus that was parked next to her Audi. She came up behind him and jabbed his shoulder with the barrel of her gun. He reached in the pocket of his warm-up pants, took out his key and pushed a button on the keypad and the trunk popped open.

"Get in," Karen said.

Ricky looked over his shoulder at her. "I'm not getting in there."

Karen swung her arm and hit Ricky on the back of his head with the butt of the Mag.

"Jesus, what're you doing?" He bent over, making a face, holding his head, rubbing it with his fingertips.

"You don't have a choice," Karen said. "Get in."

He lifted his leg up, put a foot in the trunk, and then pulled himself up and in. He fit with no trouble. There was enough room left for a bag of golf clubs.

"I'll give you a piece of the action," Ricky said.

Karen could see he was nervous now. "Just give me the keys."

He tossed them to her.

"I'll split it with you," Ricky said.

Karen said, "You don't have anything to split."

"What do you want?" Ricky said.

"I've got what I want," Karen said.

Ricky said, "You think it's going to end here? You're out of your fucking mind. I don't care where you go, I'll find you—"

She slammed the trunk closed. She could hear him kicking the sheet metal inside.

"Get me out of here." Panic in his voice now. "Help!"

Most new cars had a release button in the trunk in case you fell in by mistake, but Ricky didn't seem to know it. Karen tapped her knuckles on the trunk lid and said, "Hey, keep it down in there." She got in Ricky's car, started it, backed up and drove to the edge of the cornfield behind the station. She had her foot on the brake, holding the car back. She could hear Ricky yelling and banging inside the trunk. She shifted into drive and opened the door, took her foot off the brake and jumped out. The Ford rolled into the field, knocking down stalks and then disappeared in the high corn.

Forty

Karen drove straight to Providence Hospital and went up to the third floor and found her sister's room. O'Clair was already there, sitting in a chair next to Virginia's bed, holding her hand.

O'Clair glanced at her and said, "What took you so long?"

Trying to be funny, showing a side of him she'd never seen before.

Virginia fixed her tired eyes on Karen and said, "You look vaguely familiar. Do I know you?"

Karen said, "How're you doing? Are you all right?" She looked terrible.

"I'm hanging in there," Virginia said.

"You mind if I have a word with my sister?" Karen said to O'Clair.

O'Clair glanced at Virginia and said, "I'm going to get something to eat. Can I bring you anything?"

Virginia shook her head. O'Clair got up and moved past Karen and walked out of the room. Karen sat in O'Clair's chair next to the bed. Virginia had a bandage under her lower lip, and her right forearm was in a cast. Karen held her hand.

Virginia said, "Why'd you come back?"

"I was worried about you," Karen said. "Why do you think?"

"I'm okay," Virginia said in a quiet voice.

She didn't look okay. She had two black eyes and her face was bruised and swollen. "I'm sorry you got involved in this," Karen said.

Virginia said, "Then I never would've met Oak."

"Oak, huh?" Karen said. "What's the story with you love-birds?"

"He's going to take care of me," Virginia said. "Nurse me back to health."

It was difficult for Karen to think of O'Clair as a caregiver. "You don't even know him."

Virginia said, "I know enough."

Karen was going to say, you thought you knew Fly and look what happened. But then she thought she knew Samir and Lou. There was no guarantee. You could never be sure.

"He's nice to me," Virginia said. "He likes me and I like him. We're talking about moving to Florida together. He's going to buy a motel on the beach. Doesn't it sound great?"

She sounded excited and Karen wasn't going to spoil it.

"You should come and visit."

Karen tried to picture herself on a beach with O'Clair, and couldn't.

"I'm serious." Virginia tried to smile. She looked like she was in pain. "Don't worry about me, I've got Oak."

"I'm happy for you," Karen said.

"What about you?" Virginia looked at her with affection. "What're you going to do?"

"Get my passport, try to explain things to Mother, and take off."

"He told me what happened in Chicago. Aren't you worried about Ricky and Samir and all those freaks looking for you?"

"No," Karen said. Johnny was dead. Samir was in the hospital, barely hanging on, and Ricky was in the trunk of a car, and even if he got out he was so inept she wasn't concerned.

"Come on," Virginia said, "I don't want anything to happen to you."

Don't worry," Karen said.

"You sure?"

"Trust me."